Sweet Strings of Love

Sweet Strings of Love

Drawn into the realm of romance, Chloe Celeste tastes the bittersweetness of life as unrequited love changes her view of the future.

Kay D. Rizzo

Pacific Press Publishing Association
Boise, Idaho
Oshawa, Ontario, Canada

Edited by Bonnie Tyson-Flyn
Designed by Tim Larson
Cover photo by Sinclair Studios
Typeset in 10/12 New Century Schoolbook

Library of Congress Cataloging-in-Publication Data

Rizzo, Kay D., 1943-
    Sweet strings of love / Kay D. Rizzo.
       p.   cm. — (Chloe Celeste chronicles ; 3)
    Sequel to: Winter's silent song.
    ISBN 0-8163-1221-4
    1. Man-woman relationships. 2. Young women. I. Title.
II. Series: Rizzo, Kay D., 1943-   Chloe Celeste chron-
icles ; 3.
PS3568.I836S94   1994
813'.54—dc20   94-18538
                                              CIP

94 95 96 97 98 • 5 4 3 2 1

Contents

1. Unexpected Guests 11

2. A Portent of Danger 27

3. Flee With the Dawn 45

4. Run Before the Hunter 59

5. Paris Bound 75

6. On the Left Bank 89

7. Along the Seine 105

8. Delicate Negotiations 119

9. On the Winds of the Storm 131

10. Wedding Bells and Fond Farewells 147

11. Cold Light of Day 163

12. As Time Goes By 179

13. Getting on With My Life 197

14. Unwelcome Surprises 213

15. In God's Good Time 231

Dedication

To Sue Haynes, whose friendship
and love endure beyond most
relative experiences.

Characters

From the glittering embassies of Europe to the sagebrush-covered hills of southern Oregon, the adventure of seeking the will of God continues for the Chamberlain family.

CHLOE CELESTE (CEECEE) CHAMBERLAIN—Loyalty and political intrigue plunge her into the direst risks as the daring, spirited young woman dons disguise to preserve the lives of her siblings.

THADDEUS ADAMS—Shattered by the realities of war, he must follow his ideals, at the risk of losing the woman he loves.

CYRUS AND CHLOE MAE CHAMBERLAIN—Dedicated to their country and their God, they struggle to protect their children against forces that could destroy both body and soul.

ASHLEY MCCALL—Lovely, wealthy, and pampered, she plays her cruel game of love—ignoring the difference between a brief fling and lasting love.

NIKOLAI MAGDONOVICH—Born to royalty, orphaned by political strife, the arrogant young aristocrat risks his life to protect the gold and the silver he possesses.

PHOEBE MAGDONOVICH—Snatched as a child from her father's arms, then orphaned by the only parents she knew, the delicate and retiring heiress must flee for her life before a relentless enemy.

CALVIN (CAL) BLAIR—This quiet, wealthy cattle rancher sets his sights on the new government nurse at the reservation and refuses to take No for an answer.

NINA COOK—Homespun and set in her ways, the retired schoolteacher defies new dangers and old memories when she befriends the determined young nurse from New York City.

Unexpected Guests

The last four measures of Beethoven's Sonata in A Major wafted throughout the stilled room. Tears of joy filled my eyes as I lowered my violin bow and glanced over at my piano accompanist. Sarge had played the entire piece without error. It took a moment for the audience to recognize the significance of the event, but then they broke into thunderous applause, accompanied by stomping and whistling. *Not exactly the sophisticated response heard at symphony concerts in New York*, I thought, *but definitely from the heart.* I bowed graciously, then gestured toward Sarge at the keyboard. The man grinned, then waved his scarred hand high in the air, a gesture of triumph.

"Encore! Encore!" the children and staff shouted.

"How about some ragtime?" one of the younger children cried.

I looked at Sarge and grinned.

"Gotta feed the masses, you know." He winked at me and broke into a rousing rendition of Scott Joplin's "Maple Leaf Rag." After coming to work at the small hospital and orphanage at the base of the French Alps, I met Sarge, a former concert pianist who had lost two fingers in the war. His joy and love for living astounded me. In a country reeling from a terrible war, he found beauty and happiness. He challenged my cynicism at every turn, forcing me to think beyond the tragedy of the day. And thanks to him, my music repertoire had broadened considerably. For the first time in my life, I was actually having fun with music—an alien concept to a serious violinist aspiring to the concert stage.

As the applause exploded following a second encore, Nurse Bouchard marched to the front of the orphanage's large assembly room and clapped her hands, demanding everyone's attention. Orphans and hospital staff alike obeyed the brisk and formidable head nurse. "It's time for our birthday girl to cut her cake." She led me through the crowd to a large table decorated with paper chains and streamers. In the middle of the table was a large sheet cake, a little lopsided but made by loving hands and frosted white by smaller but equally loving hands. In the middle of the cake, one large emergency candle flickered.

Nurse Bouchard handed me a large kitchen knife. "Due to the shortage of candles, we decided that one candle would represent every twenty years you've lived."

"But I'm only nineteen!"

Everyone laughed.

"Ah, who's counting?"

"For convenience' sake, we'll call you twenty, all right? So, as I was saying, at the rate of one candle every twenty years, you'll get to blow out your second in, let me see, 1939."

"I'll be too old by then to blow out anything!"

"Now, just a minute, young lady. Watch who you are calling too old!" Dimples formed in the woman's cheeks as she flashed a teasing smile at me.

"Oops! Sorry."

"Forty and proud of it!" She laughed. "Now make a wish."

"Wish. For what should I wish?"

Mimi, a fourteen-year-old resident of the orphanage and a favorite of mine, suggested, "A handsome prince to come and take you away to his castle!"

"You've been reading too many of Nurse Michelle's novels." Nurse Bouchard shook her head and sputtered, "The only princes around here have mortgaged the family castles in order to travel to America in search of wealthy American heiresses."

"Miss CeeCee fits the American part." Mimi giggled.

"Knowing CeeCee," Auriel, my brother's fiancée interjected, "she'd reject any prince who could not afford to keep her in hand lotion or install adequate indoor plumbing in that drafty old castle."

Everyone laughed while I blushed. "OK, OK, I deserve all the teasing about my complaints about the outdoor facilities and the cold-water showers. As to the hand lotion, I wouldn't need so much if warm water flowed from the tap as it's supposed to."

"Aw, come on." Sarge swaggered over to the group crowded around me. "Forget the privy and cut the cake."

The children in the group cheered his suggestion. I closed my eyes and made my wish, then blew out the candle. One clean slice through the cake, and I returned the weapon to Nurse Bouchard. "Don't say it," I teased. "I definitely was not cut out to be a surgeon."

Knowing how often the head nurse slipped suggestions that I should study nursing into our conversations, everyone laughed.

She handed me a chipped saucer with the first piece of cake on it. I thanked her and asked for a second. "I'd like to take one to Jamie at the hospital," I explained. "Since he couldn't come to the party, I want to take the party to him."

"Maybe Nurse Auriel would prefer to take it to him," Mimi whispered.

"Not tonight. This is my evening with my big brother." I glanced at Auriel and grinned. She winked and smiled. Balancing the two plates in my hands, I made my way through the crowd and out the door. It wouldn't be dark for another half-hour, but the light was fading into a misty twilight. As I made my way across the hospital grounds, I paused to admire the halo of sunlight bathing Mont Blanc's snowy crest. Jamie saw me coming and met me on the veranda.

"Let's eat alfresco," he suggested, taking one of the plates from my hands. "It's quieter out here, and the smell of fir trees instead of disinfectants is a little more pleasant."

"Good idea." I followed him to the veranda and sat down beside him on the steps.

"So, tell me, Cricket, has it been a good nineteenth birthday for you? Not quite the birthday celebration you would have had in London with the folks or with your socialite friends." He cut a forkful of cake. "Not exactly Wedgwood china, either, is it?"

I glanced down at the cracked and mismatched saucers and

at the tarnished fork in my hand. "If anyone had told me a year ago that I'd be where I am today, doing whatever it is I do, I would have laughed in his face."

"Don't belittle your work here in the hospital and at the orphanage. You do more good than you think."

I shrugged but didn't try to stop him. At that moment, I needed to feel that I had purpose in my life.

"Both at the hospital when you do private nursing for surgery patients and at the orphanage, reuniting children with their war-scattered families."

"But when I look at all the little children I haven't been able to help, I feel so frustrated."

He gazed toward the mountaintop. "You expect too much of yourself, Cricket, but you'll learn." He fell silent. The wind murmured through the branches of the fir trees surrounding the hospital. "I'm going to miss you when you go home." He paused again and sighed. "Do you ever regret coming down here?"

"Only when I step into the shower."

"You and your cold showers!"

"Do you know what it's like to have a dozen twenty-four-inch icicles dangling down your back when you finish washing your hair?" I eyed his short-cropped hair meaningfully. "No, I think not!"

He laughed and ate the last bite of cake on his plate. "Thanks," he said, handing me the saucer. I stood to my feet indignantly.

"And you expect waitress service too?" I extended one hand. "A tip, Monsieur?"

He stood up, stretching to his full six-foot height, and kissed me on the forehead. "Your tip, Mademoiselle. Now, get back to your party. Your fans are waiting for your skillful rendition of 'Turkey in the Straw.'"

"How very bourgeois of you." I arched an eyebrow at my brother.

"Bourgeois? Ooh-la-la! Sounds like you've been reading political missives from a certain young radical in Paris," he teased.

"If you're referring to Thad's newspaper essays—"

"More like boring tomes. Admit it, CeeCee—"

"Well, he is more of an intellectual than I."

Jamie guffawed. "Aw, come on. That socialist garbage goes against everything American—and you know it. You do understand how your father makes a living, don't you? An oil executive, remember?"

"Oh, pooh!" I switched my shoulders back and forth. "Thaddeus is making quite a name for himself in Paris, I'll have you know."

He gave a wry smile. "Well, I hope the American government will let him back into the country when he finishes all his postulating."

"You're joking—aren't you?" I stared at him in stunned surprise. I'd never thought about the legal problems Thad might encounter once his socialist leanings had gone public. "You don't think—"

"Aw, Cricket, I'm just teasing. I'm sure your Thaddeus Adams will wise up sooner or later. And when he does, he'll be a great brother-in-law."

"What? Brother-in-law?" I took a swing at my brother. He ducked. "I'm not—he's not—we're not—how could you suggest such a thing?" Indignant, I felt the heat rising in my face. "Thad's a friend, that's all. If anything, we stand a better chance of becoming cousins-in-law when he marries daffy Ashley than becoming husband and wife!"

In the middle of my protest, a green-and-silver Rolls-Royce roared onto the hospital grounds. Jamie and I glanced at one another, then back at the shiny vehicle.

"Who's that?" I asked.

"Wow! That is an Alpine Eagle, four speed. It won the 1914 Austrian Alpine Trail race," Jamie said admiringly.

"I thought it was a Rolls-Royce."

He looked at me and grimaced. "The model, dear, the model. The company made only a dozen that year. Then the war started and—" He shrugged his shoulders and strode toward the vehicle, calling over his shoulder, "Probably tourists who lost their way."

Curious, I followed behind, at a slower pace.

The uniformed chauffeur, a short, paunchy man somewhere in his late thirties, killed the engine, hopped out of the car, and spoke in broken French. "I am looking for Dr. James McCall. Can you tell me where I might find him?"

Jamie extended his hand toward the man. "I'm Dr. McCall. How can I help you? Is there a medical problem?"

"No, Monsieur. I am Valery, at your service." The chauffeur bowed, then opened the passenger door. A young boy around age fourteen burst out of the car. He gazed about the hospital grounds, his upper lip curling with disdain. My attention was drawn back to the automobile when a gloved hand appeared from the interior of the car. The driver grasped the extended hand and assisted a young woman from the vehicle. She appeared to be near my age, perhaps a little younger. I couldn't tell.

She wore her hair pulled back in a tidy chignon, like mine. Unlike mine, not a strand of hair was out of place. Her cream-colored linen suit was immaculate, with hardly a wrinkle. Her wide-brimmed travel bonnet, with its pale beige plumes clustered around the crown, rippled in the breeze as she gazed doe eyed at Jamie.

"Dr. McCall, it is a pleasure to finally meet you." She pursed her full mouth into a demure pout. While her gestures seemed confident, I detected a shy reserve in her eyes.

As I silently watched the exchange, I noticed that her features looked strangely familiar. My brother bowed graciously. "You have me at a disadvantage, Mademoiselle. I don't believe I know your name."

Her laugh was like a crystal wind chime in a gentle breeze. "But, of course. How foolish of me. I am Phoebe Magdonovich, daughter of the late count and countess of—" She faltered, her eyes glistening with tears. "I'm your stepsister. Cyrus Chamberlain is my father." She gestured toward the young man strutting back and forth in front of the car. "And this is Nikolai, my half brother."

Jamie and I exchanged startled glances, but he managed to regain his composure more quickly than I. "Welcome. Welcome to Chamonix." Then, taking my hand, he drew me to his side. "This is CeeCee, er, Chloe Celeste, my sister—" He paused in confusion. "—your stepsister. We have a younger brother, Rusty, er, named Cyrus after your father. He's in London with our parents. But you already knew that, didn't you?"

The young woman smiled indulgently. "I am so glad to finally meet you both. I know so little about either of you. My mother moved to Europe when I was but a baby." Then, noting the uncertainty on our faces, she added, "I do hope our unexpected arrival will not inconvenience you in any way. If there's an acceptable inn nearby, we could stay there for the night."

"Oh, forgive me." Jamie took Phoebe's elbow. "You must be exhausted from your trip. But, first, tell me what prompted this visit. I thought Cyrus instructed you to stay at the American Embassy in Switzerland until he could come for you."

At the mention of the embassy, the boy turned his face away from us while Phoebe and the chauffeur exchanged nervous glances. "It became uncomfortable for us at the embassy after our mother passed away. She died of consumption, you know." Phoebe withdrew a linen handkerchief from the beaded purse dangling from her wrist and dabbed at her tears.

"I'm so sorry." I touched the sleeve of her jacket. "It must have been most difficult for the two of you, losing her while so far from home."

She nodded and sniffled. "We were on holiday in Venice when the war broke out—Mama thought Italy's warmer climate would ease her lung infection. When she realized she wouldn't be getting any better, we moved north to Switzerland, where we lived until the war ended. Just before Mama died, she contacted your father. And you know the rest of the story, I believe."

Undaunted by Phoebe's evasive response, Jamie persisted. "Don't misunderstand me, Phoebe. I'm delighted to have you here. But I still don't understand why you chose to leave Switzerland before Cyrus came for you."

Phoebe's mouth tightened while Nikolai strutted over to us. "It's quite simple, really. My sister and I are titled nobility, or I should say, I am titled. The Bolsheviks have a price on our heads—they intend to kill us."

"Hmm, interesting." Jamie shot a quick glance at me, then drawled, "You'll have lots of time tomorrow to clear up any questions CeeCee and I might have. And, of course, I will cable Cyrus of the change of plan." He pointed toward the hospital. "In the meantime, Nikolai and Valery, you two can bunk in the doctors' quarters with me. And, Phoebe, CeeCee will find you a bed in the nurses' dormitory."

Phoebe clutched her suit jacket in horror. "Dormitory? You sleep in a room with other persons?"

I laughed. "About seven other persons, to be exact."

"B-b-but that won't do. That simply won't do." She looked nervously at her younger brother, then at Valery. "I've never shared sleeping quarters with anyone, not since I outgrew my nanny, at least."

Nikolai sighed impatiently. "Isn't there something available more suitable to my sister's station and sensibilities?"

Jamie assumed what I called his learned-physician look. He stroked his chin and ran his tongue along the inside of his mouth, ruminating on the situation. "Well, there is a fine inn on the edge of town that might still have a room available." He pointed toward the town of Chamonix.

Valery shook his head vigorously. "No, no, I don't think it would be wise to go farther this evening. You must make do, Miss Phoebe, with the inconveniences."

The woman and the chauffeur exchanged glances that I couldn't interpret.

"You will, of course, need to use my bed," I warned, "since we have no extras right now."

All three turned toward me in surprise. By the looks of distress on their faces, you would think I had suggested Phoebe sleep on the hospital veranda. I swallowed my urge to laugh. "I'm on private duty tonight in the hospital, so you will have the bed all to yourself."

Phoebe sighed in relief. "It seems I have little choice. You will put clean linen on it for me?" she asked with an air of condescension.

I bristled. *Who does she think I am? Her lady-in-waiting?*

I gave her a sugary smile. "You'll find everything you need in the trunk at the foot of my bed. Just help yourself."

She glared her response, then turned to her chauffeur. "I will need my valise and my steamer trunk."

No "thank you"? No "so nice of you"? No "oh, CeeCee, you are such a dear? I don't know how I'll ever repay you"?

"Yes, ma'am." The chauffeur touched the rim of his hat respectfully.

Nikolai tapped Valery on the shoulder. "Better move the car behind the hospital, don't you think? Out of sight?"

After a moment's hesitation, the chauffeur responded. "Yes, yes, sir. That's a good idea. I'll do that as soon as I carry Miss Phoebe's luggage to her, uh, quarters."

For the first time since the British luxury car drove onto the hospital grounds, I remembered the birthday party in progress— and in my honor. The same thought must have occurred simultaneously to Jamie.

"Oh, CeeCee, why don't I take Phoebe back to the dormitory, and you return to your party? You may want to alert Nurse Bouchard of our unexpected guests." He turned to Phoebe. "Of course, you three are welcome to join the birthday celebrations for my sister. It's her nineteenth."

"I would, except I am exhausted from our journey." She gave me another supercilious smile. "Please excuse me." The chauffeur and Nikolai also begged to be excused. As an afterthought, they mumbled a happy birthday. *Ooh, Nurse Bouchard is going to love this*, I thought. *She just loves surprises.*

"I really should get back to the festivities. I'll see you at breakfast." I headed toward the assembly room, thankful for the escape.

Jamie picked up Phoebe's valise and guided Phoebe in the direction of the nurses' entrance. "Your bed is the first one on the right?" he called after me.

"Yes, and as I said, there is clean linen just inside the trunk." I turned and grinned. "Be sure to acquaint Phoebe with the, er, facilities." I know that my dimples showed in spite of my valiant attempt to conceal them. *If my dear stepsister objects to sleeping in the same room with other people, what will she do when she finds out about the primitive facilities?*

"Right." He rolled his eyes. I hurried into the assembly room to enjoy as best I could the last part of my special evening. Before the party broke up for the night, I suggested to Sarge that we play "Turkey in the Straw." I knew that from somewhere on the hospital grounds, Jamie would hear the tune and understand the significance.

My second surprise of the evening was much more pleasant—a birthday gift from the children and staff.

"Open it, Miss CeeCee," Mimi cried. "I helped pick it out."

Eagerly, I lifted the lid on the box, folded back a layer of tissue paper, and shrieked with delight. "Oh, the dirndl from Marie's shop. I love it. How did you know I wanted that dress? When I went back the next day to buy it, it was gone!" I lifted a dark-green-and-white dirndl from the box. I had first seen the dress the day I took the older girls shopping in town.

Mimi and her friends giggled. "I know. We went back and bought it to surprise you. Please try it on for us."

"I promise I'll wear it to church this week; will that do?"

After the party, Auriel took my gift to the dormitory while I went directly to the hospital. An Italian soldier who'd joined the French army had undergone foot surgery that day to remove gangrenous toes and needed special nursing attention. He was already asleep by the time I arrived on duty.

I made myself as comfortable as possible in the wooden straight-backed chair beside his bed.

After midnight it started to rain. By three, the spring downpour had turned the world beyond the hospital's diamond-shaped windowpanes into an impressionistic work of grays and blacks. I shook my watch, questioning its accuracy. *Has it been only five hours since I came on duty?* I sighed. *The last five hours are always the longest.* The sounds of the ward were familiar—labored breathing, coughing, moaning, someone mumbling in his sleep.

In the soft light from the kerosene lamp on the bedside stand, I studied the sleeping soldier's smooth olive-toned face. *He can't be more than seventeen.* I looked at the man's chart. *Twenty-one? Huh!* I'd discovered that many of the injured men at the clinic had lied about their ages in order to enlist in the Great War. *Talk about living with the sorry consequences of one's decision!* I sighed. *Enrico Fellini, you should be at home, flirting with local girls or learning a trade, not battling an infection that could very well could take your life.*

A lazy smile spread across his lips as if he'd heard my thoughts. I adjusted the covers around his shoulders before tiptoeing to the nurse's desk, where Michelle sat engrossed in an American novel. I peered at the title, *The Romance of Calamity Jane and Dead-eye Dick,* and smiled to myself at the tense worry lines creasing her forehead.

"Excuse me," I whispered.

"Oh, CeeCee!" she gasped, "you scared the liver out of me."

I chuckled. "Sorry." I scanned the desktop for my Bible and my diary. "I thought I left my—"

"They're over there on the medicine cabinet. I spilled a little of the cough medicine on the desk this evening—" She shifted uncomfortably.

"Thanks." I walked around the desk and retrieved the books. "Quiet night."

"Yes." She glanced toward my Bible. "A perfect night to curl up with a good book."

I nodded and tiptoed back to my patient's side. Placing the Bible on the stand, I adjusted the wick of the lamp to increase the light. Making myself comfortable, I traced my finger over the gold lettering on the cover of my personal diary. "Chloe Celeste Chamberlain—1919." I tugged at the blue satin ribbon page marker. The leather-covered book, a gift from my aunt and uncle in California, fell open to May 17.

My birthday. Eventful enough this year? Memories of earlier birthdays flickered through my mind. *Who would have thought last year at my birthday party at home in New York City that I'd spend part of my nineteenth birthday in France with an Italian soldier? And in a place where the simplest of physical comforts would be a luxury?* I glanced down at my hands, chapped by frequent dousing in cold water. A wave of self-pity washed over me as I studied my cracked, broken nails and splintered cuticles. *Who would have thought—*

A groan from my patient brought me back to the present. *Stop it! No pity brigade here. Chloe Celeste, you can leave this place any time you please, which is more than can be said for your patient here. Talk about being stuck!* Briskly, I adjusted the journal on my lap and removed a stubby pencil from my skirt pocket.

Dear Emily. I'd been addressing my secret missives to my favorite poet, Emily Dickinson, since I had received my first journal as a preteen. *Here I am helping out in the hospital again. A number of the staff are sick with bronchial infections. Must be the weather. As usual, I'm as healthy as a horse. Not that I'm complaining. And, most of the time, I enjoy helping out.*

Nurse Bouchard asked me to "pinch-hit." I laugh to myself every time I hear the very correct French nurse use the very American idiom. The woman has a mission to turn me into a nurse. And who knows? She might succeed.

I glanced at my watch again. *Not even four o'clock yet?* I closed my notebook and slipped my pencil back into my pocket. Stretching my neck backward, then from side to side, I tried to relieve the kink in my neck. Next, I tried massaging the sore spot, all the while fighting the urge to close my eyes for a moment or two. Settling back into the chair, I closed my stinging eyes for just a moment to moisten them.

"O-o-o-oh, my foot hurts." The young man's groans lurched me awake. "Mama, it hurts. It hurts." I leapt to my feet and touched Enrico's forehead with my hand. *Feverish!*

I leaned closer and whispered, "You're fine. I'm right here for you." Dipping a clean washcloth in the basin of cool water, I bathed his forehead.

Then I stepped beyond the dividing curtains and called to Michelle, "Enrico's awake. He needs you."

"It's time for his next medication. I'll be right with you. I'm with bed three."

I knew the patient in bed three, a young Belgian soldier who'd lost both legs by throwing himself on a grenade to save the life of his captain. We'd talked many times about his war experience. Now the captain, whose life he had saved, was home enjoying his family, but the soldier was imprisoned by his anger and his injuries.

Throughout the ward, the other patients stirred, calling the nurse, asking for bedpans, for drinks of water, for pain medication. *Concentrate,* I told myself. *Enrico is your responsibility.*

Michelle will take care of the others. I moistened the cloth and bathed his forehead again, all the while speaking in low, soothing tones.

Through gritted teeth, Enrico moaned, "I don't understand why my foot hurts so badly. Didn't the doctor amputate the toes like he said he would?"

"Remember how Doc McCall told you you'd feel the toes for a couple of days? Like the toes were still there? The nerves are playing tricks on you."

The soldier gave me a wry smile. "The mind's a funny thing, isn't it? Before, when I first woke up, I could have sworn I saw my mama."

"You saw me, I'm afraid. Does she have red hair too?"

"Not hardly. It's black as a raven's wing." He laughed. "Just shows you what the mind can do."

It took fifteen minutes before the nurse could administer the pain medicine to Enrico. "When one wakes up, everyone does," Michelle complained. "We sit for hours with nothing to do; then all of a sudden the place erupts into chaos! Never fails!"

"Power of suggestion," I quipped. "Like children, one needs a drink, and suddenly, everyone's thirsty."

Slowly, the effects of the medicine calmed Enrico, and the pain lines in his brow faded. After I placed a freshly rinsed cloth on his forehead, he grasped my hand. "Thank you," he whispered.

"My pleasure, Private Fellini." I lifted his head and turned his pillow. "There, that should make you feel a little more comfortable. Now, why don't you try to get some more sleep."

Obediently, he closed his eyes.

After I emptied the water from the basin into the pail at the foot of the bed and wiped the basin clean, I paused to admire the first vermilion rays of morning glow behind the mountain. *Mama always says, "Red skies at morning, sailor take warning."* At the thought of my mother, I felt a twinge of homesickness. I didn't get homesick often, but when I did, I hurt.

It had been a confusing evening, one of extreme highs and frustrating lows. I didn't like feeling so confused and frightened. *Frightened? Why should I suddenly feel afraid?* I didn't know, I just was. I picked up the Bible on the medicine stand—Mama's Bible. Settling once again into the unyielding wooden chair, I opened the pages, searching for a place to begin reading.

"Please read aloud," Enrico said.

I glanced over at my patient in surprise. "I thought you were asleep."

"No, not yet. I used to read the Bible to my mother. She couldn't read, never went to school. My little sister Lena reads my letters to her now."

"What would you like to hear?"

He answered without hesitation. "Psalm 91. I used to repeat the chapter from memory in the trenches during German attacks." He talked as I searched for the chapter. "I'd close my eyes, cover my ears, and try to imagine myself safe at home reading the words to Mama." He snuggled down under his covers like a little boy.

"Here we are, Psalm 91." I smoothed the pages. " 'He that dwelleth in the secret place of the most High shall abide under the shadow of the Almighty. I will say of the Lord—' " I read on, absorbed in the poetry of the passage. I'd forgotten how truly beautiful the lyrical passages of the psalms were. It had been but a few weeks since I had decided to give religion another try. This time I would take it slowly, analyze every belief—no emotional outbursts or dramatic conversions for me. It would be a religion of the head—logical, practical, reasoned.

As a child, I had believed what my parents believed. But as I grew older and saw the horrors of war, the unfairness of life, as I listened to and read the words of prominent philosophers of the times, including a certain young idealist named Thad, I began to doubt all those tales of a loving God. I began to question the miracles and sacrifice of a Man named Jesus Christ. And I looked skeptically at the promise of living forever in some perfect land, a land without pain, disappointments, regrets.

At last, I reached the end of the chapter. " '—and shew him my salvation.' " I sighed and closed the book. *Lord, I admit that even now, I have my doubts about You. I don't want to, but I still do. Help me. Help me to see. Help me to know for certain.*

I stood up and stared wearily out the window. A sudden movement outside caught my eye. A man was running along the side of the building. As he passed the window, he turned toward me. We stared at one another in surprise. *Valery?* He stumbled, caught himself, then disappeared into the clump of fir trees behind the hospital. *Where would he be going at this hour of the morning?*

Knowing that the path he took dead-ended at the gorge, I watched for the chauffeur to return. When he didn't, I grew more curious. Ten minutes passed, fifteen, twenty. I felt a tap on my shoulder and turned.

"Hi, I'm here to replace you." Nurse Evelina yawned. "You can go now. Your shift is over."

Thanking her, I collected my belongings and tiptoed from the ward. Overwhelmed by my need for sleep, I lost interest in the chauffeur's bizarre behavior.

It wasn't until I felt the cold metal doorknob of the nurses' entrance beneath my fingers that I remembered I had no place to sleep. My stepsister occupied my bed. *Wonderful! Now what do you expect to do?* I groaned. I hadn't thought far enough ahead to realize Phoebe would still be asleep when I got off duty in the hospital. I cast about for ideas of where I could sleep until my bed was available. *On a chaise lounge on the veranda?* I shivered and hugged myself against the damp morning air.

From where I stood, I could see the rear bumper of the Rolls-Royce. An image of its broad brown leather rear seat filled my mind. I ran to the parked car and climbed inside. Finding a green plaid woolen blanket folded in the back seat, I wrapped it around me and fell asleep.

A Portent of Danger

Down the center of the road, Mimi and the children marched straight toward me, singing "Turkey in the Straw." Sarge followed, rolling the upright piano with one hand and accompanying them with the other. Behind me, I heard the uneven rumble of an approaching vehicle. I whirled about to see a green Peugeot racing toward me. I shouted and waved to the children, "Get out of the way!"

They laughed, waved back, and continued marching on their collision course with the speeding automobile.

"Look," I screamed, "watch out for the car. Get out of the way!"

They laughed but maintained rank. I whirled about again and charged the descending automobile. Shouting and waving my hands frantically at the driver, I begged him to stop. He honked his "ooga" horn, but instead of braking, he accelerated toward me.

My brain said, "*Jump, CeeCee. Jump to safety,*" but my feet refused to move. So I braced myself for the impact. But the driver swerved around me and aimed his vehicle directly at the children.

"No! No!" I screamed, crying and running toward what would soon be the site of a terrible tragedy.

"No! No! No!" I felt someone grab me by my shoulder and shake me.

"What do you think you're doing? You don't belong in here!"

I started at the gruff voice and cried out in terror. I opened my eyes, but my unfamiliar surroundings were a blurry haze.

"Where—where am I?"

I heard a second shout—this one Jamie's voice. "Hey, what do you think you're doing? Unhand my sister!"

I pressed my hand against my forehead. Nothing was making sense.

The gruff voice shouted in my face, "What are you doing in my car?"

My eyes snapped open. I didn't recognize the stranger, who continued to shout at me. "I said, What are you doing, snooping around in my automobile?"

My sleep-fogged eyes cleared, and I saw Nikolai's infuriated face. He seemed angry enough to drag me from the car by my collar. If I'd been a male, I think he might have.

"I-I-I'm not snooping. I was sleeping."

Suddenly Nikolai shot into the air in front of my eyes. His mouth flew open, his face paled, and his eyes bugged. Jamie held the boy by the collar, dangling him six inches from the ground. "Don't you ever put your hands on my sister that way or speak to her in such a manner again! Do I make myself clear?"

Nikolai nodded, angry tears filling his eyes. He gulped and gurgled, "Yes."

"Sir! That's yes, sir! Do you understand?" I'd never before seen Jamie angry at anyone. I stared, uncertain what might follow.

"Yes, sir," the boy gasped, his coat collar cutting off his oxygen supply.

Realizing the gravity of the boy's condition, Jamie dropped him to his feet. "Explain yourself, young man!"

"I came out of the hospital to find your sister snooping in our automobile." A petulant whine filled his voice.

I clicked my tongue in disgust. "Look, I'm sorry. I was napping in your precious car, that's all. Your sister is still sleeping in my bed, if you remember. I worked all night."

"Oh, well," he complained, "you should have asked first. This is a very expensive automobile."

"Be reasonable!" Jamie snapped. "Did you want her to waken you to beg your permission?"

"Yeah, well, uh, I guess not." The boy stuffed his hands into his coat pockets, his pout darkening.

Jamie took a deep, uneven breath. "If you're hungry, the kitchen is open now." I knew his anger hadn't cooled.

I folded the blanket and placed it beside me on the seat; then Jamie helped me from the car. Nikolai eyed us both with distrust. In spite of his attitude, I felt a little sorry for the boy. His bravado was the only thing that stood between him and a very difficult world. Hoping to ease his discomfort, I said, "The cook makes a delicious porridge to satisfy the appetites of the Americans here who are in the habit of eating larger breakfasts."

"Ameri—" Nikolai muttered derisively. One glance at Jamie, and he swallowed the rest of the word and followed us into the dining hall. He remained silent throughout the meal, picking apart a croissant and inspecting each piece before eating it.

Jamie eyed the boy with disdain and started to say something, but I silenced him by placing my hand on his. "It's not worth it."

"So, where's your chauffeur this morning?" Jamie asked a little later.

"Still sleeping," Nikolai mumbled.

"Afraid not." Jamie shook his head. "He got up in the middle of the night and went out—I figured to the outhouse—but he never returned. I was looking for him when I found the two of you."

I shot a worried glance at Jamie. "I saw the man walk past the hospital window when it was barely dawn. When he saw me, he ran into the woods."

"What? Why didn't you tell me? This is terrible!" Nikolai leapt to his feet and dashed out of the building. Jamie and I looked at one another and shrugged. Slowly my brother rose to his feet and straightened.

"I suppose I'd better go find out what this is all about."

"Wait." I took a last gulp of milk and jumped up from the table. "Let me go with you."

We strode to the Rolls-Royce to find Nikolai frantically unbolting the rear seat from the floor. The blanket I'd so carefully folded lay in the dust on the road.

"It's gone! It's gone! He stole the diamond tiara and the golden urn!" Wild eyed and close to tears, Nikolai whirled about and shriveled down into the seat, his arrogance replaced by fear. He stared, ashen-faced, at the convertible's closed canvas roof. "He stole my mother's diamond tiara and the urn."

Poor kid, in a foreign land, no parents upon which to rely. I knew he wouldn't appreciate my sympathy, but I felt compelled to try to make him feel better. "Maybe he went into town for something and will be back later this morning."

"We could go look for him if you'd like," Jamie suggested, ambling toward the driver's seat.

Nikolai shook his head slowly but did not look at us. "No, he's gone. He won't be back. Now, what are we supposed to do?"

"Hey." Jamie held up a folded piece of paper. "This was stuffed into the door handle. Here, it's addressed to you." He handed Nikolai the note.

Nikolai snatched the paper from Jamie's hands and read it silently, shaking his head and muttering, "I can't believe this. I can't believe this. I can't believe Valery would do this."

Without a word, Nikolai thrust the note into Jamie's hands, climbed out of the car, and ran toward the doctors' quarters. As an afterthought, he turned and called, "Don't tell my sister yet about Valery's defection."

Jamie opened the note and read it aloud. "Your Lordship, by the time you read this, I will be on my way to a new life. I've been planning this for a long time. Consider the tiara and the urn payment for the services my family faithfully rendered to yours for four generations." Jamie paused and studied the paper for a few seconds.

"Is that all it says?"

He shook his head. "I considered taking the Rolls as payment but decided against it. A fancy car like that would be too easily traced. So, good luck, and please forgive me. As aristocrats go, you're no better or worse than any other, but the old guard is gone; the old traditions are dead. And I simply do not want to risk my life trying to protect yours, not when I can finally breathe the air of freedom. Sincerely, Valery Kerchenko."

A postscript followed. "One last warning. I wouldn't linger too long in France, if I were you. They can't be more than two days behind you."

I peered over my brother's shoulder. "What is that supposed to mean? Who are 'they'?"

"And what does he mean about risking his life?" Jamie scratched his head. I shrugged in response.

"That feisty young pup has a lot of explaining to do." Jamie started to follow Nikolai, but I grabbed his wrist to stop him.

"Give the boy a few minutes to absorb what has happened before you interrogate him."

"I suppose waiting a few minutes won't hurt."

"Yeah, if only he were a little less arrogant, a little easier to get along with." I groaned.

Jamie gave a derisive laugh. "I guess I wasn't too easy to get along with for a while after my mother died either. I know I gave Mama a rough time. And when our dad died in the mining explosion, I was unhappy for a long time."

"So, what happens next, after you get your answers?"

"It's according to what the mystery is all about. But one way or another, I guess Phoebe and Nikolai are our problem now. One of the first things I'll do this morning is go into town and send a cable to your father and see what he suggests."

"My father?" I folded my arms across my chest. "Why don't you ever call Cyrus 'Dad'?"

Jamie frowned. "I don't know—just never got into the habit, I guess. When I came east to the boys' school, Grandma McCall did a lot to keep our real father's memory alive for me. It was easier with Chloe. I don't even remember my real mother's face except in Aunt Drucilla's family photo albums." He paused and stared into the deep green forest skirting the hospital grounds. "Chloe has always been there for me."

"That's how I feel about Cyrus." I thought of the kind, gentle man with the bushy mustache and the deep bass laughter whom I called Daddy, and suddenly, I missed him terribly. I tried to imagine what it would be like calling someone other than he "Father." I couldn't. "Isn't life strange, the way paths cross? Mama runs away from her home in Pennsylvania, meets your mother on the train west, cares for you after your mother dies of consumption, marries our father, who dies in a Colorado mining accident, then marries Cyrus, and they have Rusty. Strange family at best. And, now, from out of nowhere, these two enter the family circle." I cast a sheepish look at my big brother. "I'm not sure I like it."

"We'll adjust. That's what families are all about." Jamie laughed. "In a few months, Auriel will be a member of our family too. Will you resent her?"

"No!" I was horrified that he'd suggest such a thing. "She is already family, as far as I'm concerned. It's those two!" I hugged myself and thrust my lower lip into a pout. The thought of having my father give Phoebe a hug or a kiss on the forehead disturbed me more than I liked admitting. I liked being his one and only darling daughter. "Nothing will ever be the same again."

"That's true," he mused, throwing his arm around my shoulders. "But that's life, I'm afraid."

"I guess we need to give them a fighting chance. We did get off to a bad start with them."

He tapped the end of my nose gently. "And love always makes room for more."

"I suppose." I leaned my head against his shoulder as he led me toward the nurses' dormitory.

"You'll adjust to the new situation, you'll see."

I pursed my lips. "And this is certainly a new situation."

He opened the door to the nurses' quarters for me. "Look, if I'm gone when you waken, don't be alarmed. I'm going to take Nikolai to town with me when I cable the folks." His face sobered. "I'm determined to get him off by himself. I've got to get to bottom of this."

"Good." I stepped inside the threshold and paused. "Thanks for listening—and for not scolding me for not being more gracious to them. You'll let me know what you find out?"

"Absolutely. As soon as I know something, you'll know it too. In the meantime, get some sleep. Use Auriel's bed if you like. She's working the day shift this week."

"Thanks." I gave a little wave before stumbling inside the building. *I'm too tired to worry any longer; I'll piece it all together later.* As I passed my bed and the sleeping Phoebe, I added, *And I'll worry about what to do with you and your nasty brother later too. My nasty brother! Eeuuww! What an awful thought.*

My second attempt at sleep was more rewarding. I didn't hear Phoebe get up, dress, and leave the dormitory. It was late morning when I found her sitting in a rocker on the hospital veranda, surrounded by an admiring horde of male patients. When she saw me round the corner of the veranda, she smiled shyly. "Nikolai and your brother went to town. They said they'd be back as soon as possible. I came out and sat down—" She rolled her eyes prettily toward the men, "—to get a little sunshine, and these gentlemen joined me to keep me company."

I eyed the men with the authority of an older sister. "I hope you men realize you are in the presence of a lady."

"Hey!" Marcus, a Canadian flier who'd lost an arm in a plane crash, retorted. "We were perfect gentlemen. Ask her. Just like we are with you, I might add."

The other men echoed his sentiments.

I chuckled, knowing they'd misunderstood my statement. "No, that's not what I meant. She's a real lady—you know, like lords and ladies, dukes and duchesses, barons and baronesses."

"Oh, I thought—" Marcus reddened. "Sorry, Miss CeeCee."

I winked. "No offense taken. But I did come to take her away from you."

"Noooo!" the men complained in unison.

"That is, if you want to go, Phoebe," I added. "I've arranged to take a group of the younger children for a short walk to the springs. It's such a lovely day, I wondered if you'd like to come along."

Her eyes brightened. "I'd like that very much, but I'm afraid these shoes aren't very good for walking."

"Neither is that silk dress. One snag from a burr, and it's over. Better put on something cotton."

Phoebe glanced down at her silk sheath and frowned. "I don't think I have any cotton dresses with me."

I thought about my faded brown dress of undetermined fiber and age hanging in my locker. "Why don't you go into the dormitory and put on one of mine? Try on my extra pair of walking shoes too. I wouldn't want you to scuff up those calfskin pumps."

She looked at me in surprise. "Why, thank you, Chloe."

"CeeCee. Everyone calls me CeeCee."

"Thank you, CeeCee." Phoebe stood up, said her goodbyes to the men, then hurried to change while I gathered the children together for the walk. I invited Mimi to come along to help supervise. After my dream last night, I didn't intend to take any chances with speeding Peugeots and singing children.

The children were lined up, each with his or her walking partner, when my stepsister appeared. She was wearing my new green dirndl. *The dirndl is my birthday present. I want to be the first to wear it.* Mimi was the first to speak. "Miss CeeCee, she's wearing your dirndl!"

The children stared at the dress, then at me. Phoebe walked toward us, smiling broadly. Struggling to maintain a smile on my face, I leaned toward Mimi and whispered, "It's OK. She must have gotten mixed up. I'll talk to her."

Mimi nodded her head emphatically.

"I see you're ready to go," I called. "Did I misspeak when I said my brown dress was hanging in the locker? It must still be in my pile of ironing."

"No, it was there," Phoebe replied, adjusting the gathers at the neck of the bodice. "I just couldn't bring myself to wear such a faded garment. I decided I could make do with this one. I hope you don't mind."

Behind me, I heard Mimi gasp, "Make do?"

I frowned at the young girl and received an entire row of frowns from her and the other children. Taking a deep breath, I faced Phoebe. "Phoebe, I'd like you to meet the children. They're the ones I must thank for the lovely dress you're borrowing from me. They purchased it for me for my birthday—yesterday."

"Yesterday?" A quizzical look came over Phoebe's face. "Oh, then, this is a new garment?" She uttered a sigh of relief. "I'm so glad. I didn't relish the idea of wearing clothing worn by another, no offense, of course. But the idea of putting garments next to one's person after another has worn them is repulsive at the very least—it makes one shudder."

I closed my eyes and shook my head. *She doesn't have any idea—Can't she see?* Every child behind me wore faded, patched hand-me-downs and was happy for them.

"I didn't realize my father was in such dire straits as to not insist that his stepdaughter dress more representatively of his position. He is with the American Embassy, isn't he?" She asked her question as if she thought Cyrus had lied to her and her mother.

"My father does nicely by us, I assure you." I glowered and turned toward the entrance of the hospital grounds. "Let's go, shall we?" *It will be useless introducing the children to her individually; she doesn't care about anyone but herself!* I'd never before been embarrassed to introduce a member of my family. I set off at a determined pace.

"Hey, Miss CeeCee," a surprised Mimi called, "the littler ones can't keep up."

I slowed, giving them time to regroup. Phoebe fell in beside me. "Did I do something to upset you?"

If you need to ask, you wouldn't understand if I told you. I ignored her question and called to Mimi. "Bring up the rear of the line so we don't lose anyone." I shouted as an afterthought, "Watch for automobiles."

"Look, I really am sorry if I offended you. I didn't mean—"

I raised my hands to silence her, staring straight ahead as I marched beyond the hospital's wrought-iron fence. "Let's forget it, shall we? And have a nice walk."

I was relieved when she remained silent for a few minutes. "You don't like me, do you?"

"How can I like or dislike you? I don't know you."

"My brother and I must have made a terrible first impression last evening, and, well, I'm sorry. We've never been out on our own before. We've lived a very sheltered existence up until our mother died."

I tried to steel my sympathies against her words. I wanted to stay angry.

She continued. "Please, forgive me. Ever since our father promised to take us in, I've been so looking forward to having my very own sister."

Oh, did you have to? Phoebe's plea put a dent in my hardening heart. I remembered how thrilled I felt at finally having a sister when I learned of Jamie's engagement to Auriel. "Starting over would probably be a good idea."

"Do you mean it?" Genuine eagerness sparkled in her eyes.

I took a deep breath. The cobalt blue sky, the brilliant sunlight glistening on the snow-topped mountain peak, the deep green of the forest, and the alpine spring flowers—I knew I couldn't stay angry on such a glorious day. "Yes, I mean it."

"Thank you."

Phoebe did her best to win over the children during the rest of the walk. While we rested beside the springs, she taught a group of little girls how to make flower chains. "Where I grew up, the flowers will not be out for another month," she told the children.

By the time we left the springs, only Mimi refused to warm up to Phoebe. To soften Mimi's mood, I suggested she set the pace on the way home, and I'd follow at the back of the group. The children set off singing "Old MacDonald," one of their favorites. As we rounded the last curve in the road before the hospital property lines started, Phoebe grabbed my arm. "CeeCee, did you see him?"

"Huh? Who?"

"Sh. Over there behind that tall fir tree." She leaned close to me and pointed her finger.

"Phoebe, which fir? There is an entire forest of firs. And whom am I supposed to see?"

"I don't know his name, but I recognize his face. He's one of the people chasing us," she hissed, her face pale.

"Chasing? Who's chasing you?"

"We told you. The Bolsheviks want to murder all of Russia's nobility. Nikolai is the nineteenth in the royal line."

"What?" My eyes widened. "You mean, to be czar?"

"I'm not in the blood line, but I am still on their list, since I'm family. If they see me, they might try to kidnap me."

I stared at her in disbelief. "Aren't you exaggerating a little?" I still hadn't seen the phantom Bolshevik.

She shook her head vigorously. I studied her ashen face for a moment. "You really are frightened, aren't you?"

She nodded. "Isn't there a back way onto the hospital grounds?"

"No. Not from here, anyway." I inhaled deeply, then exhaled slowly, trying to think logically about our situation. "The best thing we can do now is act as if everything is normal. First, you're not dressed in your usual garb, so he might not recognize you. Second, if necessary, we're close enough to the hospital to scream and run if he tries anything."

The children had switched to "Frére Jacques."

Phoebe cleared her throat and swallowed hard. "You're probably right. But how did they find us so fast?"

"That's easy. Your chauffeur led them right to you, in that Rolls of yours. It doesn't blend in with its surroundings very well."

She groaned. "My knees are shaking so badly, I can't stand up."

"Oh yes, you can, and you will!" I grabbed her arm, resisting the urge to glance toward the clump of trees where she'd seen the stalker disappear. "Start singing with the children!" I opened my mouth and bellowed along with the children nearest us. Then I hissed, "Sing, or I promise I'll—I'll pinch your arm."

Phoebe stared at me in surprise. "You'll do what?"

"Pinch your arm—and I mean it. Now, smile and sing, do you hear?"

She nodded, her green eyes round and terrified. I laughed to myself. *I think she's more afraid of me than of the Bolshevik at this point.*

Swinging my free arm, I threw my head back and sang us into the hospital compound. Once inside the gates, Phoebe tried to free her arm from my hand, but I refused to let go. "Not yet," I warned. "He could still be watching."

A group of ambulatory patients waved from the veranda, where they were playing cards. The dinner bell rang, and the children ran ahead to the dining hall. Phoebe stumbled beside me as I sauntered over to the veranda. "So who's won the most buttons today?"

Lucky, a young man from Kentucky, snorted, "Not me, I'm afraid. But—" I couldn't miss the twinkle in his eye, "—if I had two pretty girls leaning over my shoulders, my luck would return."

"It takes more than luck, my friend," Sarge interrupted, gathering the booty from the center of the table, "to defeat these gifted hands." He wriggled his fingers in the air, then glanced at me. "We still have a date tonight, don't we? A little Joplin, perhaps?"

"Or Debussy?"

"Maybe Chopin."

"It's a deal."

"So, did you have a nice walk?" Marcus inquired.

"Hey, you're the one with the zippy convertible I saw Doc driving this morning." Oren, a young Belgian soldier, winked at Phoebe. "That's one incredible auto car."

"Thank you," Phoebe mewed. "It was my father's before the war."

"You mean the one Doc McCall was driving this afternoon?" Lucky squinted over at his friend.

"There it is now. Old Doc's handling it like a professional." Marcus pointed toward the entrance to the hospital grounds. The tone in his voice expressed the awe evident on each of the men's faces. "That is an incredible machine."

The Rolls-Royce, its camel brown convertible top up and the side windows battened in place, circled the yard slowly, then stopped near the wrought-iron entry to the hospital.

"Oh no!" I ran to the driver's side of the car. "Jamie." I opened his door. "You can't park the Rolls here. Phoebe spotted one of the Bolsheviks watching the grounds today. We need to hide the car in the barn or somewhere."

Jamie pursed his lips as he glanced toward Nikolai. "So they're here already. Figured they were. Good."

"Good?" I couldn't believe his reaction. "Phoebe says they're killers. If they see the car, then they'll know where to find them."

"Precisely. That's exactly what we want." Jamie grinned at Nikolai. To my amazement, Nikolai grinned back. The two climbed out of the car and closed the doors. Then Jamie threw his arm around my shoulders and started walking toward the hospital. Phoebe and Nikolai fell into step beside Jamie.

"I don't understand," I protested.

"You will. I promise. I'll tell you all about it later. By the way, the folks send you their love and are looking forward to seeing you soon."

"Me? You mean us, don't you?"

"You."

"What?" I abruptly stopped walking.

"Just keep smiling and walking, Cricket. We want our phantom friends to see us behaving normally, without suspicion." He spoke through his toothy grin.

"But—"

He jerked me closer to him and forced me to keep walking. "Just do as I say, sister dear." His voice hardened. "I've learned that these guys take their orders very seriously. We saw two in town—one watching the railway station and the other, the police station."

"You still didn't tell me why you said 'you' in the singular before."

He threw his head back and laughed. "You never forget, do you? You're an English bulldog with a bone."

"You're doing it again."

"All right." He leaned closer to me. "Cyrus says we have to get the two of them to the American Embassy in Paris as soon as possible. The quickest way to do that would be by train, if the goons weren't watching the station, the hospital, and the main street in town. But since they are, Nikolai and I have come up with an alternate plan."

As we approached the veranda, Marcus called out to Jamie, "Dr. McCall, how does the Rolls drive?"

"Like a magic carpet."

"Better than an American Packard?" Lucky asked.

Jamie laughed. "Now, Lucky, can any vehicle measure up to the 'silent boss of the road'?"

The soldiers from England and Europe booed while the Americans cheered.

"Aw, come on, Yank," Marcus argued. "Nothing compares to the British-made Rolls-Royce. You know that."

A French soldier added, "It took an army of French Renault cabbies to turn the Germans back from Paris, if you remember right."

Lucky snorted. "Renault! Make sense—it took any army of Renaults. If you'd had a Packard, you would have needed to send only one to do the job."

"Boo!" We entered the hospital, leaving the men to argue cars.

"Listen, you three go upstairs to my office, where we can be alone. I'll go find Auriel. We'll need her help in this scheme."

"What scheme?" I stomped my foot.

Jamie laughed. "Some things never change." He turned and left.

"The office is at the top of the stairs." I strode toward the staircase.

Phoebe tugged at her brother's sleeve as we climbed the stairs. "What is going on?"

Nikolai stuffed his hands deep into his pants pockets. "Doc will tell you in a minute. I'm still not sure I agree with him, though."

I glanced back over my shoulder. "Did you find Valery or the stuff he stole?"

"Are you serious?" the boy snarled. "He's probably halfway across the English Channel by now. I would be if I were he."

Phoebe's eyes lighted up. "Do you think he went to England?"

"Tsk! Of course not!" Nikolai gestured peevishly. "It was just a figure of speech! He could be on his way to Monte Carlo or Lisbon, for all I know."

When we reached the door to the doctors' office, Nikolai held it open, letting his sister and me pass through before him. "We'll never see the tiara or the urn again."

Nikolai leaned against the wall while Phoebe and I sat down in the two straight-back wooden chairs in front of the desk.

"When you saw the two men in town, did they see you?" Phoebe wrung her hands nervously.

"Of course. Everybody saw us driving that vehicle. No one could have missed it." His face revealed utter misery. "You wouldn't believe the number of people who stopped Doc to admire the dumb thing. Why couldn't Father have bought something a little less flamboyant?"

"Well," Phoebe huffed, "it's not as if he knew he was going to die or that we'd be running and hiding from these anarchists!"

"Sorry," Nikolai muttered.

"I wish Jamie would hurry back!" I jumped to my feet and paced to the window. "Can't you tell us about this great plan of yours?"

"It's not my plan!" he protested.

The office door swung open. None of us had heard Jamie and Auriel come up the stairs. Auriel sat down next to Phoebe. Jamie offered me his chair behind the desk. I refused. "I'd rather stand, thank you."

He nodded and sat down. "Where do I begin?"

"Try the beginning?" I couldn't hide the edge in my voice.

"Relax, Cricket," Jamie soothed. "Are you sure you don't want to sit down?"

I shook my head impatiently.

"Because the Rolls is so visible, we had to concoct a plan to spirit the three of you out of here without those goons knowing when and where you've gone."

"You keep saying 'you' and looking at me." I frowned. "I don't like the sound of that."

"Phoebe and Nikolai can't travel alone. They don't know the country, and neither of them can drive an automobile."

"I could learn," Nikolai interjected.

"We've already discussed this, Nikolai. You don't have time. Besides, the Bolsheviks are looking for a boy and a young woman. You'd be easily identified."

"What about you, Jamie? You speak French, drive a car, and know the country a lot better than I," I reminded.

"The plan is very simple, really." He sighed, his patience growing thin. "We're going to pull a switch on our mysterious guests. And, Cricket—" Jamie turned to me. "—you will make a cute farm boy."

"A farm boy?"

Jamie nodded. "That's right. A farm boy."

"You are joking, aren't you?"

He shook his head and grinned.

"I can't dress up like a—"

"And why not? Your mother did, to run away from Granddaddy Spencer."

"That was different. She was—" I knew I was defeated. His plan made sense; he couldn't leave the hospital for any length of time. With Dr. Paul Best returning to the States due to his war injuries, Jamie and Dr. Bietz had been left to operate the hospital alone until a replacement could be found.

"If I could go with you, I would." Jamie took my hands in his and whispered, "Cyrus was really anxious over Phoebe and Nikolai's safety. They've been so mollycoddled all their lives that they have no survival skills."

"But I don't think I—"

"Oh, Cricket, you're strong. I've seen you in action. You're going to do just fine."

"I'm not so sure about that."

"As Cyrus always says, 'Those who are strong must always look after the weak.' " Jamie massaged the back of my hands with his thumbs. "That's one reason I stayed here after the Armistice. Someone has to care."

"But I don't want to go back to London yet. I still have too much to do here. I'm making real progress finding little Antoine's grandparents. Just last Tuesday I heard from the Red Cross in Reims, and they say—"

Jamie touched his finger to my lips. "You knew you'd have to leave sooner or later."

My eyes misted. "I know, but not now, not like this. I'm scared."

He drew me into his arms, patting the back of my head as I rested against his chest. "You know you'll have all our prayers with you." His strong, steady heartbeat reassured me more than his words. "Listen, we've got a lot to do before you leave tomorrow morning—such as teach you how to drive Dr. Bietz's Renault. And you still don't know the plan. So, what do you say we get busy?"

"Will I get to say goodbye to the children?"

Jamie shook his head. "We can't risk it, I'm afraid."

Seeing the pain in my eyes, Auriel placed her hand on my arm. "May I make a suggestion? When you get back to London, write to each of them. They'll love getting your letters."

Jamie turned toward Phoebe and Nikolai. "Why don't you two separate your clothes into two piles, absolute necessities and things you can live through the next few days without. We'll ship them to London for you." He shook his finger in their faces. "Remember, no fancy dress clothes. You're traveling in disguise. Nurse Bouchard will outfit you while I teach CeeCee how to drive a Renault."

Flee With the Dawn

In the darkness, I stumbled from my bed. Someone was moving about at the far end of the dormitory. *It must be Nurse Bouchard,* I thought. *What am I doing up at this hour anyway?* Then I remembered the plan and braced myself against the temptation to crawl back under the blankets.

Hearing my stepsister's gentle snore, I reached across the narrow aisle and shook her shoulder. "Phoebe," I whispered, "it's time to get up. Come on; wake up."

She groaned and rolled over to face the wall.

"No, you can't go back to sleep," I insisted. "We've got to get ready to leave for the train station."

She sat up slowly, the moonlight from the window behind her outlining her form.

"Don't go back to sleep, you hear?"

She stretched, yawned, and mumbled something in Russian.

Grabbing my shower supplies from the top of my bureau, I hurried to the shower room. *Your last cold shower for a while,* I thought. Somehow, I wasn't as thrilled as I thought I'd be. *But, then, it isn't the cold showers you mind leaving, is it?* I took my shower and washed my hair. Before returning to the dormitory, I sat down in a dry corner of the shower room and opened my Bible to Psalm 139.

Today, I really need this. Even though I didn't have much time, I wanted to take the time to read something from His Word. *If ever I needed divine help, it's today.*

The words underlined by my mother's own pen spoke to me

as if she were right in the room. "Whither shall I go from thy spirit? or whither shall I flee from thy presence? If I ascend up into heaven, thou art there: if I make my bed in hell, behold, thou art there. If I take the wings of the morning, and dwell in the uttermost parts of the sea; even there shall thy hand lead me, and thy right hand shall hold me." A shiver skittered up and down my spine as I read verses 9 and 10. What gorgeous poetry! *Where will the day's journey end? In London or Paris or—* My imagination ran wild with the possibilities. I rubbed the goose bumps on my arms, but the quaking inside didn't vanish as easily.

Dear God, if ever I've needed You in the past, I need You now. I'm frightened. I need You to slay the wicked as You promised. I took a deep breath and closed the Bible. As I rose to my feet, an envelope fell to the floor.

Thad. I looked down and smiled at the familiar handwriting. *It would be so nice to—Why not? Why didn't I think of it sooner?* As I picked up the envelope and touched it to my lips, an idea germinated in the back of my mind. *Once I drop off Nikolai and Phoebe at the American Embassy, I'll be free to come and go as I please. No one's chasing me.* The thought of seeing and talking with Thad pleased me more than I would have imagined.

The possibility teased my imagination as I hurried to the dormitory to dress. After buttoning the patched cotton work shirt Nurse Bouchard had rescued for me from the rag bag, I hauled on a pair of faded blue bib overalls. *This is insane. We'll never get away with this.* The bulky work socks and heavy shoes felt leaden and cumbersome. *I'm going to have blisters before we even board the train.*

Quickly I stuffed my nightgown into the lightweight military rucksack Jamie had given me the night before. Groping for my brush and hairpins, I dropped them into the brown cap Nurse Bouchard had found for me to wear, then hurried to the line of sinks in the shower room.

My hair was still damp when I brushed it back into a tail. *Good! That will help it stay in place better.* My nightmare was having my long red mane tumble out of the cap at the worst possible moment and give us away to our pursuers. I braided the tail, wound it on top of my head, then pinned it tightly in place. After pulling the cap down over my hair, I examined the results in the wall mirror over the sinks. *This is never going to work! I can't believe I agreed to this—as if I had a choice!*

In the dim gas light, I had to admit Nurse Bouchard was right. Between the oversized shirt, the bib overalls, and my angular figure, I could pass for a boy of fourteen or fifteen. I smiled to myself. *Mama, when you hear about this, you're not going to believe it.*

I thought about her fleeing her home at the age of sixteen, dressed in her younger brother's clothing. *She must have been terrified—or desperate.* I hugged myself to quell the butterflies in my stomach. *I think I know how you felt, Mama.*

On the way back to the sleeping room, I ran into a partially awakened Phoebe heading toward the showers. She gave a yelp; her eyes widened with fright.

"Sh, it's me, CeeCee."

"Oh." She grasped the front of her robe. "I thought you were one of the Bolsheviks coming to get me."

"Well? What do you think?" I whirled around in a circle.

She studied me for so long that I squirmed under her gaze.

"You look fine. But you need to move more like a man. You know, clump, clump, clump."

"Oh," I wailed. "I'll never pull this off."

"Don't worry." She giggled. "Just think like a man, and this plan just might work."

"Think like a man." And just how does a man think?

She started toward the shower room.

"Wait." I caught her arm. "I don't care what Jamie says. Take along at least one dressy outfit. After all, we will be in Paris, you know, the City of Lights and love and—"

Phoebe looked doubtful. "I don't know. You think so?"

"Once we're on the train, we'll be safe. Besides, I have a friend who lives there. Who knows what can happen?"

Her eyes brightened. "Paris. I've always wanted to visit Paris again. Have you told her you're coming?"

I giggled. "My friend's a he. His name is Thaddeus. And, no, it will be a total surprise."

"That would be so much fun. My mother and the count fell in love in Paris, you—"

At the sound of someone walking past the dormitory, we stopped talking and grasped each other's hands for a second, her eyes revealing the same fear I felt.

"See you later," she whispered, scurrying into the showers. Back in the dormitory, I placed my hairbrush in the faded carpetbag Nurse Bouchard had found for me. Even my well-worn luggage would fit the character I would play. I slid the Bible, with Thad's letter in the back cover, into the case and clasped the case shut. *There!* I was pleased with myself. *A rucksack and a carpetbag. That should please you, Dr. James McCall. And I still will be allowed to preserve a few vestiges of my femininity.*

But I was wrong. The two cases didn't please my brother. When I met him in the dining room a few minutes later, luggage in hand, he groaned. "I warned you to travel light! If you have to carry those two pieces very far, you'll wish you'd listened."

"They're not very—" I started to protest but was saved the necessity of defending myself by the arrival of Nikolai, who was wearing an expensive Edwardian wool suit and a felt bowler hat. He was lugging two large portmanteaus and dragging a small steamer trunk.

"The trunk goes with us in the Rolls." Jamie eyed the boy's garments critically. "And the cases look too expensive. You'll need to empty the contents into the duffel bag I left at the foot of your bed this morning."

Nikolai protested weakly but finally conceded that a poor French farmer would not be carrying Italian leather luggage.

"Did you try on the work clothes that you'll change into later?"

Nikolai squirmed. "I really don't think I—"

Jamie aimed his finger at Nikolai's nose. "That's just it, you don't think. You will do as I say. Now, you high-tail it back to the physicians' quarters and get those clothes. When you change, you'll need to do it quickly to keep up the act." Jamie turned toward me. "CeeCee, don't let him out of this room if he doesn't cooperate. And, Nikolai, understand, you will do whatever

CeeCee tells you to do on this trip, no questions asked. Is that clear?"

When Nikolai started to protest, Jamie loomed threateningly over the boy. I'd never before seen this side of my big brother—so intimidating. I felt a little sorry for the boy, though I suspected that later I would thank Jamie for his bullying. Jamie stuffed his hands in the back pockets of his trousers, his legs spread aggressively, his neck lowered stubbornly. "If he gives you any trouble, CeeCee, let him fend for himself. Your task is to make sure you and Phoebe get through safely."

Knowing my brother, I knew he meant every word. The tension eased when Phoebe clattered into the room wearing a pink-flowered silk chiffon dress, pink calfskin shoes, and a large floppy hat adorned with roses made from dyed feathers. The whole effect made me laugh.

"I can see you have the right idea, Phoebe." Jamie grinned. "Now if you can act as well as you look, we'll make this scheme work."

The tattered carpetbag Nurse Bouchard gave Phoebe looked even more worn next to her fine array. "I think I have everything in here that I'll need until we reach London." She dropped the case on the table in front of Jamie. Her expression revealed eagerness and excitement, a contrast to Nikolai's petulant pout. She looked at her little brother. "What? What's wrong?"

Jamie narrowed his gaze. "Absolutely nothing. Isn't that right, Nikolai?"

"Yes, sir," he mumbled while grabbing his luggage and placing it on a table at the far end of the dining hall, before returning to the doctors' quarters. Jamie shook his head and walked across the cafeteria to the windows, staring out at the predawn darkness. I sat down at the nearest table and yawned, then laid my head in my arms. *If only I could catch a short nap.* When Nikolai returned, I lifted my head enough to see Phoebe rush to her brother. Together, they huddled over the table, whispering and glancing over their shoulders periodically.

Finally Auriel arrived. She waved when I glanced up, then hurried to Jamie's side. I lay my head back down and closed my eyes.

Suddenly Sarge and Nurse Bouchard burst into the dining room. His excitement and energy contrasted with her grave concern.

"Lucky's in place," Sarge announced, his eyes dancing. "He and a few of the patients have set up quite a sophisticated relay intelligence system. They've been keeping watch over our intruder all night long." He tugged at the jacket to the chauffeur's uniform with his maimed hand. In spite of Valery's wider girth, the jacket pulled tightly across the military man's broad shoulders. "So, how do I look?" He saw the incredulous look in our eyes and shrugged. "Hey, the hat fits anyway. But I had to give up on the trousers. The waist was too wide, and the pant legs too short." He glanced down at his gray gabardine pants. "These will have to do. Everything's ready with the automobiles." Sarge looked at me, grinning. "And who's this ragtag young buck? A spy?"

"Be careful," I warned. "I'm this far from running back to the dormitory and changing into a skirt and blouse." I measured an inch with my thumb and forefinger.

"Hey!" He waved his hands defensively in the air. "I think you look terrific. Well, not terrific exactly; maybe the word is *convincing*."

"Thanks. I need all the encouragement I can get."

The worry in Nurse Bouchard's eyes softened at Sarge's ebullience. She walked over to me and put a hand on my shoulder. "Don't let this buffoon unnerve you, child. You'll do just fine, as long as you keep that hat in place."

"And walk like a man," Sarge interjected.

I stood up and placed my hands on my hips. "And show me, Mr. Smarty Britches, just how does a man walk?"

Sarge laughed and strode to the far end of the dining hall, then back again.

"You mean like this?" I exaggerated his swagger.

Jamie called to me across the room, "I think you need a little practice, Cricket."

Auriel poked my brother in the ribs. "Stop picking on her. I think she looks great. If you don't leave her alone, you'll have her spooked."

Sarge snorted. "One look at that gorgeous red hair of yours, and it will take more than baggy overalls and a pair of farm boots to fool the men of Paris."

My face reddened, and everyone laughed at my discomfort. Sarge shook his head, the smile fading. "Seriously, kid, I'm going to miss our concerts."

I nodded my head. "I will too."

"And don't worry." His voice softened. "I'll make sure the trunk containing your violin gets safely to London."

I cast him a look of gratitude. Only Sarge would know the trepidation I had experienced the evening before as I packed my precious violin in my steamer trunk and fastened the latches. I'd never before trusted my instrument to anyone.

Sarge cleared his throat. "I guess this is goodbye, dear friend. We're all going to miss you around here—the children especially."

"And I'll miss them too—and you. If you ever get to New York, you'd better come see me, you hear?"

He nodded and swallowed. "Who knows? I'm like the proverbial bad penny. I show up when everybody least expects it."

"You've been a good friend, Sarge. And just in case you didn't know it, I learned a lot from you." My eyes filled with tears as I stood on my tiptoes to kiss his cheek. "I'll never forget you."

"Enough is enough!" Jamie gestured toward the first rays of dawn coming through the dining-room windows. "It's time to get this show moving. OK, Sarge, grab those empty portmanteaus and CeeCee's trunk. I'll take the other two trunks. They'll go in the back seat of the Rolls with Phoebe. We want to make them visible."

Nikolai and Phoebe exchanged a look of concern when Jamie hoisted her trunk onto his shoulder. Jamie looked surprised at the weight. "I'll have to come back after the other one," he admitted. "All right, it's time for act one to begin. Play it up big."

Phoebe shuddered. "I don't think I can do this."

Jamie snarled, "Yes, you can, and you will. It's your only chance, remember? Now, give all the arrogance you can muster."

"You and your sister can certainly be bossy!" she said in dismay.

Jamie laughed. "Well, you're half right. CeeCee can be bossy, at least!"

"Me?" I punched his arm playfully.

He laughed again and headed toward the door. Phoebe took a deep breath and followed him outside while Sarge urged the reluctant Nikolai to follow. Nurse Bouchard remained behind while Auriel and I strode a few steps behind the entourage.

As Jamie and Phoebe rounded the corner of the veranda, Jamie called out in a voice louder than normal, "Are you sure these trunks will all fit into the back seat?"

Phoebe shrugged with all the style of a disinterested aristocrat. "Of course! They'll have to. I wouldn't think of living without even one little necessity." She flung her hand toward the vehicle and glanced at the pretend chauffeur, who'd already opened the back door of the vehicle and was depositing one of the trunks onto the seat. She turned to Jamie. "Just set those trunks anywhere. Our man will take care of everything."

Jamie set the trunk on the ground beside the car. "These are certainly heavy enough." He wiped his brow, glaring at Nikolai. The young boy stood silently, looking sullen and scared. I wanted to poke him to get him to do or say something.

Phoebe's delicate laughter filled the early-morning air. "I tried to convince you to leave the luggage for the chauffeur to carry. It's hardly your place to act as our servant, brother dear."

Jamie brushed aside the remark. "I really don't mind helping."

"Really! You Americans can be so egalitarian. Before you know it, we'll hear the United States has gone Communist."

Nikolai started at his sister's words and glanced over his shoulder toward the forest, where the interloper was hiding. Auriel intercepted his look and threw her arms around the boy's neck. "Oh, Nikolai, we are so glad you stopped to see us on your way to Paris. Give our love to the folks. And be sure to tell them that we'll see them next month."

He nodded stiffly but remained silent. Immediately Jamie strode over to them and pounded the young boy on the back. "That's right. We sure did enjoy getting acquainted with you two. When I get to London, you and I should play a little tennis at Father's club, don't you think?"

This time, Nikolai mumbled something I couldn't hear. Jamie stretched, then placed his arm on Nikolai's shoulder, urging him toward the hospital. "Well, if your chauffeur has everything tied down, I think you're ready to leave. Why don't you come back inside and grab a bite to eat before you go."

Jamie, Auriel, Phoebe, and Nikolai led the way back inside the building, with Nurse Bouchard and me following. Sarge stayed behind to buff the silver fixtures on the automobile with a chamois cloth he'd found under the front seat.

Once inside the dining room, Jamie led Nikolai into a room next to the dining hall to change clothing while Auriel donned Phoebe's clothing and Phoebe became a French milkmaid. I looked down at my strange get-up, then at Auriel's with envy. As she dropped the slippery silk dress over her head, the garment fit her slight figure as if it had been custom fitted for her. After I fastened the buttons at the back of the neckline, I helped her restyle her hair, then pin the wide-brimmed hat in place.

"By the way," I whispered, "I left your blue velvet-and-taffeta dress in your locker." I emphasized the word *your*. "It's yours, forever and ever." Before she could reply, I stepped back to take a look at her. "You look lovely, from your head to your— Uh-oh! The shoes."

She still wore her sturdy nurse's shoes and gray cotton hose. Quickly, Auriel put on Phoebe's silk hosiery and French-heeled pumps. With Auriel's look complete, I restyled Phoebe's heavy brown hair into two braids, one coiled over each ear like earmuffs. "I feel like a scullery maid," she confided, her voice filled with distress.

"That's good!" I giggled. "You look like one."

Phoebe clamped her lips into a thin, disapproving line.

It's time to shift the conversation to a friendlier topic. "Hey, you played your role beautifully out there. I was impressed."

She eyed me, uncertain whether to accept the compliment or to stay irritated.

"I have a feeling this one will be a trifle more difficult," Auriel admitted as she smoothed her hands over the skirt. "How do I look?"

I eyed her from all angles before answering. "Perfect. Don't you think so?" I looked at Phoebe.

Phoebe gave Auriel a sullen glare. "That's my favorite dress. And Mums paid an outlandish price for the hat."

"Wonderful," Nurse Bouchard called from the far end of the room. "I'm sure Miss Auriel will wear it in good health. If you're finished dressing, ladies, I'll let the men out of their closet."

I laughed. I hadn't realized she'd been standing guard for us while we changed clothing. She knocked on the door and called for Jamie and Nikolai. When they emerged, I laughed at the sight of Nikolai dressed in torn overalls and a drab shirt similar to mine. Jamie looked somewhat better in Nikolai's suit jacket, though the seams looked ready to burst.

Jamie tossed the trousers onto the closest table. "A little short for me," he explained. As he adjusted the derby on his head, he added, "A little tight."

I laughed. "I always knew you had a big head."

He gave me a withering stare. "I think that's it." He took a long breath. "Let's go through the plan one more time. Sarge will drive Auriel and me to the train station in the Rolls-Royce as if we are Phoebe and Nikolai. We hope our unwelcome guests will tail us, thinking they're following you. We'll board the morning train for Paris. Before we reach the Lyon station, we'll change into our medical attire and give the men the slip during the fifteen-minute stop at Lyon."

I hadn't heard that part of the plan before. When I frowned in concentration, Auriel squeezed my hand reassuringly.

"In the meantime, CeeCee, you, Phoebe, and Nikolai will drive the Renault to Lyon and catch the afternoon train for Paris. Auriel and I will spend the day sightseeing in Lyon, then return to the station in the evening to drive the Renault back to the hospital. If our pursuers are still with us, by then, they should be totally confused."

"And you will sell the Rolls-Royce and send us the money?" Nikolai asked.

Jamie smiled patiently. "Yes. And I will deliver the money myself. Oh, that reminds me." He reached in his pants pocket, withdrew a small leather money pouch, and handed it to me.

"Here, CeeCee, this should get you through to London."

I had unclasped the carpetbag latches in order to slip the pouch inside, when Jamie's hand on mine stopped me. "I'd feel more comfortable if you wore it under your shirt. The pickpockets in Paris would love to fleece a naive farm boy of his luggage."

I nodded and started to reclose the bag. *Oh no, I almost forgot.* I reached inside and pulled out the Bible, taking a moment to slip Thad's letter from it and into the case.

"Here." I stuffed the Bible into Jamie's hands before I changed my mind. "You'll want this back."

Jamie paused, then returned the book to me. "You can keep Mama's Bible until I get back to London. I'll use Auriel's a little longer. Which reminds me, let's have prayer before you go."

We formed a circle, like our family had done so many times over the years. Nikolai and Phoebe looked at us, then at one another, uncertain. We bowed our heads.

"Dearest heavenly Father, we thank You and praise Your name for the way You've led us in the past. Through accidents, illnesses, even war, You have faithfully been with us. Go with us today as we play out this strange charade. We don't understand what is happening, but You do. So we leave it all in Your tender care. Amen."

Jamie took my hands and kissed my cheek. "Let us know right away when you get to London. We'll be praying for you, Cricket. Remember, God keeps His word."

"I know." I choked back the tears.

Auriel placed her arm on mine. "I know you're going to be fine."

I nodded. "You've been so kind to me and so patient. I'm going to miss you. I'm leaving here a totally different person from when I arrived."

Nurse Bouchard, Auriel, and Jamie looked at my clothing and laughed. I followed their gaze and reddened. "Beyond the clothing! Nurse Bouchard, when I spouted my outlandish theories, you didn't preach at me or try to convince me I was wrong. Instead, you showed me genuine Christian love. I appreciated that."

I kissed her, then kissed Auriel. "And, you, sister dear. You're everything I ever wanted in a sister and lots more. I can hardly wait until you get to London so I can help you plan the wedding."

Auriel's face glowed with anticipation. "That will be such fun!"

"And, Jamie, thanks for not rushing me with this religious stuff. I'm getting there, a little at a time. But I do have one confession to make to you before I leave."

My brother lifted a eyebrow in surprise.

"I was furious with you for ordering Paul to stay away from me. I really did care for him, you know."

"I know. Do you forgive me?"

I paused and gave him a wry smile. "I'm not sure yet. Yes, I guess you were only doing it for my own good. I'll forgive you."

"I'm glad. He was my best friend, so it was difficult to do." Jamie sighed and took one of my hands in his. "I guess it's time to say goodbye. If I could, I'd be the one taking the risks. You know that, don't you?"

I nodded, clutching the money pouch and the Bible in my hands. "I know. And I'm sorry I gave you such a rough time about wearing this outfit."

"I don't blame you. I can't imagine anyone easily convincing me to masquerade as a woman either."

Nurse Bouchard laughed. "Doctor McCall, you'd make an ugly woman."

"Oh, I don't know. I think I'd be quite fetching in a bonnet like that." He pointed at the floppy straw-and-feather concoction on Auriel's head. "But, you're probably right. I'm sure I could never look as beguiling in it as my lovely fiancée."

I kissed Auriel and Jamie goodbye a second time before they rushed out of the building. Nurse Bouchard followed them, leaving Phoebe, Nikolai, and me alone to our thoughts. In a few minutes, the orphans would be flooding through the doors for breakfast. We had to leave before they arrived.

While waiting for word from Lucky, I replaced the Bible in the carpetbag and fastened the clasps. Then I turned toward the wall, unbuttoned my shirt, and slipped the pouch into my lace chemise. My breath caught in my throat when I heard the Rolls-Royce rumble away from the hospital. *This is it. They're gone. Now there's no turning back—we have to go through with it.*

Looking at Phoebe, then at Nikolai, I recognized that the strained, haunted looks on their faces mirrored mine. I gulped back a bitter taste rising in my mouth. Seconds later, one of the patients poked his head into the room. "Lucky's given the all-clear signal. The goon followed the Rolls just like Doc said he would. You can leave any time."

I thanked him and picked up the rucksack with one hand and the carpetbag with the other. "Come on. Let's go."

As we passed the open kitchen door, the cook called, "Wait. You can't go without this." She handed me a large wicker basket. "A lunch. It's a long ride to Paris."

The size and weight of the basket suggested it held one gigantic meal. I thanked her, then pushed open the exit door. "Wait here until I bring the car around. Phoebe, you get into the back seat and lie down out of sight. No one's looking for two farm boys traveling together."

Dashing across the yard to the barn, I threw open the double doors. I stashed my luggage on the rear floor of the Renault before cranking the engine to life. *I can do this*, I told myself. *Jamie says a Renault is the easiest automobile on the road to drive. I can do this.*

As I backed the little vehicle out of the barn, I had to admit that it did handle well. One last look at the place where I'd found so much happiness, and I shifted into first, then drove as close to the back door of the hospital as I dared. Before I came to a complete stop, Nikolai burst out of the building and yanked open the passenger's door. "Will any of this fit in the boot?"

I shook my head. "No, it's full of spare tires. Jamie says we'll probably need every one of them before we reach Lyon."

Opening the car's rear door, he added his and Phoebe's luggage to mine. Then he signaled to Phoebe, and she rushed from the building in a flurry of tattered skirts. As her foot cleared the running board, he slammed the car door shut behind her, ran around to the passenger side, and jumped in, placing his duffel bag on the floor between his feet.

"I'm sure there's room for that in the back seat, Nikolai."

"No," he insisted. "I want it right here with me."

"Fine." I shrugged. *This is going to be a delightful trip; I can tell.* "Let's go." I shoved the engine into gear, and the little car jerked forward. As we rounded the side of the hospital, Mimi and a group of her friends bounded out of the orphanage, heading for the dining hall.

"Stop!" She waved her hands and shouted, "Where are you going?"

"No!" Nikolai grabbed my arm. "Doc McCall said not to stop for anyone, remember?" Normally I would have thought it humorous to have Nikolai call Jamie by his professional title, but I didn't find his reminding me of my brother's orders the least bit funny. I growled, pasted on a P. T. Barnum smile, and waved goodbye to the disappointed girl. As I drove out the front gates of the hospital grounds, I glanced back to see Mimi standing there in the yard, gazing after us.

Please forgive me, Mimi, for not saying goodbye.

Run Before the Hunter

The crisp morning air washed cool across my cheek as I memorized the blue of the sky, the deep greens of the forest, and the mountain peaks with their whipped-cream toppings. In spite of my reason for traveling, it was a good day to be going somewhere and doing something. In the passenger seat beside me, Nikolai sat hunched and silent as we chugged along the winding road toward town. This was fine with me, since his comments usually irritated, rather than helped.

As I drove, my thoughts drifted to the hospital and the orphanage. I remembered the confused look on Mimi's face when I failed to stop on my way out of the compound. *I must write to her as soon as I reach London.*

Already, my days at the hospital were taking on a sepia tone in my memory. Helping to locate missing parents for the children had been satisfying. But in caring for the postoperative patients during the previous few weeks, I'd discovered a new calling. *Won't my parents be surprised?* I thought. *Me, the one who went into hiding at the first sign of illness.*

I thought of all the friends I'd made and left behind— Sarge and his courage, Nurse Bouchard and her commitment, the children and their insatiable desire for love, Paul and, what? Had I really expected anything more from our friendship than friendship? I didn't know.

I hate goodbyes. I'm always saying goodbye. Sometimes I wonder if caring for other people is overrated. If only I could breeze through life, untouched by the people I meet, people like Mimi,

Paul, Sarge, Nurse Bouchard— Even as the thought entered my mind, treasured memories brushed it aside.

Suddenly I realized that the Renault had drifted to the left side of the road. I swerved back to the right and laughed. *We might survive this if I can remember to drive on my side of the road!* I laughed again.

"What's so funny?" Nikolai's gaze met mine briefly.

"Nothing you would understand. The map Jamie made for us is lying on the floor by your feet. Why don't you navigate for me?" I gestured toward the floor.

The boy leaned down and retrieved the piece of paper from the floor, and I returned my attention to the road. "I need to know which road to take after we leave town."

We heard a small voice from the back seat. "May I sit up yet?"

I glanced over my shoulder at Phoebe curled up on the rear seat. "No, not until we leave Chamonix."

"Watch out!" Nikolai grabbed the dashboard.

A doe and two fawns had leapt out of the woods and onto the road. Clutching the steering wheel with a death grip, I swerved to avoid the animals. A loud pop sounded as the automobile's left rear tire slammed against a sharp rock on the side of the road. "Oh no!"

"What was that?" Phoebe's head popped up behind me.

I groaned. "Our first flat tire of the journey," I explained as I wrestled the car to a stop.

"I thought you knew how to drive," Nikolai snarled.

"Look, brother dear. Let's get something straight right here and now." I glared at him. "I did not volunteer for this little adventure. So, tread lightly with me, or you may find yourself walking to England! In the meantime, you and I have a tire to change."

"Me? But I—"

"Now!" I steadied my breathing, regaining my composure. "I'll get the jack out of the toolbox while you fetch a tire from the boot."

"You can't—" He gave me a challenging look. We stared at one another for a couple of seconds. Without looking away, I yanked open my door.

"Now, if you please."

Uncertainty flickered in his eyes. He heaved a long, dramatic sigh, then carried out my orders. I climbed out of the car and located the necessary tools in the toolbox attached to the running board on my side of the car. *At this rate, this trip is going to be interminable!*

I noticed that Nikolai had intently watched my every move as I changed the tire. Once we were on our way again, I suggested, "Nikolai, the next blown tire is yours to change."

Instead of an outburst of resistance, a half-smile flickered across his face. *Maybe what this kid needs is responsibility.* I smiled to myself and eased the car around a sharp curve in the road.

Beyond the next curve, the quaint little town of Chamonix came into view. By now, Jamie and Auriel, along with their unsavory pursuers, should have boarded the train for Paris. I felt a tap on my arm.

"You'll need to make a left turn at the next intersection." Nikolai pointed at the pencil drawing. "It looks like Doc wants us to skirt the town."

"That makes sense, since any number of people could identify this vehicle as Dr. Bietz's. It's not as if there's an abundance of motor cars out here in the provinces." Seconds later, I spied the turnoff.

The narrow mountain road outside of town was rough, but the side road on which Jamie directed us was far worse. The ice heaves of spring had left ruts and potholes deep enough to break an axle. So I had to lower my speed to a crawl and grip the steering wheel with all my strength to keep the vehicle from shimmying all over the road.

Beyond Chamonix, the road improved, allowing me to relax. We rode in silence, absorbed in our own thoughts. Occasionally, I glanced over at Nikolai's narrow, pinched face. He never looked my way or seemed to alter his expression, just stared ahead at the empty road. The dark shadows under his eyes suggested he hadn't slept well. *A lot of pressure for a kid his age,* I thought, trying to stir up feelings of familial love toward him. *Maybe in the same situation, I'd behave even worse. Maybe—*

My growling stomach reminded me that we'd been traveling for several hours. I remembered the basket of food on the seat beside Phoebe. "Getting hungry?" I called out to Nikolai.

He jerked his head as if he'd been dozing. Without looking my way, he nodded.

Running along both shoulders of the road was a white rail fence. "There's a pasture up ahead on the right." I pointed toward the large oak tree in the middle of the field. "That oak could give us shade. Are you up to climbing fences?"

"I guess."

To say we were hungry would be an understatement. Within ten minutes, we'd inhaled nine sandwiches and finished off a half dozen hard-boiled eggs. Our focus was then on the three hefty slices of chocolate cake the cook had packed. Nikolai took his slice of cake and wandered toward a nearby clump of trees. As I watched the boy walk away, I thought of my little brother Rusty. The two boys were as different as possible, Rusty with his easygoing temperament and Nikolai with his dark, sullen arrogance.

Savoring the last bite of the cake, I licked the frosting from my fingers, then leaned my head against the tree trunk. *What a beautiful day.* I closed my eyes. *If only I could take a short nap—*

A shout from the far end of the field jerked me alert. *Oh no, the owner of the field—it's not that we're hurting anything.* Gazing down the field, I saw a man waving frantically at us. *I suppose we are trespassing.*

Phoebe looked fearfully toward me. "What's he saying?"

"Who knows? He probably thinks we'll steal his acorns or something," I muttered, rising to my knees to collect the blue gingham dinner napkins. "I suppose we'd better go before he calls the local gendarme. Where's Nikolai?"

She shrugged. "He disappeared over that way."

The man ran toward us, continuing to shout and wave as he ran. Not wanting to have to apologize for using his tree and his pasture for a picnic spot and risk his detecting my gender, I stuffed the empty containers into the basket and stood up. Phoebe rose to her feet also.

I picked up the basket. "Why don't you fold the blanket and head back to the car while I find Nikolai?"

Another quick look at the advancing farmer, and she agreed without comment. I lumbered a few feet toward the clump of trees where I'd last seen Nikolai, only to freeze in my steps. Like a lightning bolt, my stepbrother burst into the clearing, terror blazed across his face. He charged across the field in my direction, glancing over his shoulder as he ran.

Seconds behind him, an enraged and determined young bull thundered from the woods. *Oh no!* I shot a glance over my shoulder at the farmer, still too far away to come to our aid.

Instinctively, I shouted, "Look out! Run!" which is exactly what Nikolai was doing. Suddenly I realized that he wasn't the only one in danger. I glanced about for a safe retreat. *The tree! I could climb the tree.*

For an instant, it seemed like a good idea, but I changed my mind when I realized that sooner or later I'd have to come down. And by the look of fury in that bovine's eyes, our standoff would probably last far longer than I'd prefer.

Once I eliminated the tree from my list of options, I whirled about and dashed ahead of Nikolai, the picnic basket and its contents farthest from my mind. Up ahead, Phoebe tumbled over the fence, in a flurry of skirts and crinolines. For once, I was thankful to be wearing men's overalls. And my stride did them justice. Within twenty feet of the fence, Nikolai flew by me.

"Run," he shouted frantically. "The bull!"

Casting a quick look behind me, I found myself staring into the eyes of a snorting beast five times my size, intent on doing serious damage to my person. *I'm going to die. I know I'm going to die!* I dropped the basket to increase my speed. The knowledge that, at any instant, I could be sailing through the air like last year's circus poster produced a burst of energy.

I hurled my body onto the barrier over which Nikolai had just disappeared. As I teetered for an instant, with one leg poised to fling over the top rail, the crazed animal smashed into the fence railing on which my other foot rested. The impact threw me to the ground in front of the stunned beast. But I scrambled to my feet and clambered over the fence, landing on top of Nikolai in the grassy gully on the other side.

For an instant, both of us were too stunned to move. A loud cackle brought me to my senses. Phoebe sat doubled over on the ground, helplessly shaking with laughter. On the other side of the fence, the farmer, who'd stopped short of the scene, was doing the same.

Rattled, the bull snorted and shook his head, attempting to dislodge the empty picnic basket dangling from his right horn. Whatever I'd placed in the basket minutes earlier was now strewn across the field.

The incensed animal charged the basket with a series of thrusts and parries, crushing the basket against the fence until only the basket's handle and rim remained intact. I wondered how long it would take the creature to decimate the barricade as well. Tiring of his wooden target, the animal looked around for a new target against which to direct his rage. Spying the farmer, the bull lowered his head and pawed the ground, giving the man time to lunge for the fence. This time, Nikolai and I were in on the laughter as the middle-aged farmer soared over the top of the fence and into a heap beside us.

However, our laughter stopped abruptly at the sound of wood splitting, and all four of us dashed for the safety of the Renault. No one took the risk of cranking the engine to make good our escape. Fortunately, for both us and the Renault, instead of charging the vehicle, the bull shook his head and staggered away, never realizing he'd been one charge from victory.

Once we knew we were safe, we checked ourselves for broken bones or cuts. "I can't believe it. You'd expect—" The man hesitated. Eying me strangely, he glanced at my face, then at my overalls as I spoke. In his eyes I could read the thought *crazy American.*

I looked past him at Phoebe, silently pleading for her to break into the conversation. Instead, she gestured toward her head, then toward me.

Oh no. My hand flew to where the hat was supposed to be. Long strands of red hair hung down around my face. As my fingers ran along the side of my head, I closed my eyes and groaned.

"It's over there where you fell." Nikolai pointed to the hat resting on the bull's side of the white fence. To the farmer, he said, "Please forgive my sister; she is a little simple." He tapped the side of his head and rolled his eyes.

The farmer looked at me, then at Nikolai, and laughed, tapping his head in the same manner.

Silently, I glared at my brother, trying to decide if I was more angry or more relieved. After giving us a lecture on trespassing, the farmer left. Nikolai snagged my hat with a long twig while I recombed and braided my hair. After pinning it to the top of my head, I jammed the hat down over it. "There. If that doesn't hold it, nothing will! Nikolai, start the engine."

He hopped from the car and turned the crank. His feet had barely cleared the running board when I shifted the car into gear, and we were on our way once more to Lyon.

One flat tire later, and we arrived in the third-largest city in France, famous for its silk. Jamie's map led us straight through the city the Romans had founded in 43 B.C. *The centurion at Calvary could have walked these streets. If only I had time to explore the area— Maybe someday.*

As the Renault bounced over the stone streets congested with donkey carts, horse-drawn wagons, bicycles, motor-driven taxi-cabs, hansoms, pedestrians, and dogs, I tried to imagine Roman soldiers dressed in shiny helmets and other military regalia, marching in formation beside us. My mind snapped back to the present when we passed a clock tower outside a gray stone cathedral. Three-thirty, only fifteen minutes before our train would arrive at the depot—and we weren't there yet. Suddenly, over the cacophony of city noises, we heard a loud crash, followed by shouts and cackling chickens. At the same instant, the taxicab in front of me screeched to a halt. I braked hard to avoid hitting its bumper.

"What in the world?" I opened the door and stood on the running board to determine the reason for the traffic jam. Nikolai did the same on his side of the car. At the next corner, potatoes spilled out of an overturned cart that had collided with a truck loaded with caged chickens. Potatoes, wooden cages, chickens, and shouting people filled the intersection.

Back up! I threw my arm over the seat and craned my neck, only to find us boxed in by the afternoon traffic. I sank back into the seat and pounded my fist on the steering wheel. "It's hopeless. We'll never make it to the depot before the train leaves for Paris."

"We've got to." Phoebe leaned across the back of the seat. "They'll find us if we stay here overnight. They'll figure out they were following the wrong couple, and they'll find us."

Nikolai had a suggestion. "We've got to abandon the car and walk to the train station. It can't be too far, since we are in the center of town."

"The Renault? Leave it here in the middle of the street?" I stared at the boy incredulously. "I can't do that."

"The police will impound it until Jamie or your doctor friend comes to claim it." He gave me a direct look, his blue eyes clear and determined. And as much as I hated to admit it, he was right. When we reached Paris, I could wire the hospital and tell Jamie where to find it.

"All right. But, first, we'd better lighten our luggage. That duffel bag of yours looks mighty heavy."

"No! I'll manage my stuff, if you manage yours." He shot a quick warning look at his sister, who sat staring into space.

I tried to reason with him. "But who knows how far we'll need to walk?"

He replied by climbing out of the car and dragging the duffel bag after him. Phoebe followed his example. As they unloaded their luggage, I killed the engine. *I should just let them go, let them find their own way! That's what I should do. It would serve them right.*

I thought of Daddy and the confidence he and Jamie had in me that I could get them safely to the embassy. And I knew I couldn't let Daddy down. *What's so important in those dumb cases, anyway? If I had my way, I'd leave everything in the boot of the car and let Jamie ship it.* Then, remembering what I'd packed—my mother's Bible, my diary, my favorite chiffon dress— I'd be worried whether I'd ever see them again. *Considering all*

*Nikolai and Phoebe have already left behind, I guess I can under-
stand their reluctance to leave the last few possessions of home.*

Clutching my carpetbag with one hand and hoisting my rucksack over my shoulder, I started down the crowded street. I
looked back to see both Nikolai and Phoebe staring after me.
"Well, come on. If we're going to do this, let's do it."

I pushed my way between dozens of excited people fighting
over the dumped potatoes and scrambling after the terrified
chickens, both of which would, most likely, fill that night's stew
pots. By the time I reached the intersection, I had abandoned
all attempts to be courteous. No one could hear my "pardon mois"
anyway.

Oblivious to the frenzy around them, the two drivers shouted
and shook their fists in each other's faces. I glanced back at the
abandoned Renault one last time and pressed on until I reached
the edge of the traffic jam. Seeing a sign pointing toward the
train station, I didn't wait for the other two to catch up with me.
One kilometer—we aren't as far away as we thought.

As I shifted my rucksack to the other shoulder and grabbed
the carpetbag with my alternate hand, I wondered how Nikolai
was doing, carrying his overstuffed duffel bag. I had no idea
how heavy Phoebe's luggage might be, and I wasn't hanging
around to find out.

I sighed with relief when I reached the red brick station. As I
stepped off the curb across the street from the depot, I spied
Jamie and Auriel standing beside the station's main doors. Ready
to lift my hand to get their attention, I stopped short at the
sight of a gaunt dark-clothed man off to one side, watching them
from behind an open newspaper. *Oh no, they're trying to warn
us that the escape plan has failed.*

Instead of crossing the street as planned, I hurried back toward Nikolai and Phoebe. I found them half a block from the
station.

"They're here," I whispered, jostling against Nikolai as if by
accident. "Turn around and follow me."

I walked to the next corner and slipped into a small cafe,
choosing a window table where I could see the passersby clearly.
Seconds later, Phoebe and Nikolai appeared outside the cafe.

As they paused, trying to decide where I'd gone, I tapped on the window and motioned for them to come inside, where they wouldn't so easily be seen.

After explaining about seeing Jamie and Auriel and the suspicious-looking man, I suggested, "I'll walk to the station and buy our tickets. Then I'll board the train as soon as possible and save a compartment for us."

Nikolai bristled. "Why you? I should be—"

"Because these men don't know me and aren't looking for me. Remember?" I turned to Phoebe, whose face was white with fear. "In five minutes, you go to the station and hide in the ladies' facility until the conductor announces the train's departure." I took a deep breath to regroup my thoughts. "Nikolai, you wait across the street from the station until it's almost time for the train to pull out; then make a run for it."

"And what if the train leaves one of us behind?" Phoebe looked visibly upset. Nikolai looked grim.

I leapt to my feet, my chair scraping against the tile floor. "We'll make sure it doesn't happen." I paused for one last warning. "If you think you're being followed at any time, don't lead them to the rest of us. Adopt a family or something."

Not waiting for further discussion, I charged out of the cafe and back down the street toward the depot. As I crossed the busy street in front of the station, I adopted what I hoped would look like a long, masculine gait, purposely marching straight past Jamie without turning my head his direction. I was close enough to hear Auriel gasp. I cast a prayer upward that our pursuers didn't.

No one stopped me or called to me as I pushed open the doors and wove my way to the ticket window. "Three overnight tickets to Paris, a compartment, please, if one is available."

The ticket agent looked me over critically and told me the price, his voice oozing with sarcasm. I reached inside the bib of my overalls, withdrew the leather pouch, and counted out the exact amount. Before returning the pouch to its hiding place, I gave the man a self-satisfied smile. "When will the train be leaving?"

"In fifteen minutes."

I leaned toward the iron grill separating us. "Sir, I need a piece of paper and a pencil, please."

The agent slid the three tickets across the counter, along with the pencil and scrap of paper. Putting the tickets in a front pocket of my overalls, I stepped out of line and scribbled a note to Jamie, telling him about the Renault. A boy hawking the evening newspaper willingly agreed to deliver the note for a price. I handed him a coin and waited until I saw him tap Jamie on the shoulder; then I blended in with the crowd heading out the door to the platform.

One glance up and down the track, and I'd located three more potential Bolsheviks scanning the faces of the passengers as they boarded the train. I pulled my hat farther down over my face and ingratiated myself into a group of university students.

Stepping onto the train, I glanced over my shoulder and caught sight of Phoebe emerging from the station. I darted a quick look at the nearest of the three black-coated men I suspected of following us and met his intense gaze. He'd been watching me. Before I looked away, I noted a jagged scar running along the left side of his jaw, drawing one side of his mouth into a lopsided, clownish grin. *I should have changed into my dress at the cafe*, I groaned. *He wouldn't be looking for a redheaded female*.

Flustered, I ducked inside the passenger car and found the nearest restroom. After slipping into my green dirndl and fine white cotton stockings, I stuffed the overalls, shirt, and boots into the rucksack and placed the leather pouch close to my heart. *There! I feel better!* I straightened when a grandmotherly woman in her seventies entered the tiny facility. Her questioning stare reminded me that I still wore the cap.

Laughing to myself, I took it off and placed it in the rucksack. One by one, I removed the pins holding my braid in place and restyled my hair into long braids. My only hope was to look so different from the skinny young man who boarded the train that no one would make the connection. Last, I pinched my cheeks, hoisted my rucksack over one shoulder, grabbed my carpetbag, and began the search for an empty compartment.

Three cars later, I found one. I'd been inside the compartment long enough to stash the rucksack under the seat and settle myself and my carpetbag next to the window when I saw a swarthy face peer through the small window in the compartment door. The man's eyes were shaded by the brim of his hat. I forced myself to casually turn my face toward the train window. For a moment, I held my breath. *Go away. Go away! Please, God, make him go away.* It took every bit of determination I had to keep from checking to see if the man had left.

I tensed when the compartment door slid open, slamming against the molding with a bang. *This is it! What do I do now?*

"I finally found you!" Phoebe's breathless voice brought tears of gratitude to my eyes. She dropped her luggage with a thud on the seat opposite me. "I almost didn't recognize you. You changed your clothes."

I gave a silly little laugh of relief. "I thought you were— One of them came through checking compartments just minutes ago."

"I know. I followed him onto the train, even asked him how soon the train would be leaving. For the first time in my life, I'm grateful that my mother insisted I learn to speak an unaccented English, American English, that is."

"You are a constant surprise." I stared at the young woman I'd imagined to be rather dull and stuffy. "And you know what? I think you actually like this Mata Hari game." I admitted, "You're good at it too."

"It's kind of like playacting, you know, like a stage actress." She blushed and settled herself on the seat across from me. "Have you seen Nikolai?"

I shook my head. "Did you pass Auriel and Jamie outside the station?"

"Yes. They pretended not to see me; I did the same. I wish my brother would hurry. I'm worried."

By the increase in steam spouting outside the window, I knew the train would begin moving at any moment.

"Nikolai!" Phoebe jumped up and started to open the door.

"Don't!" At my command, she returned to the upholstered seat across from me. "The best thing we can do is sit here and wait patiently. If one of those spies comes snooping around again, we need to look like a couple of country girls traveling to

Grandma's house."

The sudden lurch of the train threatened to toss both of us onto the floor. "You're right," she admitted as she settled back in the seat and slid over to the window. "It's just that Nikolai is all the real family I have left. It's been pretty rough for both of us these last few months since Mama died. Most of the time, Nikolai has watched over me, instead of the other way around, as it should have been."

She turned toward the scenery passing by outside the window. "I haven't been fair with him, expecting him to take charge and make such major decisions."

"You mean, like coming down to Chamonix instead of staying at the embassy in Switzerland?"

She nodded. "Things were getting more and more difficult for us there. We were virtual prisoners. When your father, er, my father, wrote and said you and your brother were so close to where we were, it seemed like an answer to our prayers."

I frowned. All this political intrigue, being pursued across international lines, being held as a prisoner in one's own embassy, distressed me. It didn't make sense to my simple, uncomplicated mind.

"Look, I have to be honest with you. I still don't understand why anyone would go to so much trouble to find you."

Her eyes shifted to the compartment door before replying. "The new government, Marxism or Communism, whatever you want to call it, is supposedly controlled by the common people, the workers. In order to rule, they must prove that the aristocracy is unfit to rule, that they've robbed and oppressed the working class."

"Are they right? Did the Russian royalty do those things?"

A petulant expression flickered across her face. "Not any more than the royalty of England or France or Spain—or America, for that matter."

"What do you mean, America? We don't have any royalty there."

"Oh?" She lifted her eyebrows. "What do you call the Rockefellers and the Vanderbilts, for instance? Americans have no right to look down their noses at the excesses of European royalty," she defended.

The memory of the elaborate parties the wealthy robber barons had thrown during the late eighteen hundreds brought a blush to my face. I remembered reading about a theme party where each guest ate his or her meal while mounted on a thoroughbred horse around a massive table so full of food that reinforcements were needed to strengthen the floor beneath it. At another party, the table centerpiece was live swans floating on a large pond. And I knew that both extravaganzas had been paid for by the labor of impoverished immigrants and their children working twelve- to fifteen-hour days making less than ten cents a day. "I suppose you're right."

We both turned when the compartment door slid open. "Tickets, ladies?"

A rotund, ruddy-faced conductor stepped inside the doorway while I retrieved our tickets from a pocket hidden in the full skirt of my dirndl. I handed them to him. "The third ticket is for my little brother. He's gone exploring. You know how curious fourteen-year-old boys can be."

The man chuckled. "Yes, children add stress as well as joy to a conductor's existence."

I laughed daintily. "I imagine so. It will take our grandmama days to settle him down after taking his first train ride."

The man smiled. "I was about his age when I rode on my first train. From then on, I knew I'd be a railroad man someday. My mother wanted me to be a priest—imagine, me a priest!" The railroad man turned to go.

The shadow of a black-cloaked man brushed past the open door. *He's back. Oh no.* I glanced quickly at Phoebe, but her face was again toward the window, so I had to think of a reason to detain the conductor on my own. I forced a cheery smile.

"If our brother gets into any mischief, please send him back here immediately," I requested, my voice sounding unusually maternal.

"He'll be fine; don't you worry. Now you ladies relax and have a nice journey."

"Thank you, sir. I'm sure we will." I smiled. "Remember, now, if Siggy threatens to derail the train, let us know."

The conductor grinned and waved. "No threat of that, Miss." The door slid closed behind him.

For several seconds, we sat silently, staring out the windows. When our pursuer didn't return, I whispered, "Did you see him? Is he one of them?"

She nodded, her eyes round and frightened. "He's the one I saw in the woods by the school."

"No wonder he recognized me. He would have seen me that day on our walk. Maybe changing back into female clothing wasn't the best idea, huh?"

She shrugged. "I don't know. These men are like Russian wolfhounds on a scent. Sometimes—" Her eyes filled with tears. "—sometimes I wish I could just give them what they want. Maybe they'd go away."

Give them what they want? The instant her strange words registered in my mind, a look of fear swept across her face. Suddenly she ran to the door and peered out into the aisle. "Where is Nikolai? I wish he were here! What if he missed the train altogether? What if the Bolsheviks cau—" Her voice broke. I looked at my lap, hoping she didn't expect me to answer the question I'd been asking myself since our train left the Lyon station.

Paris Bound

"I'll tell you what. I'll go find him for you." I'd awakened to find Phoebe curled up in the corner, sobbing. Nikolai still hadn't appeared. *OK, I'm worried too*, I admitted. *Searching for him is better than sitting here and doing nothing.*

"No! Don't leave me alone." Her voice rose in fright. "We need to stick together. What if one of those men came back while you're gone?"

"Well, we both can't leave here at the same time. We'd have to carry everything with us and risk losing the compartment." Though I had no intention of letting Phoebe know, I silently agreed. I didn't want to face our adversaries alone either. Then I thought of two basic unavoidable situations. "Sooner or later, we're both going to have to go to the facilities and to the dining car to eat."

"I know," she wailed. "And that is going to be necessary sooner than I'd prefer."

I cast her a wry smile. "I know what you mean. I'm so thirsty that my mouth feels like I've been eating sand. We'll just have to take turns, like it or not."

Since her needs appeared more pressing than mine, I insisted she go first. Extracting the leather pouch from my bodice, I handed her some coins. "Here, get something to eat in the dining car."

Phoebe blushed and pushed the money back at me. "No, no, I don't need any money. I have a few francs of my own."

"Oh, all right." I was surprised—there'd been no mention of

any money but what Jamie had given me before we left the hospital. "While you're there, look around, not only for Nikolai, but to identify our pursuers. It may help us later to know how many there are, if we have to flee quickly."

"What about you?" she asked as she stood up and grabbed her tattered carpetbag. "You said you were thirsty."

"I'll go after you get back." I eyed the bag clutched in her hand. "You can leave that here if you'd like. No one will bother it; I assure you."

"No, I'd prefer to take it with me. My, er, cash is in the bottom of it."

"Then take the money. Why lug something around when you don't have to?" I extended the coins toward her once more. "You can pay me back later when we reach Paris."

Opening the door, she shook her head. "No, I'd prefer to use my own money, thank you."

Sighing, I glanced out between the green velvet curtains at the gathering dusk. Daylight faded into indigo blue, and the lights across the valley began to twinkle on. *So peaceful— If I were an artist, I think I'd use pastels to depict this scene. I'm sure Thad would—*

I hadn't thought about Thad's art for weeks. He hadn't mentioned it in any of his letters from Paris either. The memory of the sketch book he gave me before he enlisted in the army filled my mind. *I hope his infatuation with Socialism isn't getting in the way of his art.* Leaning back against the seat, I continued watching the changing panorama outside the window. *It's going to be so nice seeing him again. Won't he be surprised when I knock on his door tomorrow?* I hugged myself and closed my eyes. *Tomorrow.*

I felt my awareness flicker. Forcing my eyes open, I blinked a few times, then closed them again. It had been a long time since dawn. Soon the gentle rocking of the train lulled me to sleep, and I didn't waken until I felt Phoebe shaking me vigorously, speaking in an agitated whisper. "CeeCee, he's not here. Wake up! He isn't on the train."

"Who's not here? Who's not on the train?" I rubbed my eyes and yawned.

"Nikolai! My brother, remember?"

"Oh yes." I rubbed the palms of my hands over my ears, then drew them slowly along each side of my jaw to my chin, covering my yawns. "Are you sure? Did you look everywhere?"

"Yes, yes, I'm sure." She paced to the door and back. "What are we going to do? I must find my brother!"

"Look, I'm sure you think you checked every possible location on the train, but think about it. You couldn't check the men's room—"

"I stood outside and watched for fifteen minutes. Then I asked a man to check whether there was a young boy inside."

"Well, maybe he's hiding in the sleeping berths."

She shook her head. "I asked the conductor. He hasn't seen anyone resembling Nikolai's description on the train. Worse yet, I wasn't the first to ask about my brother."

"You mean—?"

She nodded. "Someone asked about Nikolai before I did."

The tiny hairs on my neck prickled. "What about in the baggage cars? Someone could hide in there for hours without being detected."

Again, she wagged her head. "The conductor had the baggage men check for me. Nothing. No one."

"What about the Bolsheviks? Did you see any?"

"I spotted five, I think. The man with the scar, the swarthy one I spoke to at the station, a brown-haired man with a graying beard and mustache, a bald man who smokes a pipe, and—" She slumped into the seat across from me. "—a young guy close to our age. He's wearing a black-and-gray striped jersey, dark pants, and a navy beret."

"Good work. Did any of them take particular notice of you or make any threatening advances?"

She frowned a bit. "Not really, but I did sense their gazes following me wherever I went."

Laughing nervously, I opened my carpetbag and removed my Bible, diary, and pencil from the case. "I guess it's my turn. No one came by the entire time you were gone—that I know of, at least." I stood up. "I slept a little."

"Slept! I had to shake you before I got any response from you.

You were so sound asleep."

"I was tired. Someone could have walked off with the crown jewels, and I'd never have known it." At the mention of the crown jewels, Phoebe winced. *Oops, probably remembering the diamond tiara the chauffeur stole.* My stomach rumbled as I opened the door and stepped out into the narrow hallway. "If I wasn't hungry earlier, I sure am now. I'll see you in a few minutes."

"Please hurry back." She tore at a fingernail she'd been worrying.

I nodded and left. Immediately, I sensed someone watching me from the shadows. After walking the length of the day car, I turned casually, doing a visual survey of the area. Behind me, I caught a flicker of movement, a blurred face reflected in the glass window between the interior of the railway car and the outside platform. I grabbed hold of the seat back nearest where I stood, fighting the temptation to dash to the door and throw it open in his startled face. Instead, I fled the opposite direction, arriving out of breath and slightly disheveled in the dining car.

Two men sat at the bar, drinking and conversing with the bartender. Even in the soft candlelight on the tables and the gas-light sconces behind the bar, I recognized one of the men Phoebe had described, the one with the beard and mustache. I expected him to look my way but realized he didn't have to. The mirror behind the bar gave him a perfect view of every move I made.

The only other patron was an elderly woman hunched over one of the tables at the opposite end of the car, drinking coffee and doing what appeared to be one of the word-cross games the *New York World* publishes regularly. Her makeup, heavy jewelry, and prewar frippery aged her, making her appear fragile and tired. *Probably can't sleep while traveling.*

I chose to sit at the first table to the right of the door through which I'd just entered and with my back to the wall. I'd barely laid the Bible and my diary down and slid the chair away from the table, when a sleepy waiter appeared beside me, a glass of water in one hand and a menu card in the other.

"I know it's late, sir, but I fell asleep in my compartment, and I am famished. What would you recommend that I order?"

In a patronizing voice, he said, "Of course, the chef has retired for the evening, Mademoiselle, but I believe we could assemble a nice little croissant sandwich with the filling of your choice."

"Ooh! That sounds delicious. Bring two brie-and-watercress croissants, please. As I said, I am quite hungry."

He nodded. "May a suggest a garden salad?"

I caught a movement out of the corner of my eye. The man I'd seen following me earlier entered the dining car. Without looking my way, he went to the bar, seating himself far from the man with the beard.

Hm, so you're the swarthy one. I think I'll call you Payne. You've been nothing but one, I might say. I chuckled at my little joke. *And your friend with the beard, I'll call him Harry.*

"Mademoiselle? Will there be anything else?"

I snapped my attention back to the ingratiating waiter. "Oh yes. The garden salad sounds good. And could I have a second glass of water, please."

"Will you be wanting coffee?"

"No, thank you." I shook my head. "But I would enjoy a pastry and a cup of hot chocolate after I finish my croissants."

"Very well, Mademoiselle." He bowed and disappeared as quickly as he'd first appeared. It took the entire glass of water to slake my thirst.

I studied my opponents over the rim of my glass tumbler. *Harry, you appear to be in your early forties. And, Payne, you're twenty-five, at the most. Don't you have anything better to do with your lives than chase two helpless girls across France in the middle of the night?* Giving the men names made them seem less threatening. I was tempted to tip my glass their way, but that might be going too far. *What if they interpret the gesture as an invitation of some kind?*

I reached for my diary, only to find the waiter standing beside me, balancing a full tray of food and drinks. The salad, the water, the croissants, the chocolate, the pastry, and the bill all arrived at the same time.

"My, such fast service." I set the diary to one side, allowing him to place the food before me.

The man bowed and gave me an insipid smile. "I am going to take a break, Mademoiselle, so I thought it best to bring everything at once."

"A good idea. Oh, please, could you tell me the time? I left my watch with my luggage."

The man slipped his pocket watch from his vest pocket. "It is exactly one twenty-eight. Will there be anything else, Mademoiselle?"

"No, thank you; this will do just fine."

Where did all the time go? First, I was watching the sunset, and now it's one-thirty in the morning. I guess I slept for a quite a while. I lifted a forkful of lettuce to my mouth. *And what in the world was Phoebe doing all that time? Looking for Nikolai, as she claims?*

I would have pondered the mystery of the lost hours longer, except my growling stomach reminded me of my hunger. I didn't look at the cost of my late-night snack until I'd finished the last bite of my second croissant sandwich. One glance, and I knew I wouldn't enjoy the chocolate and the pastry.

"I wonder if they call highway robbery 'railway robbery' when it occurs on a train?" I muttered. I must have spoken louder than I realized, for the two men chatting with the bartender glanced my way for the first time. Never moving his head, Payne stared into a coffee cup the bartender had delivered earlier. He didn't have to. I knew I'd never been out of his vision.

OK, boys, it's going to be a long night for all of us. I imagine neither of you has slept much in the last twenty-four hours. I chuckled. *Can't say the same for myself.* Opening my diary, I began to write.

Dear Emily, you'll never believe where I am or what I'm doing tonight. I'm giving new meaning to your words "I like to see it lap the miles . . ." My, my, you are really full of humor tonight, CeeCee, dear. *By morning, this locomotive will have licked up the miles all the way to Paris—* I paused to nibble on my pencil. *—and to Thaddeus. He has no idea I'm coming. Won't he be surprised?*

I slipped the envelope to Thad's letter from the back cover of the Bible and studied the return address—1120 Boulevard de Montparnasse. As I sipped my hot chocolate, now lukewarm, I reread his letter, especially the parts about the cafe called La Rotonde. "Montparnasse is a fabulous blend of artists, writers, and political philosophers. They call it the American Left Bank, though many Russians, Poles, and Latins live here as well. The riverbank is lined with bookstalls and bistros, all alive with the brightest of our postwar avant-garde intelligentsia." *Sounds pretty boring to me, sitting around in a cafe all day doing nothing more than sipping coffee and griping about society.*

The next section of the letter I didn't like. I'd read it so often I knew it by heart. Even as my eyes skimmed the words, I tried to justify my feelings about it. *It isn't that I think I have a claim to him. It's just that he's my friend, and I worry about his judgment in women. I'd hate to see him end up with an empty-headed floozy.*

"In the evening, pretty American girls sashay along the street in their shimmy dresses, following the action from cafe to cafe." *Well, at least he's no longer writing to me about my dear cousin Ashley.*

Without moving my head, I glanced over at Payne, catching him in the middle of a yawn. I chuckled to myself. *You're going to need more than one cup of coffee to outwit me; I'm wide awake.*

I returned the letter to its envelope and placed it in the back of my diary. Opening my Bible to Psalm 91, I skimmed the familiar words. ". . . deliver thee from the snare of the fowler, and from the noisome pestilence." *How appropriate! The snare of the fowler. You guys are pretty foul, you know, and are definitely noisome pests.* I read on. Phrases like "terror by night . . . arrow that flieth by day . . . pestilence that walketh in darkness . . . destruction that wasteth at noonday" sent shudders up and down my spine. It was as if the psalmist were also a prophet.

"There shall no evil befall thee, neither shall any plague come nigh thy dwelling." I considered shouting the words aloud, in bold, defiant tones. *No, that wouldn't be smart, would it, Father?* I read through the rest of the chapter. Was it only two nights before that I had read these very same words to Enrico? *Strange. Forty-eight hours seems like an eternity.*

The train hissed and chugged to a stop in what seemed like a hundred small towns along the route to Paris. The old lady in the corner looked up from her word-cross and smiled at me. I returned her smile. Finally the man I dubbed Payne stood up and, without looking my way, exited the dining car in the opposite direction of my compartment. Relieved, I took a deep breath. With him gone, I only had to worry about old Harry, who still sat at the bar drinking coffee.

Five minutes passed, and the train eased out of the last station. We were once again on our way. I decided to take advantage of the fact Payne was temporarily out of the picture. Slipping the correct change from my leather pouch, I stood and walked over to the bar to pay my bill. Harry shaded his face from me as I placed the money and the tab on the bar.

"Monsieur, the waiter told me to—"

"Oui, Mademoiselle." The bartender, who appeared to be in his early thirties, smiled and winked at me. "A little late for such a pretty young lady to be up and about, eh? Perhaps you need help sleeping?" he added, his lips curling into a suggestive leer.

Of all the— I shot him an Arctic glare. "Please see that my waiter receives the change for his services." I turned on my heel, returned to my table, scooped up my Bible and the diary, and headed back toward my compartment. Rocking with the train motion, I staggered through a maze of extended elbows and trouser-clad legs to the back of the darkened passenger car.

Slipping out onto the connecting platform, I paused to see if Harry had followed me. I smiled to myself when I saw the old woman enter the far end of the passenger car. *Good*, I thought, hurrying down the aisle of the next passenger car, *I have a head start*. The fear that one of our pursuers would try to throw me off the train in the middle of the night hadn't left my mind since I'd left the compartment.

When I finally reached the last sleeper car, I checked behind me again. This time, I saw no one following me. *Good! I'll do a little exploring before going to bed.* I rushed to the back of the car and through the door leading to the baggage car. The door behind me slid closed as I stepped from one platform to the next, the two floor surfaces shifting in opposite directions. Three chains strung across the opening on each side guarded against someone falling from the platform—*or being pushed*, I thought.

The thought goaded me to action, and I grabbed a brass railing from each car to steady myself. With the crisp night breeze lifting the tiny hairs on my arms, I tried the doorknob. It was locked. I shook the knob in frustration. *Oh, well, so much for becoming the first female Pinkerton agent—or France's equivalent, anyway.*

At the sound of the door behind me sliding open, I whirled about in terror and found myself face to face with the little old lady from the dining car. The soft light from the hallway behind her bathed my face but shrouded hers in darkness. I stared in surprise. "Are you lost, ma'am?"

Before she could reply, the shadow of a large man loomed over her—it was Harry. She turned her head for a moment, then in a feeble, bewildered voice, she said, "Oh, my! I do seem to be in the wrong place, don't I?" When she staggered slightly, I reached out to her.

"Here, let me help you find your compartment. What is the number? Do you remember which car it was in?" I forced my way inside and slid the door closed behind me. When the door clicked shut behind me, I sighed with relief, knowing that I was relatively safe again. *Oh, thank You, Lord, for rescuing me from this night terror.* I looked up at Harry's face, made more sinister by the deep shadows.

"Excuse us, sir, but my friend here seems to have lost her way. Could you please let us pass through?"

The man grunted and turned sideways so we could slip past him. I took the woman's arm and guided her into the next car. "Let me help you find your way to your compartment."

"What a sweet young woman you are to worry about an old lady like me," the woman murmured gratefully. I wanted to hug her and thank her for preventing my possible demise but was afraid I might alarm the poor dear.

Patting her hand, I walked past the door to my compartment, never glancing in its direction. Behind us, Harry silently watched as we bridged the gulf between the last two compartment cars.

The woman chatted about going to visit her great-grandchildren in Paris. She told me I reminded her of her favorite granddaughter, Sybil. Then she shook a gloved finger in my face. "You really are much too young to be traveling alone, my dear, especially at times like this. You know, the war and all."

"Oh, I'm not traveling alone. I'm with my stepsister and stepbrother," I confided, giving her upper arm a gentle squeeze. My eyebrows shot up in surprise at the inordinate firmness of her arm muscles.

The woman laughed self-consciously. "From milking three cows every morning for forty years."

Uncomfortable that she'd read my thoughts, I mumbled, "I imagine that would do it."

"There it is. That's my berth." The woman pointed to the far end of the third sleeping coach. "Now, I remember. Imagine, I walked right past it and didn't know it. Getting old isn't a picnic, you know."

"I doubt it has much to do with age. All these railway cars look so much alike."

"Thank you so much, dearie. You're a good girl; your mother should be proud." She patted my arm, then opened the curtain to her berth. "Sleep well, dear."

After wishing her good night, I hurried back to my compartment, hoping old Harry had given up on me and gone to sleep. I slipped into my compartment, expecting to find a trembling and frightened Phoebe curled up in the corner. Instead, I found her asleep. She didn't move a muscle or flicker an eyelid when I closed the door behind me. As I shoved my case out of my pathway, it thudded against the leg of the bench. Even when I changed out of my dirndl into a soft cotton dress that would be more comfortable for sleeping, she didn't stir. *You were gone for over an hour. What did you expect? That she'd wait up for you? Like you waited up for her?*

I placed my diary and Bible on top of my carpetbag and snuggled down on the bench seat opposite hers. Like a brightly painted toy circus train chugging around its little track, the events of the day paraded through my mind, over and over again. I'd just see the caboose roll past when the engine would reappear. Around and around and around and around and—

I awoke to the sounds of Phoebe stirring. Still wearing the faded outfit Nurse Bouchard had given her as a disguise, she stood clutching her carpetbag, her hairbrush in one fist and a small brown velvet jewelry case in the other.

"Good morning," I mumbled, closing my eyes against the sunlight filtering through the cloudy sky outside our window.

"Oh, did I waken you? I'm sorry. My hairbrush slid to the bottom of the case, and—" She cast about for words. "—I had to retrieve it."

Rubbing the sleep from my eyes, I responded, "I'm glad you found it." I rolled over, my back to her, hoping to get a few more minutes of sleep once she left the compartment. I'd almost drifted off when she spoke once more.

"Do you think since we know we're being followed anyway, it would be safe to dress in, uh, our own clothing?"

"I don't know. I don't want to think about that right now. I don't want to think of anything right now."

"You do know that we're less than twenty-five miles from Paris, don't you?"

"What?" I shot up from the seat. "Why didn't you say so?" I reached for my carpetbag from under the seat and started to unlatch it—but it was already open. I frowned, staring at the unlatched case for a few seconds. *I know that I— Was I that sleepy? Hmm!*

"See you in a few minutes. I need to, uh, go to the necessary room."

I hardly knew that she'd left the compartment until she'd been gone for several seconds. Pushing aside the mystery of my opened case, I located a change of clothing, slipped into my shoes, and padded down the hall to the closest ladies' facility. Except for the leather pouch I wore next to my skin and my fresh underclothing, I left everything else behind. *No one is going try to move in with us now*, I figured.

Draping my clothing over my shoulder, I turned the porcelain handle of the water faucet. I gathered a handful of water and splashed it on my face. Assuming Phoebe occupied one of the two stalls behind me, I asked, "Have you thought anymore about how we'll locate your brother once we get to Paris?"

A moment later, a woman in her late twenties emerged from the stall, her clear blue eyes filled with questions. "Were you speaking to me?"

Blushing, I responded, "I'm so sorry. I thought my stepsister was in here." Refusing to give up on the assumption, I peered under the second door and shook my head. "Hmm, that's strange. Where else would she have—"

"Oh, don't worry. Wherever she went, she'll be back soon." The stranger shrugged. "There aren't too many places one can disappear to while traveling aboard a speeding train."

"I suppose you're right. But still—"

"You're American, aren't you?" the woman inquired.

"Yes, yes, I am. How did you know?"

She lifted one eyebrow and grinned. "Your mannerisms are so Yankee." When I frowned, she added, "That's a compliment. My fiancé is an American. I met him in Paris, during the war. We're going to be married and live in Queens, New York. Do you know where that is?"

I smiled and nodded. "I live across the river in Manhattan."

"Oh, imagine that. We'll almost be neighbors. My name's Yvonne, Yvonne Perrine."

"It's nice to meet you, Yvonne. I'm CeeCee Chamberlain." I extended my hand to her.

"CeeCee, do you mind if I ask you some questions?"

"No, that's fine."

"Is CeeCee a nickname?"

I nodded. "It's short for Chloe Celeste. My mother's name is Chloe Mae and—" I tried to explain.

In her excitement, she interrupted. "Are you staying in Paris for a while? Or are you traveling farther today?"

"It's a little complicated, I'm afraid. I hope to visit a friend of mine while I'm in the city; then I'll go on to meet my parents in London."

"Ooo-la-la, he is a male, yes? I can tell by your blush."

I glanced away in embarrassment. "He is a male, yes. But we're only friends, I assure you."

"Uh-huh!" She laughed knowingly. "Only friends."

"It is true," I insisted. "Why does everyone imagine Thaddeus is more than a friend to me? Can't a man and a woman be mere friends? Nothing more?" Yvonne was the latest of many who assumed Thad to be more to me than what he was—a friend. I didn't try to hide my irritation.

She placed her hand on my wrist. "Don't be offended. All the world loves young love, especially after the big war, now when so many people's lives have been devastated by tragedy. It gives hope for the future."

"I-I'm sorry. I didn't mean to—"

Her grin widened. "That is OK. Isn't that how you Americans say it? OK? So where do you plan to meet this young man of yours?"

"He lives on the Left Bank, on Montparnasse."

"Yes, I know the area—everyone knows the area. Is he an artist? A writer?"

"An artist."

"Ah, how romantic!"

"And you, Yvonne, do you live in Paris?"

She shook her head. "I'm going with Ralph to the American Embassy so we can secure a visa for me. When the authorities refused to let me emigrate to America after Ralph returned to America on the troop ship, he sailed all the way back for me. Isn't that beautiful?" Her face glowed with happiness.

"How lovely. He must be one special guy."

"Guy? What does that mean? Is it another American idiom?"

"Yes, I suppose it is. It's slang for *man*."

"Oh, slang. Is also idiom?"

I laughed. "I suppose so. I never thought of it that way."

"You Americans have many slang words, don't you? I studied English at the university, yet when Ralph speaks to me, I must ask him, all the time, what he means."

"It must be confusing." I turned to enter the stall. "I, too, must visit the American Embassy on business. Maybe I'll see you there."

"That would be nice. Goodbye, CeeCee Chamberlain. I hope we meet again soon, in America."

"Me too."

She gave a little wave and opened to door to the hallway.

"Good luck with your artist."

"Thank you." I waved back.

A few minutes later, I returned to my compartment, expecting to find Phoebe impatiently awaiting my return. Instead, the room was empty. She was gone. Her carpetbag was gone. My luggage sat neatly arranged on the floor beneath the window. My Bible and my diary lay on the bench where I'd slept. I looked about the room for any evidence that Phoebe had ever been there. There was none. I opened my cases and looked inside. While nothing seemed to be missing, I knew instantly that someone had searched them.

As I changed into my soft gray wool flannel suit, I tried to make sense of my discovery. *Where in the world did she disappear to? Maybe she's in the dining car, getting a bite to eat.* I retrieved my hairbrush and hairpin case from the carpetbag. *How did this get open last night? I know I closed it before leaving for the dining car.*

I lifted it. It seemed a bit heavier than it was the day before. *What is going on here?* I opened the case and dumped everything onto the seat, examining my possessions carefully. *Everything's here*, I mused. The case slid from my lap to the floor with a thud. I turned the soft-sided case upside down—a leather bottom. I dropped the case again. Thud!

Peering inside, I saw nothing. Hmm! I slid one hand along the inside walls of the case, then across the bottom. I would have missed the tear in the lining, except my fingernail caught on a ravel. When I tried to free the nail without breaking it, the heavy buckram lining on the bottom of the case shifted. *What in the—* Long, amateurish stitches held the piece of fabric in place.

Carefully, I removed the stitches and pushed the fabric panel aside. My fingers rested on top of what felt like a velvet case almost the exact size and shape of the base of the carpetbag. I removed the chocolate brown case from the bag and pressed the tiny brass button to unfasten the latch. The lid popped open, and I gasped.

On the Left Bank

"What in the— Where in the— How in the—" I glanced about the compartment, searching for answers, any answers. The sound of the door opening jolted me to action. I snapped the case shut and dropped it into the carpetbag. The quizzical look on the conductor's face told me he'd seen my furtive movements. And I'm certain that my face mirrored the sudden unreasonable fear I felt.

"Mademoiselle, I am so sorry to have startled you, but I needed to catch you before we arrive at the station. When your sister left the train, she asked me to give this note to you." He handed me a folded piece of stationery.

I opened the note and read, "Dear CeeCee, I am sorry to tell you this way, but Nikolai and I think it is best if we find our own way to England now that everyone is on our trail. I have left a few things in your bags for safekeeping. I hope you will guard them for me. They belonged to our mother and mean a lot to Nikolai and me. Again, please forgive me for not taking you into our plans, but I'm sure you can understand why. Sincerely, Phoebe."

Understand? Actually, I don't understand a thing! Daddy isn't going to like this, but I did the best I could. How was I to know Nikolai would get sep— Nikolai? She found him? But last night she told me— I exhaled through my clenched teeth. *"Dear God, what is going on? I'm so confused."* I stared at the note for several minutes and didn't know when the conductor left the compartment. But when I looked up, I was alone again.

I ran to the door and pulled down the shade, then removed the velvet case from the bag. Slowly I opened the lid and stared once more at the contents. The matching set of ruby-studded diamond necklace, bracelet, and earrings glistened in the early-morning light. I'd never held anything so incredibly beautiful in my hands. The jewelry's ornate silver settings indicated that the jewelry was quite old.

I struggled to make sense of all that was happening. Slowly, as I recalled the events of the last few days, things began to fall into place. I remembered reading in the newspapers a few weeks before about Russian nobility escaping the country during the revolution and taking their riches with them. The article had also explained how the Communists were determined to reclaim the wealth for the country and its impoverished people. I stared at the jewelry in disbelief. *So this is why our pursuers have persisted? I've been risking my life for jewelry?* I slammed the case shut and hugged it to my chest. *I don't want this stuff. I've got to get rid of it!*

Until I could decide what to do, I returned it to its hiding place inside my carpetbag. With shaking hands, I adjusted the panel of buckram over the case, then stuffed my clothing on top of it. I clasped the carpetbag shut and set it on the seat beside me.

I don't understand. If she didn't trust me enough to share with me her plans to leave the train early, why would she entrust me with her jewelry? My gaze fell on my rucksack. Suddenly suspicious, I lifted it. *Oh no, not more of the stuff. This bag is definitely much heavier than it was yesterday.*

I released the drawstring and turned the bag upside down. My clothing fell out onto the bed, along with three books I'd never before seen— *Sonnets From the Portuguese*, by Elizabeth Barrett Browning; *A Tale of Two Cities*, by Charles Dickens; and *The Diary of Samuel Pepys*. I opened the front cover of the book of sonnets and yelped. The inside pages of the book had been carved out to house what appeared to be a bar of solid gold. I grabbed the other two books and discovered each held matching gold bars. *This is hardly a spur-of-the-moment plan. Someone knew exactly what he or she was doing.* A new thought raised the little hairs on the back of my neck. *If Phoebe entrusted me with this, there must be a whole lot more stored in their luggage.*

Of course, now I can understand why she wouldn't leave her case behind when she left the compartment and why Nikolai kept his duffel bag between his feet in the front seat of the car. It all makes sense. If the chauffeur knew the extent of the wealth those two carried, maybe he wasn't such a cad after all for taking only what he did.

I don't know how long I would have stared at the shiny metal if I hadn't heard footsteps stop outside my door. When the doorknob moved, I leapt to my feet, letting the books fall to the floor with a bang.

Throwing myself against the door, I slid the brass bolt into place. I knew the fragile lock wouldn't successfully keep out anyone determined to enter, but it might afford me time. I scooped up the books and returned them to my rucksack, dumped my clothing on top, and drew the string closed. *I don't know if people can really die from fright, but if they can, I must be close. Oh, dear God, what have I gotten into? Please, please help me know what to do.*

Whoever tried to open my door gave up after two attempts. I tiptoed to the door, pressed my ear against the thin wood panel, and listened until his footsteps receded down the hall. Leaning my forehead against the door in relief, I prayed, *Thank You, Lord. I guess You saved me from another of those arrows that fly by day.*

When the whistles blew, announcing our arrival at the Gare de Lyon, I jumped in surprise. A moment later, the conductor marched past my door, calling out the stop.

I had already jammed my Bible, brush, and diary into the carpetbag before I realized my hair still lay in tangles about my shoulders. Brushing it as quickly as possible, I twisted it into a chignon, then pinned it into place, hoping it would stay until I could better secure it. I pawed through the carpetbag until I found my gray felt cloche. *Please behave. I've more on my mind today than hair fashion.*

As other travelers disembarked, I peered out my window at

the crowded railway platform. It took but a moment to locate two of my pursuers, Payne and the man with the scar on his face. I didn't need to open the door to my compartment to know that Harry and the bald man with the pipe would be waiting for me in the hallway.

I will try to postpone making any moral judgments over the rightness or wrongness of Nikolai and Phoebe's behavior, but I can't walk out onto that platform before something changes. However, the first thing I need to do is get rid of this stuff. I refuse to run all over Paris, a target for a bunch of wild-eyed radicals. And I won't risk my life for a couple of greedy relatives either. All right, let's start all over again.

Opening up the two cases, I dumped everything onto the bed. The books and the jewelry case landed on top. I set them aside. Then I sorted the clothing into two piles, one containing the things I would need, and the other, things I could do without. At the last minute, I switched my cream-colored silk chiffon dress from the "do without" stack to the "needed." Carefully, I placed the jewelry and the books in the bottom of the rucksack, then covered them with the "needed" pile of clothing. The farmer's overalls refused to fit, no matter how hard I crammed, so I yanked the pants from the rucksack and fired them into the corner. "Fine! I never liked you anyway."

After tightening the drawstring and knotting it, I filled the carpetbag with the rest of my belongings and clasped it shut. "Now, I think I can face the enemy!" I tossed the rucksack over my shoulder. The heavy bag caused me to stagger. *Nice of my darling brother and sister to share the load.* Picking up the carpetbag with my other hand, I exited the compartment, trying not to think about how I must look, dressed in an expensive wool suit and carrying tattered luggage. I glanced at my hands as a porter helped me down the steps onto the platform. *Gloves, I forgot to bring along a pair of gloves and a purse! Every woman in the train station carried a purse of some kind.*

"Did you say something, Mademoiselle?" the porter asked.

"N-n-no." I reddened. I'd been unaware I'd spoken aloud. "I could use the services of a redcap, however."

The porter tipped his cap, then lifted his hand and whistled.

A redcap barely in his teens appeared out of nowhere and rushed to my side. He sized up the value of my luggage with a well-trained eye before insolently querying, "Will you be needing a cab, Mademoiselle? Or is someone meeting you curbside?"

I tilted my nose into the air as I'd seen my Bostonian grandmother do so many times and waved my hand graciously toward the depot. "If you would be so kind as to carry these to the luggage-holding desk. I presume you have such a service here?"

A look of annoyance replaced the one of arrogance. "Yes, Mademoiselle, follow me."

As I followed the redcap across the crowded platform, I pretended not to notice that two of my pursuers, the one I called Harry and the man with the scar, followed in my wake. The other three appeared to be frantically searching the faces in the crowd, probably looking for Phoebe or Nikolai. *Hmmph! Fooled you this time, huh?* I frowned. *What am I saying? Now they'll all follow me!*

At the luggage desk, I tipped the redcap, then turned to the attendant behind the desk. "Monsieur, how much does it cost to store one's luggage for a few hours?"

"We store luggage by the day, Mademoiselle."

"Am I the only one who may retrieve them?"

"No, Mademoiselle. I relinquish them to whomever holds the claim check."

"Good. Do I pay you now or when I come back for them?"

"You must pay for the first twenty-four hours. Then, later, if necessary, you pay the rest."

A quick look over my shoulder, and I could see Harry weaving through the crowd, his eyes focused on the two cases. I opened the carpetbag and slipped Thad's letter out of the Bible. Then I reclasped the bag, placed the exact number of francs on the counter, and handed the bag and the money across the counter to the attendant. In a loud voice, I said, "Please be certain this is stored in a safe place. It contains things very precious to me."

CeeCee, my conscience nagged, *don't tell lies. I'm not*, I argued. *Mama's Bible is very precious to me. And, besides, Jamie would be furious if anything happened to it.*

The agent had me fill out my name and address on a numbered card, which he attached to the case. Then he handed me a card with the matching number. "Just present this to whomever is on duty," he instructed.

"Thank you. I have one more question. Could you direct me to a leather-goods shop? I forgot to bring along a purse." I shrugged helplessly. "And how can a lady survive without her purse?"

"Ah, my wife! You wouldn't believe the things she carries in her purse. But then again, perhaps, you would." The agent nodded good-naturedly and pointed toward the exit. "Go to your left two blocks. There is a fine leather-goods shop on the Rue de Leon."

"Thank you so much." I placed the claim check inside my leather pouch, slipped the pouch under my suit jacket, and refastened the buttons, cringing at the slight bulge it added to my midriff. Picking up the heavy brown rucksack as if it were ten pounds lighter than it was, I clutched it to my chest. "To the left? Two blocks?"

He nodded and turned his attention to the next customer. I knew without looking behind me that Harry had heard every word. *If he knows where I am going and why, and if he thinks the valuables are back at the station, perhaps I'll be safe until I can reach the security of the American Embassy.*

I strolled along the busy avenue, looking into the shops along the way. Once in a while I would catch the reflection in a shop window of one of the two men following me. I found the leather-goods shop and purchased a black leather purse to match my walking shoes and a pair of black leather, wrist-length gloves. I was tempted to transfer the leather pouch containing my luggage-claim check to the purse but changed my mind, thanks to Jamie's warning about purse snatchers.

At the last minute, I bought a large petit point carpetbag, which could hold the rucksack. With my new purse still filled with butcher's paper and my rucksack hidden in the carpetbag, I left the shop feeling a little more fashionable than I had when I entered. Hailing a taxi, I went directly to the American Embassy. Once there, I gave the receptionist the name of the man Jamie had said to contact, Mr. Donald Higgins.

The balding undersecretary, wearing round, metal-rimmed glasses, welcomed me with a cool reserve. "Your father cabled that you'd be arriving. Are your brother and sister with you?"

"I'm afraid not. We became separated during the journey."

He arched an eyebrow. "Really! We've been in communication with our embassy in Switzerland, and there seems to be a problem of some kind. We're supposed to hold them for questioning."

"Oh? I'm sorry, but I can't help you." I shrugged. "I would like to send a cable to my father in London, though. He asked me to deliver them safely here, and I don't exactly know what to do next."

He nodded. "Of course. And we will expect you to stay in our guest quarters, here at the embassy, as a courtesy to your father, of course." His pencil-thin mustache twitched. "Here, let me take that bag for you."

Before I could reply, he lifted the bag a few inches, then dropped it to the floor with a thud. "What do you have in here? The public library?"

"It is rather heavy," I demurred, but offered no explanation.

"Yes, I see that." He walked to the hall and signaled to a young marine. "Ensign, carry Miss Chamberlain's case to the guest wing, room 357. She'll be along in a moment."

Remembering that at the embassy in London, a chambermaid often unpacked guests' luggage for them, I rushed to the doorway. "Tell the maid not to bother with the case. There's nothing in there that will need any special care."

Noting the undersecretary eyeing me suspiciously, I giggled nervously. "I have a letter in there from my boyfriend, here in Paris. You know how curious hired help can be."

He nodded. "The cable room is down this hallway to the right. Did you encounter any difficulties during your journey? Other than misplacing your sister and brother, that is?"

"For some reason, we were being followed."

"Why would someone be following you?"

I shrugged. "Who knows?"

Once my cable was sent, Mr. Higgins escorted me to my room. "You will, of course, dine with Mrs. Higgins and me tonight in the dining hall."

"Thank you anyway, but I have other plans." I spotted my new carpetbag sitting unopened in the middle of the massive hand-carved oak bed. "Remember the young man I told you about? He has a room on the Left Bank. And I thought I'd—"

The man clucked his tongue disapprovingly. "You are a little young to travel to that part of town alone. I doubt your father would approve."

"I am sure that I'll be fine once I find Thaddeus." I placed my hands on the door, indicating that I wished him to leave the room. "And if I leave right away, I'll be there before the morning ends and, who knows, I may be back in time for dinner after all."

Reluctantly, he left, soundly protesting my plan to tour Paris on my own. As I closed the door behind him, I admitted to myself that he was right. Mama and Daddy would not be pleased. *But what am I supposed to do? Come to Paris and not see Thad?*

I hurried to the bed and opened the bag. Nothing had been disturbed. After removing the jewelry box and the three books, I glanced about the room, searching for hiding places. Hiding the books was easy. They fit nicely behind a ten-volume set of the complete works of William Shakespeare on the floor-to-ceiling bookshelves. After placing the jewelry box under a corner of the down-filled mattress, I removed part of the cash and the claim check from the leather pouch and put them in my purse. The rest, along with the pouch, I stuffed under the mattress with the jewelry.

With that responsibility off my shoulders, I placed the rucksack and its contents on a high shelf in the carved oak wardrobe, grabbed the empty carpetbag and my new purse, and headed for Paris's famous Left Bank.

I'd just stepped outside the embassy building into the clear morning air when a cab stopped beyond the nine-foot wrought-iron fence and deposited a young couple at the curb.

"Hold that cab," I called, holding onto my hat and running across the brick driveway.

When the woman turned to see who shouted, she squealed, "Mademoiselle CeeCee!"

"Yvonne? Is that you?"

"Mon ami, it is so good to see you again. Excuse me, let me introduce Ralph." She introduced the redheaded, red-faced man standing beside her. "We married at the courthouse this morning, an hour after I arrived in Paris. You are the first we have told."

"Congratulations. I'm so happy for you both."

"Will you come to a little wedding celebration we are planning this evening? We're inviting a few of Ralph's war buddies. You're the only person I know in Paris, outside of Ralph, of course." Her eyes sparkled as she snuggled against his arm. "You can bring your special friend with you, if you like."

"Well, I can see if he'd like to come."

"Oh, please." She pulled a card from her purse and handed it to me. "Here's the address of the hotel where we're staying. Seven or so will be fine."

I glanced down at the card, trying to think of a reason why I couldn't be there.

"Do come, please?" The young bride smiled hopefully at me.

The cab driver interrupted before I could reply. "Mademoiselle, do you want me to wait for you or not?"

I peered in through the open door. "Oh yes, please. Just a moment." Then turning to Yvonne and Ralph, I said, "I'm sorry, but I really must be going. Perhaps I'll see you both this evening."

"Perfect." She danced excitedly. "Didn't I tell you CeeCee Chamberlain will make a delightful neighbor in the United States?"

Ralph smiled and shrugged. "Yvonne has no concept of the size of New York City."

I laughed. "Neither did I when I first moved east from San Francisco."

As we said goodbye, I shot a quick glance about me to see if I could spot anyone following me. Except for an old lady selling flowers from a cart on the corner, the area was empty. Ralph helped me into the cab and closed the door. As I settled against the leather seat, for the first time since leaving Chamonix, I felt the heady elixir of freedom. *Maybe having Phoebe and her nasty brother desert me was to my advantage. Thanks to them, I am truly on my way to see Thad. He is going to be so surprised!*

"Where to, Mademoiselle?" Even the cab driver's gruff, insolent tone couldn't spoil the glorious day before me. I withdrew Thad's letter from my purse and read the address aloud.

"Is it far?"

"Eh." He shrugged in the typical Parisian fashion. "What is far? Nothing is far in Paris."

My excitement climbed when we left behind the sedate government buildings with their manicured boulevards and entered what I considered to be the real Paris. The city was all Thad's letters said and more. I had the urge to leap from the cab and twirl about the cobblestone street in ecstasy. Instead, I slid from one side of the seat to the other, trying to catch a glimpse of every fountain, every cafe, and every bookstore.

We stopped at a busy intersection, where a white-gloved policeman directed the midday traffic. While we waited, I spied a lavender dress in the window of a small boutique on the corner. Suddenly my stylish gray flannel suit and sensible cloche felt stodgy and confining.

"Wait! Stop! How much do I owe you?"

The cab driver's bushy eyebrows formed one grand scowl line across his forehead. "Excuse me? This is not Montparnasse, as you asked."

"I know, I know. How much?" I opened my purse and extracted some bills.

The driver started to protest.

"How much?" I demanded.

Directly in front of the taxi, the policeman blew his whistle and waved for the driver to move. Disgusted, the driver quoted me a price. I tossed him the money and hopped from the car. Dodging automobile bumpers, bicyclists, and horse-drawn vehicles, I wove my way to the sidewalk. I paused in front of the little shop to admire the frock. The soft gathered skirt of cotton plisse, reminiscent of my dirndl, was covered with tiny, hand-embroidered rosebuds. Instantly, I fell in love with the peasant-style bodice, gathered at the sleeves and the neckline with braided silk threads. *Should I splurge? I think I can swing it. And I did mention in the cable to Daddy that I need more cash. Of course, I'll need the appropriate hat, hosiery, and shoes— I'll do it.*

I marched into the shop and asked the salesclerk if I might try on the dress. Once I was installed in the dressing room, the clerk helped me into the dress.

I obeyed when she told me to hold my breath while she tightened the six-inch-wide purple cotton belt. By the time she fastened the last of the hidden hooks, I wondered if I'd ever breathe freely again. But as I studied my reflection in the mirror, I had to admit that the effect was most pleasing.

"Oui, Mademoiselle! The dress was made for you, yes?"

"I love it!" Hairpins flew in all directions, when, in a moment of recklessness, I pulled the cloche hat from my head. A similar move at the pins securing my chignon, and my hair tumbled about my shoulders. Quickly I removed what pins remained and shook my head vigorously.

"Mademoiselle!" The clerk clapped her hands with delight. "I have never seen such incredibly beautiful hair."

I swished back and forth in front of the mirror, studying myself from every angle. Even I had to admit that the contrast of my red hair against the lavender bodice was attractive. It had been so long since I had felt truly pretty—since the evening Paul Best had almost kissed me. I paused and bit my lip, remembering his outrageous description, "You're a titian-haired goddess."

"Wait," the clerk whispered, "I have just the right—" She left the dressing room, returning seconds later. Standing directly behind me, she tied a purple satin ribbon around my neck.

I frowned. "I don't know—"

"Wait." She placed a white picture hat on my head. "Pull your hair back on the side and let a few tendrils dangle around your face and, voilà! Perfection."

"I was hoping to look more modern somehow."

"No, no, no! Paris is overrun with modern young women. Everywhere one looks, one sees bobs, headbands, and shimmy dresses." The woman shook her head. "Take advantage of your natural grace and style. Unique and refreshing—that's what you are, my dear."

She turned me to face her. "What a delicate blush you have, and such smooth skin. No rouge needed here."

I smiled self-consciously. She fussed, puffing the sleeves and smoothing the gathers in the skirt. "Your young man will appreciate the difference between you and the shimmy girls that have invaded the city since the war, I assure you."

"My young man? I didn't say anything about—"

She smiled knowingly. "Your eyes revealed what your lips failed to say."

I blushed. "How much will all of this cost?"

While I styled my hair, she gathered up my clothing and placed it into my new carpetbag, then tabulated the price of my purchases, which, at the last minute, included white silk stockings and a pair of white leather ballet shoes minus the ribbons.

"These are lovely pumps," she said, as she placed my black leather walking shoes in my carpetbag, "but too bulky for such a delicate dress."

I agreed. By the time I counted out the total cost, I winced, realizing I'd spent far more of Jamie's money than I had intended. *If Daddy doesn't wire any money, I may become a permanent resident of this city.* As I turned to leave the shop, the woman called me back. She held in her hands a delicate white crocheted shawl. "Please, your new outfit needs one more item. The night air along the Seine can be nippy in the springtime." She draped the shawl about my shoulders.

I shook my head. "I can't afford to spend more mon—"

"It is a gift—" Her eyes grew soft and misty. "—to young love and to Paris in the springtime."

My mouth dropped open in surprise. "I can't take this from you; your employer will be upset."

Smile wrinkles formed at the corners of the woman's dancing eyes. "I am my employer. Please allow me to exercise a little whim. You see, my daughter would have been your age if she'd survived."

"Survived?"

"The influenza." The woman reached out and touched one of the tendrils dangling beside my face. "Her hair wasn't quite as red as yours—more strawberry blond."

"I'm so sorry." I swallowed hard. "Thank you so much. I'll treasure the shawl always."

"When one day you use it to cuddle your babies, think of a sentimental old dressmaker in Paris."

Ignoring the usual reserve Europeans prefer, I gave the woman a quick hug and left before either of us shed the tears filling our eyes. As I burst through the door onto the street, I bumped into an old woman, her hands full of bundles and shopping bags. I reached out to steady her, wondering why she looked vaguely familiar.

"My, my." The woman's voice crackled as she spoke. "If it isn't my young friend from the train. Remember? You helped me find my berth in the middle of the night?"

"Oh yes. I thought I recognized you. You're here in Paris visiting your granddaughter, right?"

She nodded enthusiastically, gesturing toward the shopping bags in her hands. Something about her smile told me she was trying too hard to be sincere. "Yes, I wanted to pick up a few things for my precious Rochelle this morning. She was so delighted to see me."

I frowned. "Rochelle, I thought you said her name is Sybil."

"It is. It's Sybil Rochelle. She prefers to go by her middle name."

I spotted a taxi across the intersection. "I see. Well, I hope you enjoy your visit with her."

"Tomorrow, Rochelle and I plan to tour the Louvre. Have you ever seen the Louvre? If not, you must."

I smiled and inched toward the curb. "I hope to before I leave for London."

She took hold of my wrist. Her grip was surprisingly strong and demanding. "But, of course, why don't you come with us? You and Rochelle would get along famously."

This woman is getting on my nerves. I tried to edge away, but she held fast, the glint in her eyes belying her grandmotherly smile. A tremble of fear coursed through me. The policeman directed traffic down my street, and the cab was already into the intersection. Yanking free of her grasp, I said, "If you'll excuse me, I'm meeting someone." I didn't wait for a reply but fled toward the street, calling, "Taxi!"

The cab stopped, and I climbed in and waved at the woman I'd left standing on the sidewalk. *Chloe Celeste, you should be ashamed of yourself, being so abrupt with that nice old lady. Mama would be horrified. Nice old lady?* I massaged my slightly bruised wrist.

"Where to, Mademoiselle?" The cab driver turned and grinned. And for a moment, he looked vaguely like the man on the train whom I had named Harry, except that his beard and mustache were salt-and-pepper gray.

I thrust Thad's letter into his hand. "To this return address, please."

Staring at the busy sidewalks, I told myself, *I am becoming terribly paranoid. Next thing I know, I'll see Mr. Scarface or Payne in uniform, directing traffic in the middle of an intersection.*

The taxi driver let me off at the address I'd given him, advising me to ask for further directions in the cafe on the corner. As I stepped onto the sidewalk, my earlier bravado faded, and I felt suddenly alone and frightened. For the first time, I asked myself what I was doing popping in on Thaddeus unannounced. I would never consider behaving in such a manner at home in London or New York.

So this is the Left Bank, the center of the artistic world. Feeling as if I had suddenly stepped into another world, I walked a dozen steps to the curb and paused. Behind me, I could hear the clomping of horses' hooves on the cobblestone street. Behind the carriage, I could hear the sound of a Renault or one of the other small cars I'd seen since arriving in Paris.

The cafe tables along the street were filled with brightly dressed women and men in drab, nondescript clothing, all drinking coffee, smoking, and talking loudly. *Oh, dear Father in heaven, what have I gotten myself into this time?* I pressed my hand against my stomach to steady my nerves. *Relax, CeeCee. You're here now; you might as well try to find him.*

Two young men wearing matching black berets and floppy sleeved, open-necked shirts sat at the nearest table, watching me. Their women friends, wearing skimpy dresses of chiffon and satin, hung on the men's shoulders like toreadors' capes.

The women glared at me as I approached the table. One of the men pushed the woman on his shoulder aside and rose from the table.

"Mademoiselle, you look lost. Allow Jacques to come to your assistance." Behind him, the rejected woman slunk into her chair, sulking.

I smiled, hoping to hide my acute case of jitters. "I'm looking for a friend of mine, Thaddeus Adams. He lives near here."

"Thad? Sure, I know good old Thad. He was just here, er, well—" The man scanned the crowded tables. I tried to follow his gaze.

The sulking brunette pointed with her cigarette. "Thaddeus is at that table in the corner," she purred in sultry French, tinged with a touch of Brooklyn.

I thanked her and headed toward the table she'd indicated, but not before I caught her look of relief and satisfaction that I was hunting for a man other than her own. Seven people—four men and three women—crowded around the table. The men all seemed to be shouting at once. *Politics, no doubt.* Two of the three women sat beside Thad, one on each side. I felt a sudden rise of jealousy. By their gestures and their adoring gazes, I knew they were captivated by more than his political thought. *Did I endure his crush on my cousin Ashley only to have him fall into the clutches of two femme fatales?* The third woman, older and with a cynical expression on her face, sat across from Thad, watching and apparently analyzing the conversation.

When I stepped up behind Thad's chair, the older woman glanced at me. Her brow arched in disdain, making me feel insignificant and provincial. Following her gaze, the woman on Thad's left turned toward me, her eyes immediately narrowing into thin slits. The men facing me stopped arguing midsentence. As Thad turned to see what or whom had interrupted his heated debate, I placed a hand on his shoulder. "Thad?"

Along the Seine

The three other men at the table leapt to their feet. As for Thaddeus, he merely gaped in astonishment. When he finally opened his mouth to speak, only babble came out. "Ba-ba-wha-wha-what are you doing here? In Paris?"

"I'm on my way to London." I searched his face for a hint whether my sudden arrival was a pleasure or an inconvenience for him, but it remained inscrutable with shock. "I'm sorry I couldn't notify you that I was coming, but the trip was rather sudden."

"No, no! I'm glad you're here." Leaping to his feet, he pushed the chair aside. "I'm so glad you're here!" He wrapped his arms around me and crushed me to him. I grabbed my picture hat to keep it from falling to the sidewalk.

"OK, OK. You can let me go now." I laughed. He'd never before been so passionate about my presence. *Maybe it's homesickness. Maybe it's Paris.*

"You're really here? This isn't a dream?" He continued to hold me, oblivious to our surroundings.

One of the men standing at the table cleared his throat before Thad remembered where we were. As he stepped back, I could see that his eyes were sparkling and dewy. "I can't believe you're here. In Paris. I've dreamed of this moment so many—" He caressed the side of my face, ginning foolishly. "You are so— I've missed you so much."

I brushed away the moisture on his cheek. "I've missed you too."

"Your letters have been my lifeline. You'll never know how—" He lowered his gaze to my lips. "Oh, CeeCee, I-I-I don't know what to say."

"Thaddeus."

I glanced over Thad's shoulder. The low, sultry tones came from the woman across the table from him. The tightly formed waves of her slick, salt-and-pepper-streaked bob looked as if they'd been painted on her head. Heavy strands of pearls hung about her neck, resting on the bodice of a low drape of satin. When she took a long drag from her cigarette, the dozen or so bracelets on her arm jangled and slid to her elbow. "Do you intend to introduce us to your little friend?"

The others at the table shot furtive glances at the woman, then at Thad and me. *This woman was holding court. I doubt she appreciates my arrival.*

Thad whirled about, his arm wrapped around my waist. "This little friend, as you describe her, is the most intelligent woman I've ever known—no offense, Gertrude." A wash of color flooded my face, but he continued, unaware of my discomfort. "But you don't ever want to get CeeCee into a philosophical debate." He glanced down at me and winked. "And even when you're sure you're right, she can convince you that you're mistaken."

The men laughed good-naturedly. However, I noticed they averted their eyes from Gertrude's gaze. The women glanced at one another and simpered politely.

One by one, Thad introduced me to his friends. Felix, Aldo, and Jake welcomed me with unabashed enthusiasm. The men didn't seem to notice the gaunt, high-cheekboned Margo's silence or the soft and dimpled Dolly's feline purr. But Gertrude, her face remaining devoid of emotion, studied me as a scientist would a laboratory insect.

I met her inscrutable gaze with one of my own. While I couldn't read her thoughts, I knew my presence represented some kind of threat to her. Felix borrowed an empty chair from the next table and muscled it in between Thad and Dolly. "Sit. Sit, little Miss American. Tell us about yourself."

Little Miss American? I reddened again and glanced over at Thad. He stared at me with unabashed joy. I tried not to read too much into his effusive reception. "Thad and I were good friends back in the States. He dated my cousin Ashley."

I arched one eyebrow in surprise when Thad took one of my hands in his and kissed my fingertips. "We used to take long walks on the beach together each morning at dawn. CeeCee has the soul of a poet."

Margo and Dolly laughed sarcastically.

"What a quaint little outfit!" Margo used her long black cigarette holder as a baton. "Find it in the provinces?"

Oh, so you know a little about me? Thad's been talking about me. I smiled graciously across the table, refusing to be baited. "Actually, I found it in the most darling little boutique, right here in Paris." With dramatic flair, I brushed a stray lock of hair from my shoulder. "I can't tell you where it was, for I know so little of the city." I flung a coy, innocent smile at Thad.

He patted my hand. "We'll just have to remedy that, won't we?"

I returned my attention to Margo. "I chose it for its uniqueness. Current trends can be so boring, don't you think? Today's dress designers would have all of us women looking like Mr. Ford's mass-produced automobiles."

The grim looks on the two younger women's faces told me I'd gone too far. Gertrude, on the other hand, smiled slightly and tipped her head toward me. I could see a spark of admiration in her eyes. I returned her partial smile with one of my own.

"So tell me, where are you planning to stay while you are in Paris?" Gertrude glanced toward Thad. "With Thaddeus?"

I managed to keep from blushing at the innuendo in her question. I gave a delicate, crystalline laugh. "Of course not. I have a room at the embassy. My father is presently on assignment with the London office, so he—"

A look of relief swept across Margo's face. "Oh, that's good, because dear Thaddeus hates to have anyone visit his garret." She shrugged her shoulders. "Doesn't he, Dolly dear? He says it distracts him from his art."

No love lost between those two felines. "Oh?" I shot Thad a facetious glance. The beads of sweat on his brow revealed how uncomfortable he felt with the sudden turn in the conversation.

He cleared his throat and pushed his chair from the table. "I hope you will all excuse us, but CeeCee and I have so much to talk about." He stood up and helped me to my feet, his gaze never leaving my face. "I'm sure she is eager to see as much of Paris as possible during this visit." He continued to hold my hand as if he were about to kiss my fingertips once more.

Gertrude interrupted the moment with, "You will be at the lecture tonight, Thaddeus, won't you?"

Thad took the carpetbag from my hands, glanced toward the woman, then back at me. "Um, er, we'll try to drop in for part of the evening."

"I hope so," the woman added meaningfully. "Comrade Rimsky will be there, remember? He's in Paris on party business and is eager to meet you."

Thad gave a disinterested shrug. "We'll do the best we can, but, well, you know Paris in the evening." He grinned at me and winked. Slipping his arm about my waist, he guided me through the maze of tables to the narrow brick sidewalk bordering the cafe.

I could feel Thad's friends staring after us as he placed my hand in the crook of his left arm. And I had no doubt we, more specifically, I, would be the topic of conversation at that table for the next few minutes. I felt a sense of elation as we strolled to the end of the block, though I didn't know why. It was as if I'd somehow freed Thad from their grasp.

"Where are we going?" I asked.

"I don't know. Having you in Paris is playing havoc with my mind. You belong on a pristine beach in Cape Cod, where things are clean and pure and innocent—not here." His momentary frown relaxed into a smile. "Remember how we used to talk for hours?"

"We still can. That's why I'm here—to be with you."

He studied my face for several seconds. "I've missed you, CeeCee. Why, I live for your letters."

I cocked my head to one side to avoid a direct ray of sunlight falling in my eyes. "And Ashley's letters? Do you live for hers too?"

He made a face. "Ashley? We haven't written to one another

in three months, at least."

"Oh." I stared down at my ballet shoe. "Neither she nor you mentioned that in your letters to me." To be honest, I'd sensed in Ashley's letters a changing of the guard, as I called her fickle affections.

"What about this Paul guy you mentioned in a few of your letters?" he parried.

"I haven't heard from him since he returned to the States." I lifted my eyes to meet his. "Besides, there was never anything between us, really." Thad held my gaze. *Why am I telling you this? We're only friends.* He started to respond, then changed his mind. After a pause, he began, "You must climb the Eiffel Tower and see the Arc de Triomphe and the Louvre and— But first we must drop off your bag in my apartment. We can't lug it around all day."

"Great."

He guided me the short distance to his building. As we climbed the six flights of stairs to Thad's attic apartment, he asked me about my work at the clinic and about Jamie and Auriel's engagement. On the fifth-floor landing, he asked why I was making the sudden trip back to London. I admitted only to being a little homesick and didn't mention Nikolai and Phoebe.

As I huffed and puffed my way up the last flight of stairs, Thad laughed. "The six flights of stairs are slightly inconvenient, but I live alone, so I'm the only one who needs to be concerned."

"I think your friend Dolly would like to change that."

His smile faded. "That's not funny." He pushed open the scarred wooden door, allowing me to enter the one-room studio. "My palatial mansion."

Light poured in through the sloping multipaned, south-facing window. Except for a scarred oak teacher's desk, a wooden straight-back chair, a narrow cot, and an easel, the room stood bare. He pulled back a curtain sectioning off the space behind the entrance. "My closet and my kitchen. To save you the embarrassment of asking, the necessary room is at the foot of the stairs. I share it with four other tenants."

I blushed. "Thaddeus, you can still do it, can't you?"

"Do what?" he asked.

"Read my thoughts."

He laughed and tossed my case onto the cot. "Your face is so open and honest; one would have to be blind."

"Oh, really?" I set my purse on the desk and planted my hands on my hips. "And what am I thinking now?"

Swaggering across the room, he adopted an insolent grin. "Now, let me see." He stopped less than a foot in front of me and studied my eyes for such a long, silent moment that I began to squirm under his intense gaze.

"What? What are you staring at, Thad?" My challenge faded on my lips as the humor in his eyes changed to wonder, then to an emotion I couldn't identify. A strange warmth flooded through me, and I held my breath, afraid that the pleasurable sensation would disappear.

Suddenly he turned away. "Hungry? Wait until you try Marie's croissants. They literally melt in your mouth."

Running his hands through his hair, he took a deep breath. "We'll pick up something to eat on our way to the Eiffel Tower. What do you say?"

"Yes, that would be fine." I shook my head to snap myself out of the strange trance.

"Then let's get out of here." He charged out of the apartment and down the stairs as if the devil's imps were nipping his heels. Unnerved by his abrupt exit, I grabbed my purse and ran after him. He purchased the pastries and hailed a taxi.

An hour later, we stood overlooking the city. To direct my attention to the gold-domed Church of Saint-Louis—the tomb of Napoleon—he placed his arm around my shoulder, his face next to mine, and pointed. For an instant, we both froze from the contact. Without a word, he lifted his hand from my shoulder as if he'd overstepped his boundary with me.

No, don't let go. I want you to stay. I placed my hand on top of his and looked up into his eyes. He arched his brow in question. I responded with a gentle smile. One corner of his mouth lifted slightly into a crooked grin; then he drew my attention to the city at our feet.

"Do you see that road?" The pressure on my shoulder increased slightly as he pointed to our left. "That road leads to the Palace of Versailles."

My mouth felt cotton dry, for I knew, without a doubt, that things had changed between us. I didn't know how, but he'd definitely changed. "Hmmph! That's where President Wilson and the others are working out the treaty with Germany, right?" I licked my lips and swallowed.

"So they say."

We strolled around the iron walkway until it seemed like he'd pointed out every famous building in the entire city, and many less-famous ones as well. It was as if both of us were loathe to sever the tenuous bond between us. Finally, reason returned. Hunger pains drove us from the tower to a park bench, where we shared the croissants he'd purchased earlier. During the afternoon, we ambled, hand in hand, through the park, talking about everything and anything.

We sat down on the green grass beside the Seine and watched a group of schoolchildren feed the ducks. Thad grew silent when I told him about my recent search for God. "I never knew what it meant to follow God and let Him lead in one's life until now. It's incredible, Thad. Mama and Daddy knew, but somehow it hadn't rubbed off on me."

I sensed Thad's discomfort with the topic. "It took time, of course. And I really had to want it to happen."

"If only it were that easy." Thad studied a distant point beyond me.

Dear God, I don't know how to do this. How can I explain You to him? I'm still learning about You, myself.

Maybe this isn't the right time. Frustrated about ruining the comfortable rapport we'd established, I switched topics. I talked about my new interest in nursing. As I spoke, I realized I was coming to an important decision in my life. "I've never felt so useful as I did working at the hospital. I'm seriously considering becoming a nurse when I return to the States."

"A nurse? I thought you hated being around sick people."

Determined to lure him into a better mood, I took a blade of grass and ran it along his chin line. "I guess the little girl's growing up."

"Hey, that tickles." He snatched the grass from my hand, stood, and pulled me to my feet. "The breeze off the river is chilly. Let's walk some more."

It wasn't until we stopped in a small cafe for a cup of hot chocolate that I caught my first glimpse of Harry. He entered the cafe seconds after we did and chose to sit only two tables away from us, near an out-of-tune piano, where a middle-aged black man played Scott Joplin tunes. The afternoon had been so perfect that I'd forgotten my problem. Surveying the area more carefully, I also spotted the bald man sitting at a table in the corner with his back to us, the smoke from his pipe swirling into the air above his head. I shuddered.

"What's wrong?" Thad reached across the table and placed his hand on mine. "Are you still cold?"

I shook my head. "It's a long story. I'll tell you about it later." *Time to change the subject.* "So, what about you? Are you still as entranced with socialism as you were? You haven't said much about it in your letters lately."

He studied my hand, turning it over and tracing the life line with his fingertips. "A good question. I'm not sure I know how to answer it right now." He paused. "When I first arrived from New York, I threw myself into the movement. Now, I don't know."

The confusion in his eyes unnerved me. I sensed that the anguish in his voice grew out of a deep inner pain. "I just don't know. I've seen—" He paused. "The scholars of our era are already calling us 'the lost generation,' so I guess I'm not alone, am I?" He snorted in derision. "Makes me feel like an infernal cliché!" He grew silent. For several minutes, we silently held hands, each lost in our own thoughts. When he did speak, his voice was husky with emotion. "In an ideal world, Communism would be the way to go—no rich, no poor, everyone equal."

"If only the world were perfect." I sighed, remembering the orphans I had left behind at Chamonix. "If only life were always fair."

"That's the problem. It isn't. Even in Communism, some people seem to be a little more equal than others."

"But in your letters and your essays, you sounded so positive."

He curled his upper lip into a sneer. "Writing about the ideals of Communism and living those ideals are two different disciplines."

My breath caught in my throat. This was the opportunity I'd been waiting for. I chose my words carefully. "Then I take it that if you were somehow trapped in a moral dilemma between the cause of Communism and capitalism, you wouldn't automatically follow the party line?"

His eyes narrowed as he studied my face, suspicion creeping into his eyes. "Why would you ask such a question?"

I withdrew my hands from his, leaned forward on my elbows, and rested my chin in my hands. "It's purely hypothetical."

He snorted again. "Usually, when people say a question is hypothetical, it is anything but."

"Just answer the question. If you had to make an ethical choice between the principles of the party and your friendship with me, where would your loyalties lie?"

"That's a strange question. I-I don't know. I like to think that I would be loyal to you, I guess." He looked bewildered.

I gave a sigh of relief and grinned. "I'm so glad you said that."

"What are you not telling me, CeeCee? I've known you long enough to know when you're upset about something."

"Upset?" I looked past his shoulder at Harry, then at the bald man.

"Come on. If you aren't worried about something, why have you been tapping your toes ever since we sat down? You always jiggle your foot when you're upset." He leaned back in his chair.

"My foot was tapping?"

"Yes, it was. And I know you. You only do that when you're agitated about something."

I glanced over his shoulder at Harry. *The man's eavesdropping! Of all the—* I scooted my chair from the table. "Let's walk so I can tell you all about it."

Eyes filled with suspicion, Thad rose to his feet and assisted me to mine. After placing a handful of coins on the table, he escorted me from the cafe. I couldn't resist a quick glance backward at my pursuers. Thad turned casually, surveying the area. "What is it, CeeCee? Are those men following you?"

I nodded and accelerated our pace.

"Why?"

"That's the long story."

A strange little smile tilted the corners of his mouth. "Do you want to get rid of them?"

"Absolutely. It's been a nightmare."

"OK." He tightened his hold on my hand. "Hang on." Without warning, he darted across the busy thoroughfare, dragging me behind. With my free hand, I held my picture hat in place on my head. We paused at the boulevard for an instant, then catching a short break in the afternoon traffic, sprinted the rest of the way to the opposite curb.

Behind us, I could see the two men standing on the curb, twenty feet apart, waiting for a safe break in the traffic. Thad and I dashed across a footbridge that spanned one of the Seine's smaller tributaries, then zigzagged between carefully manicured shrubbery higher than my head.

When we reached the ramp to the gray stone traffic bridge arching the main river, a gust of wind caught my picture hat and sent it sailing into the air. I lunged for it, but Thad dragged me in the opposite direction. We slipped and slid down the grassy bank and, at the last instant, ducked under the wide gray stone bridge spanning the river.

"My new hat," I wailed, casting one last glance over my shoulder. My voice carried the length of the arch.

"Forget the hat," Thad growled.

In the darkness, I stumbled over the sprawled legs of a drunken man lying on the narrow concrete causeway beneath the bridge.

"Oh, excuse me," I gasped, catching myself in time to keep from falling.

The man mumbled and lifted a green wine bottle to his lips. Thad pulled me deeper into the shadows until the only light illuminating our way came from the other end of the bridge. Adrenaline washed through me like a blast of cold water.

"What are we—" I gasped for air.

"Sh." He placed his hand gently over my lips and pressed me flat against the moss-covered masonry with his body so that the abutment obscured both of us from view. My hands were sandwiched against his chest.

"Sh! One of those men just peered around the end of the bridge," Thad hissed. I tried to look, but I couldn't lift my head away from the moss-covered wall. Thad's hand remained firmly pressed against my mouth.

A bellow echoed off the stone archway. It was the drunk. "Hey, whatcha think y'er doing? Go away. I don't want company."

In broken French, the interloper asked, "Did you see a man and a woman run past here?"

Thad's heart pounded against the palms of my hands as we stood, poised, ready to run.

The intoxicated man laughed. "Before or after the parade of green giraffes?"

Motionless, we listened to the clatter of traffic passing over our heads. After a few minutes, Thad gently withdrew his hand from my mouth, his fingers lingering on my lower lip. "Are you all right?" he whispered.

I nodded, the terror inside me still acute.

"I'm sorry about your new hat," he whispered, his breath rustling the tendrils along the side of my face.

Breathless from his close proximity more than from the run, I lifted my eyes slowly to find him staring at me. I feared that my eyes revealed much too much of my feelings. And while the shadows obscured most of his face, I saw enough to know he was experiencing similar emotions. I moistened my suddenly dry lips. "I don't care about the hat."

Pressing his hands against the wall behind me, he searched my eyes for several seconds, then, his voice raspy from emotion, asked, "What do we do now?"

"About the men chasing us?"

He shook his head slowly and took a half step backward, his hands still pressing against the wall beside me. "They're not what concerns me at the moment."

I laughed nervously. "I don't know what you mean."

Shifting his weight backward, he captured my hands in his and placed a series of light kisses on my fingertips. "I think you do, my dear."

I felt a tiny jolt of pleasure and closed my eyes to savor it.

"What about Paul?" he asked.

"Paul?" My eyes flew open in surprise.

He continued kissing my fingers as he spoke. "From your letters, I sensed you truly cared for the man. Do you still?" He acted as if my fingertips were the most intriguing substance on the planet. "Is your heart—unattached?"

How do I explain about Paul? Yes, I still care for him very much. But not in the way you think.

Thad spoke before I could reply.

"CeeCee, I know what it's like to love and lose someone—Ashley. I don't want to be hurt again. But, more importantly—" He paused and blew a stray curl from my forehead. "My feelings for you have been growing stronger with every letter."

I struggled to interpret his words. *Is it possible, really possible?* For so long, I'd refused to admit my feelings for Thad to anyone, least of all myself. Even when those around me began to suspect, I had denied caring for him.

"In my enthusiasm for being with you again, I don't want to presuppose that you feel the same about me."

Can't you tell how I feel about you? You've read almost every other thought I've had today. Can't you tell? A wave of shyness flooded over me. *How can I deny caring for you as I do? How many times have I seen your face in my dreams? But I can't just throw myself into your arms.* I started to laugh at that thought. *You're already in his arms, stupid, and have been for ten minutes.*

He bristled slightly. "What is so funny?"

I smiled slowly and whispered, "I don't think that's a problem."

Thad froze for an instant. His hands tightened around mine. "Are you saying—"

My shawl slipped to the ground as I slipped my hands out of his and placed them lightly around his neck. "As you so aptly stated earlier, 'I think you know, my dear.' "

He laughed an easy, rich laugh and slid his arms about my waist. "Ever since the day at your parents' home in Manhattan, I've dreamed of this moment."

"You mean the time Rusty walked in when we were saying goodbye?" A smile splayed across my lips.

"Uh-huh." By now, our lips were just a breath apart.

"Rusty's across the channel in London this time," I teased.

"Uh-huh." His lips touched mine as gently as the flutter of butterfly wings. For an instant, I wondered if I'd imagined the kiss. Then he kissed me again. This time, I had no doubt. Then a third time our lips met.

I threw my head back against the moss-covered stones and savored the moment. Dizzy with happiness, I felt deliciously comfortable in his arms. For an instant, the memory of Paul flashed through my mind, and suddenly I realized that Paul had been right all along. He'd known that one day, I'd be grateful that he didn't kiss me that night beside the orphanage.

"Oh, my darling, is this really happening?" Thad voiced my thoughts exactly. He brushed the tangle of curls tenderly away from my neck and placed a kiss on my ear lobe. "I can't believe this. That you're here, in Paris, in my arms!"

I didn't try to reply—I knew I couldn't.

"You are so precious to me, Chloe Celeste." He eased out of my arms. Suddenly bereft of his warmth, I gave a little cry.

"Where are you going?"

"I love you." Grasping my upper arms firmly, he planted a brief, solid kiss on my surprised lips. "For that reason, we need to get out of here right away. The men chasing us will have given up finding us by now." He picked up my shawl from the ground and draped it about my shoulders. "Let's walk along the river while you tell me what this mystery is all about."

The afternoon light faded as we strolled hand in hand beside the Seine, along with a number of other couples. As I talked about the last forty-eight hours of my life, I doubted that the secrets the other couples shared were at all like the tale I shared with Thad. The more I told him about my bizarre adventure, the more alarmed he became.

"Do you mean to tell me you've been playing hide-and-seek with agents of the Communist government for the last forty-eight hours?"

"That's exactly what I'm telling you."

"These thugs are part of the reason I'm having a difficult time with their philosophy. These men mean business; they are willing to snuff out a life on a whim." He squeezed my hand. If I'd been frightened before, now I was terrified.

He continued. "They won't hesitate to kill you, if necessary, to reach their goals. But I don't understand, with your step-sister and brother gone, why they are still tailing you."

I winced. "That's the rest of the story. Before I left the train this morning, I discovered that Phoebe had left a little something in my luggage. Three gold bars and a set of diamond-and-ruby jewelry." I steeled myself against his reaction.

He gave a low whistle. "Now I understand. Boy, are we in big trouble!"

Delicate Negotiations

The last rays of sunlight danced on the rippling water as we paused beside the river. "And where are these items now?" Thad leaned his elbows on the top railing of the iron guardrail, facing the murky water. Standing beside him, I looked up into his eyes and tried to explain about the switch I made at the railway station and about hiding everything at the embassy. "So you see, the gold and the jewels are completely safe until I decide what to do with them."

"If the embassy personnel haven't searched your room," he responded cynically.

"But they're Americans." I was horrified at the implication.

"And Americans can't become greedy or make shady deals with foreign governments? Don't be naive. I saw more graft and greed at the U.S. headquarters during the war than I hope to ever see again." Pain flickered across his face, and he avoided making eye contact as he continued.

"What do you think made me search for something better? I saw officers sell army rations on the black market for profit while little children, weak from starvation, begged at the army headquarter's main gate. And when I reported the theft, I was reprimanded and told to keep my mouth shut if I didn't want to go home 'in a box.'" He stared unseeing at the river.

"Did you say anything to anyone when you got home?"

"Oh yes." He gave a bitter laugh. "But the press doesn't want to know any details that might tarnish the military's shiny coats of armor in the eyes of the adoring public."

Thad's mood darkened until he was lost in his own nightmare. Trying to call him back to me, I wrapped his arm around my shoulders and turned to face the water, folding my arms tightly across my chest to ward off a growing chill. Then I turned to the only Friend I could think of who could take away Thad's pain. *Dear Father, I don't know how to reach Thad and pull him back, but You do. You know what he saw and how he's been wounded. I know You are the only One who can heal him. Please do. And help me to trust You with those I love instead of thinking I need to have all the answers.*

For a long time, we stood frozen in our own thoughts. I watched a lamplighter across the river as he moved from lamppost to lamppost, lighting each of the yellow-flamed torches. The answer to my prayer came in a whisper through the shade trees lining the walkway. I leaned my head back against Thad's shoulder and let the moist evening breeze gently caress my face. *"Peace I leave with you, my peace I give unto you: not as the world giveth, give I unto you. Let not your heart be troubled, neither let it be afraid."*

While the sky turned to indigo, more couples joined us on the walkway edging the river.

At last, Thad turned to me. After studying me a moment, he moved directly behind me and wrapped both of his arms about my waist. I snuggled into the warmth and protection of his presence. Resting his chin on top of my head, he breathed, "What are you going to do now? About the contraband, I mean."

"I don't know." I shrugged. "I suppose I'll have to retrieve the bag from the train station. I'd leave the case there, except I need a change of clothing. And Jamie's Bible."

"Well, whatever you decide to do, I'm not allowing you out of my sight until I know you're safe in your father's care." His arms tightened about me. "Even then, I'm not sure I'll be willing to let you go."

"That's nice. You make me feel so safe and warm."

If I'd previously doubted my feelings for Thad, I had none now, nestled in his arms.

In a heady voice, I whispered, "The Seine River must be the most romantic river in the world. And I think Paris is the only city in the world where you could get away with such a public display of your affections, Mr. Adams."

"I haven't misread your signals or overstepped my bounds, have I?" I detected a note of caution in his reply. "I don't want to do anything that might injure what we have together at this moment. I can't risk losing you."

I turned slowly to face him. "This is all so new to me; I'm not sure I can accurately answer your question." I studied the chiseled cut of his chin. "I still feel kind of shaky from your kisses." I closed my eyes, fearful that he might laugh at my naiveté—especially after he had associated with urbane French women.

"This has all happened so fast. At one moment, I feel like we're two strangers finding one another for the first time; then at the next moment, I feel as if I've known you forever."

He ran his hands nervously up and down my arms. "You know, of course, we can never go back."

"Go back?" I looked at him in surprise.

"Back to being only friends. It won't work."

His words pained me. I'd treasured his friendship for almost two years—I couldn't imagine my life without it. "So where do we go from here?"

He hesitated. "I hope forward, slowly, one step at a time."

My heart rushed a beat. I remembered something my mother had once said during one of her mother-daughter chats. *"As beautiful as young love might be, it's nothing compared to an old love that's been allowed to grow slowly and purely."* Until that moment, I hadn't even partially understood what she was trying to tell me. And while I still wasn't sure anything could surpass the growing passions I felt for the man holding me in his arms, I did know that I, too, wanted to do whatever I could to protect the love we had. "I'd like that."

In a surge of emotion, he crushed me to him and buried his face in my tangled curls. "For the first time in months, I feel alive again."

I could have stayed in his arms forever, except the gentle breeze had turned cold. A river fog moved in, concealing all but the nearest features of the landscape.

"We'd better go." His voice broke. "I don't feel comfortable—not with those goons obscured by the fog."

"But the fog obscures us too," I pointed out.

"Nonetheless, no one would see us or hear us if they tried to nab us. I think we need to pick up the bag you left at my apartment, pick up the other one at the railway station, then take you back to the embassy, where you'll be safe."

I thought for a moment, trying to find a hole in Thad's plan. "I suppose you're right."

He took my hand and led us toward the boulevard. "I had a meeting tonight, but now that's the last place I want to be."

"Me too." I threw my head back and laughed. The last of my hairpins fell, freeing my confined locks. I shook my head and flipped my curls around my shoulders. Pulling away from Thad's grasp, I whirled on the grassy slope with the ease of a ballerina. "Isn't life utterly fantastic?" I asked, my breath coming in short gasps.

I grabbed his hands, urging him to twirl with me. Instead, he pulled me to him, kissed me soundly, then growled, "I've got to get you to someplace safe." He set off at a pace that forced me to run to keep up.

I started to protest, then fell silent, finally understanding what he'd been trying to tell me most of the day.

"CeeCee, you're so beautifully innocent. I'm determined to keep you that way."

I appreciated the darkness that hid my blush.

When we arrived at his apartment building, Thad insisted I stay downstairs in the building's entryway while he retrieved my case. He returned almost immediately and hailed a cab, which took us directly to the depot. We didn't mention what had happened between us again. Except for my hand comfortably held in his, it was as if we'd done what he said we couldn't do—gone back to simply being friends.

My excitement mounted as we walked across the waiting room's marble floor. I attempted an air of disinterest while my gaze swept the area for a familiar face. From behind the luggage counter, a paunchy, balding clerk smiled ingratiatingly. "May I help you?"

Thad turned to me. "The ticket?"

"Oh yes." I opened my purse and pawed through the few items I'd collected since purchasing it that morning but found no ticket. I looked at Thad in horror, then ransacked the purse once again. "It's gone. The ticket's gone. But when? Where?"

"Did you leave it somewhere? At the apartment, perhaps?"

I shook my head vigorously. "No, I didn't even open my purse while I was in your apartment. I know I had it before I left the embassy. And I remember seeing it when I counted out the money for my new dre—" Suddenly I knew. "Why, that nice old lady! I never suspected she was one of them."

"What? What old lady?"

"The one on the train. I literally ran into her again outside the boutique. She must have picked my pocket, or in this case, my purse."

Thad turned around and told the luggage clerk what had happened. The clerk shook his head. "I couldn't give the bag to you without the claim check."

"This is impossible! I understand that you can't give me the bag. All I am asking you to do is check to see if anyone has claimed it." I felt my temper rising as I struggled to describe the case to the clerk.

The clerk looked down his long, narrow nose at me. "Mademoiselle, I do not need to check. The bag isn't there. An old woman, seventy or so, picked it up this afternoon."

"Wonderful! Now, what am I supposed to wear in the meantime?"

Thad ignored my question. He leaned on the counter. "Was she alone?"

"No, Monsieur. A young man with a long, hideous scar on his cheek accompanied her."

Thad's face blanched. "A scar running from the corner of his eye to the edge of his lip?"

I stared in surprise at Thad. *How do you know about the scar-faced man?*

The clerk nodded. "That's the man."

"André Zabinsky and Comrade Korsikoff. This is getting worse and worse." Thad closed his eyes. "By now, they will have connected you to me."

"Who will have connected us?"

Thad shot a suspicious glance at the clerk and led me away from the counter.

"The cell I belong to here in Paris." He gave a bitter laugh. "It looks as if I may need government protection as well."

"Thad, I'm so sorry. I didn't mean to mess up your life like this."

He sighed. "It can't be helped now. You say all that was in the case was your spare clothing? And a Bible."

"Not just any Bible, but the one my real father gave to Mama. And, of course, Emily."

"Emily?"

"My diary, Emily."

"This is a classic!" He snorted in disbelief. "Are they ever going to be angry when they open the case and find feminine frills instead of a fortune! A Bible and a diary."

"I'd really like the diary and the Bible back!"

"Did you ever mention me in your diary?"

"Many times." *Oops, talk about honesty!*

"Oh!" he groaned. "Now I know I can't go back to my flat. They'll never believe that I wasn't involved with your escape."

"Oh, Thad, I'm sorry. I really am sorry. I didn't think—"

He placed his hand on my arm. "And why should you? You live in a simpler world, one filled with honesty and loyalty, not intrigue and greed. It's not your fault that you got dragged into this, nor is it mine. But dragged we are, like it or not. So we might as well make the best of it."

"Somehow, I sense them watching us, even though I can't see them."

"How stupid!" He ran a hand distractedly through his hair. "This is the most likely spot for them to look after they lost us this afternoon. They know you'd eventually come back to pick up the case. I should have thought of that!"

"Don't blame yourself. I didn't think of it either. And as yet, we haven't seen any of them."

He shook his head slowly and ground his teeth together. "I never dreamed you were dealing with this bunch. Boy, your relatives must have swindled the government out of quite a booty if they sent these thugs to retrieve it."

We strolled across the high-domed waiting area to a small sweet shop. "Glance about slowly. Do you see anyone you recognize here in the station?" He patted my hand and laughed as if he'd said something clever. Through clenched teeth, he hissed, "Smile. Remember we're just another couple, enjoying one another's company."

I pasted a smile on my face and giggled in the way I'd seen my cousin Ashley do so many times over the years. "Oh, Thaddeus, you are such a card."

"And you are such a little pumpkinhead." He tapped the end of my nose with his finger. "I know what you're doing to me."

I batted my eyes and bobbed my head from side to side. "I don't know what you mean." I giggled in a high, irritating trill again.

"You are playing an excellent Ashley McCall, aren't you? You're never going to let me forget that I actually fell for her charms."

While I hadn't consciously mimicked Ashley to irritate him, I liked knowing that it did. I stared wide-eyed up at him, my mouth open in wonder. "How can you say that? This is the real me, didn't you know?"

His smile dropped. "You aren't even funny."

"A-ha," I giggled, batting my lashes again. "I promise I won't tease you about Ashley if you promise never again to call me 'pumpkinhead'!" My last five words came out clear and definite. "And, while we're at it, don't call me red, chili pepper, Tabasco sauce, or any other euphemism for the color of my hair!"

Thad burst out laughing. "I didn't mean to—"

"Come on, how stupid do you think—"

He waved his hands in surrender. "Honest! I didn't even think of it. But now that you mentioned it. Hmm."

I tilted my head and arched my brow. "I'm serious. Don't do it."

He tipped my chin upward. "How about my titian-haired—"

"No!" I gasped. "Especially not that."

"How do you know what I was about to say?"

"I just do. And I especially don't want you to call me that!"

"As you wish, Mademoiselle." He stood facing the opposite direction as I. "What about the man over there reading the newspaper?"

I shook my head.

"Then let's get a taxi and head for the embassy." We stepped out of the building into the cool night air, where a queue of taxis waited.

Thad opened the back door to the first one and helped me into the car. "To the American Embassy."

The car lurched forward, throwing us back against the seat. We rode in silence for several blocks.

Suddenly Thad caught my wrist. "I love you, Chloe Celeste Chamberlain. Do you know that?" His voice grew raspy. "I love you."

"I know. And I think I love you too."

"Think? Only think?" He cradled me in his arms until the taxi pulled up in front of the embassy gate, when he hurriedly kissed me a second time. "The next few hours might be crazy for us, but no matter what happens, remember, I love you."

His premonition of trouble sent a shiver through my body. I nodded, my eyes wide with fear. As he started to open the door, the door was snatched from his hand. The door jerked open, and two hands hauled him from the vehicle. I shrank against the far door in terror. *Run!* I told myself. *Run for your life!* But before I could open my door, a terrifyingly familiar face loomed over me.

"Daddy?" I gasped.

"Get out of this cab immediately, Chloe Celeste!" Fire flashed from his eyes. "After everything else, I find you cavorting about Paris with this, this, reactionary!"

"Reactionary? Thad? Daddy, this is Thaddeus, remember?"

"Sir, I think you—" Thad began.

My father swung around toward Thad. "Don't think. Just be quiet!"

"But, sir—"

"You're a man of the world, Adams. As a gentleman, it is your job to protect my daughter's honor!"

"Daddy!" I was horrified. The only other time I'd seen my

father so angry was when my Uncle Philip had implied that my mother wasn't a lady for being a midwife to the indigent.

The frightened cab driver leapt from the car and flung open my door. Obviously he didn't want to be involved in what might be a political incident. My father tossed the man a handful of bills without asking the tab for our ride. The cabby stuffed the money into his pocket without counting it, jumped into his car, and pulled away from the embassy gate as fast as his Renault could go.

"Daddy!" I ran to my father's side. "How did you get here? In Paris?"

"Sir, I am terribly sorry." Thad cast a gesture of conciliation toward my father.

"You should be. She's barely nineteen years old. She's never been on her own in a big city before—"

"Daddy? Thad?" The two men ignored me.

"I should have been more conscious of how our behavior, touring Paris without a proper chaperon, might be misconstrued."

"Misconstrued?" I shouted to deaf ears. "If anything, it's my fault. I dropped in on him unannounced!"

"I am sorry, sir. I would never do anything to purposely hurt your daughter or her reputation. I care for her deeply."

"Daddy! Thad!" Neither man looked in my direction. "Will you listen to me?" I shouted, stomping my foot on the pavement like a two-year-old.

They turned simultaneously toward me, their mouths open in surprise.

"Thank you," I said in a normal, controlled tone. "I am not a child to talk about in the third person. I can defend my own choices, you know."

My father, his fists clenched to his sides, growled, "So, explain. Where have you been all day? And all night?" He eyed Thad with a look of vengeance.

"It all started when I found the gold and the jewelry in my luggage this morning."

"Gold? Jewelry?" Daddy took my arm and led me toward the embassy. As an afterthought, he turned and gestured to Thad. "You come too." Then, looking at me, he repeated his questions.

"What gold? What jewelry?"

The three of us walked through the arched entry into the brightly lighted foyer. Daddy directed us into a small sitting room and closed the door behind us. He waved Thad and me over to the settee by the window but remained standing himself. "All right, we're alone now. What gold? What jewelry?"

I took a deep breath and told him everything that had happened after Phoebe and Nikolai had arrived at the hospital. I told him about "Harry" and "Payne" and the other men who had followed us from Chamonix. I described the old lady who had picked my pocketbook and how we had hidden under the bridge from our pursuers. I conveniently left out the kisses we shared. If Mama had been there, I knew she would have read the guilt on my face, but Daddy just nodded sagely.

When a knock sounded on the closed door, Daddy snarled, "Who is it?"

"Reggie," was the reply.

"Come on in," my father called. "We're talking about you."

When the door opened, Thad and I gasped in unison. "Harry?"

"Meet Reginald Duquin, the man you called Harry. And Reggie, meet my daughter, CeeCee—" He paused. "—and her friend, Thaddeus Adams." My father walked over to the man in the doorway. "Reggie's on our side. I arranged to have him follow you and protect you from those political hoods. Surely you know I wouldn't just send you and my other two children off on your own without any protection?" He glared at Thad. "He was doing a good job, too, until you two dashed across the traffic, almost getting yourselves killed."

I extended my hand awkwardly. "It's nice to finally meet you, Har—Reginald." The bearded man grinned and shook my hand.

"I thought we were both in big trouble when you ran into Comrade Korsikoff, and she led you to her berth."

"She acted befuddled, like she'd gotten turned around in her directions. Besides, I thought the sweet old lady was a godsend to protect me from you and the bald man with the pipe."

"You identified Felix Potterbaum too?"

"And André somebody, the man with the scar—"

"Zabinsky," Reggie interrupted.

"There was a swarthy guy I called Payne."

Reggie looked at my father, then back at me. "The man is a pain, but his name is Vaughn, Vaughn La Strada. He operates on both sides of the fence—sells himself to the highest bidder."

I thought a moment. "There was one more whom Phoebe mentioned spotting, a young man wearing a black-and-gray striped jersey and dark pants and a navy beret."

Reggie and my father exchanged glances and shrugged.

"Oh, well, maybe he was just an amorous Frenchman attracted to a pretty face."

Daddy didn't acknowledge my comment but turned to Reggie. "CeeCee tells me that there's more of the smuggled booty upstairs in the guest room where she'll be sleeping tonight. Perhaps you'd better retrieve it before some unsuspecting hireling comes across it and thinks he's died and gone to paradise." Turning to me, Daddy ordered, "Tell him where you hid the stuff."

I gave the man directions to the books and the jewelry case, then fell silent until the door closed behind Reggie. "How was I supposed to know Harry, er, Reggie, was one of the good guys?"

My father strode across the room, his hands folded behind his back. "He's military intelligence."

"Isn't that an oxymoron, sir?" Thad mumbled under his breath.

I gave Thad a dirty look, hoping my father hadn't overheard his sarcasm. But he had. In a cool, level tone, my father replied, "—and my friend."

Thad reddened. "Sorry, sir."

Daddy stopped pacing directly in front of Thad and glared down at him. "You have quite a few opinions for one so young, don't you, son?"

"Yes, sir. I'm sorry for voicing them, under the circumstances."

"And under what circumstances would you feel your remark would be appropriate?" Before Thad could answer, Daddy continued. "Believe it or not, there are still a few honest and trustworthy men in the world."

"I'm sure there are, sir. I didn't mean—"

Another knock sounded on the door. My father silenced Thad. "Later. We can debate the issue later. Come in."

Reggie entered and placed the treasures on the library table in the center of the room. My father strode to the table and opened the velvet box. The diamonds and rubies sparkled in the light from the electric wall sconces. At the sight of the jewels, Thad inhaled sharply.

"Wait," I mumbled, "it gets better."

Daddy opened the cover of the top book, *Sonnets From the Portuguese*; then he opened the second and the third. The gold bars gleamed in the room's incandescent light. "Well, there it is, Reg, all of it, I hope."

"The Russian agent said something about a ruby-and-diamond necklace set this morning, but he didn't mention the gold bars." The military man lifted the necklace from the box. "Says it's worth forty or fifty thousand, at least."

Thad and I shot a glance at one another. *People have been killed for less.* When I started to shake, Thad placed his hand on mine.

My father whirled about and glared at us. Instantly, Thad removed his hand from mine and folded it in his lap.

Daddy hefted one of the gold bars. "My guess is, the agent didn't know about these. My, these critters are heavy!"

"I know," I interjected. "I carried them from the train station."

"Wait," Reggie said. "I have something for you." He exited the room and returned almost instantly. "I found these in a trash can outside the railway station this afternoon." Tears filled my eyes when he handed me my Bible and my diary. "Thank you so much," I gulped. "I thought these were gone forever."

On the Winds of the Storm

Cyrus Chamberlain crying? I searched my father's pained-filled eyes for understanding. "I'm sorry I caused you to worry. I never dreamed you'd make it from London to Paris so quickly."

He grunted and pulled me into his arms. "Diplomatic privileges, my dear. Besides, the moment your mother heard about the problem, she was determined to come and battle the entire Communist movement to protect you."

I laughed. "That sounds like Mama. How did you convince her to stay behind in London?"

"Rusty. He needed her—and she knew it."

"Good. And, Daddy, Thad isn't the bad guy you think he is. Quite the contrary, he was concerned about my reputation and my physical safety at every turn."

When I explained to my father how Thad himself would be in danger if he went back to the Left Bank, Reggie took him to see the ambassador. I was pleased to have a few minutes alone with my father.

Like a young child, I pressed my ear against my father's chest and listened to the deep, reassuring resonance of his voice. "I am so grateful you're safe. I worried myself sick after Reggie found your Bible and your diary; I thought the worst had happened."

"I missed you so much, Daddy." I snuggled deeper into his arms, feeling the warmth and protection only a loving father can give.

"I'm still angry at Phoebe and Nikolai for dumping this stuff on you. You could have been killed. When I get back to London, they're going to hear about it from me."

I straightened in surprise. "Phoebe? Nikolai? You found them?"

"Found them? I spent most of the afternoon unraveling the mess they'd gotten themselves into! They were arrested by the customs officials in Calais for trying to smuggle gold out of France without declaring it, and somehow the Communists learned of it. When I got there, I had to agree to turn over Phoebe and Nikolai's fortune to secure their release from jail."

"Jail?"

He nodded.

"What all did they try to smuggle?"

"Oh-ho-ho," he chuckled, "this little cache you unknowingly carried is a drop in the bucket compared to what they were carrying. Unmounted jewels, Swiss bank notes, two golden urns, —just as a start." He hefted one of the gold bars. "And, now, what do I do with this stuff? Since it wasn't part of the deal, I wonder—would it be right for them to keep it? It will only be turned over to the Communists—after France gets its cut, of course."

"Good question." I ran my fingers across the velvet jewelry case and thought about the moral dilemma my stepsister and stepbrother had created. "Where are Phoebe and Nikolai?"

"Somewhere between Dover and London. Your mother wired me from Dover that they'd arrived safe, reasonably sound, and furious with me for making them surrender everything, including the treasure chest of unset jewels."

"Poor Mama. I don't envy her trip back to London. Those two can be a pain, let me tell you, especially Nikolai."

"I agree." Daddy sighed. "The boy has a will of iron. It was only the threat of a five-year jail sentence for smuggling that persuaded him to sign the papers."

"So what happens next?" Holding my breath, I studied the shade on the small table lamp.

My father shook his head. "I have a feeling that life as we knew it will never be the same again."

"No, I mean with Thad. Will they keep him here?" *Oh, dear God, I can't even say it, but I have to know*. "Put him in jail for subversive activities?"

"I don't know." He placed the gold bar inside the book and closed the cover. "If he cooperates, they'll probably be lenient. I hope they'll credit his actions to being young and foolish."

A rush of anger brought color to my cheeks. "Why do people over the age of thirty automatically link the words *young* and *foolish*? Thad lived by his conscience, that's all. Is that foolish?" My reaction was stronger than warranted, but I couldn't contain my frustration. I turned away from my father. "And, now, is it foolish for him to be man enough to admit he was wrong?"

My father stepped up behind me and squeezed my shoulder. "CeeCee, I have nothing against the boy. He hasn't done anything more foolish than the things I did in my youth. But he is young." He paused, and I could feel his concern. "Remember, twenty years old for a man is much younger than the equivalent is for a woman."

"Oh, Daddy! Don't be so Victorian!"

He chuckled. "I remember saying something similar to your Grandfather Chamberlain when I was your age. And in the process, I had to learn some hard lessons, CeeCee, because I scorned my father's advice."

I don't want to defy you, Daddy—I just want you to understand how I feel. Gulping back my tears, I choked out, "Can't you see that I really care for him?"

"I can tell, and that's what worries me. I just want to protect you from unnecessary heartache."

I whipped about and opened my mouth to speak, but a lock of my loose-flying hair plastered itself across my mouth. Irritated, I brushed it aside. "I don't understand. Mama was barely eighteen when she married my father. You were what, twenty-two, when you married your first wife, Phoebe's mother?"

"Precisely. Thank you for making my argument for me. While your mother might have been ready for a marital commitment at eighteen, Pamela and I were not, and the results brought incredible pain to both of us—and now, to Phoebe and Nikolai."

Fighting a flood of angry tears, I threw myself into the closest chair. "I don't think I want to talk about this any longer." My fingertips worried the carved mahogany armrests.

I averted my eyes from my father's sad, yet tender gaze. "Perhaps you're right. We'll have plenty of time to talk about private family matters when we return to England in the morning. In the meantime, if you'll excuse me, my darling—" He planted a kiss on my forehead. "—I've decided to take the gold bars and the jewelry to the ambassador, if he is finished speaking with Thaddeus, that is." He scooped the small fortune into his hands and strode from the room, leaving the door ajar.

I stared into the black marble fireplace across the room and shuddered. *Finally, Thad and I find each other, only to be torn apart yet again—this time, possibly forever.* I tried to recall the warmth I'd felt wrapped in Thad's arms, the sensation of his breath on my neck, his lips pressed to mine. But the memories failed to comfort me. *What is going to happen to us, Lord? I just know Mama and Daddy are going to spoil everything—if the United States government doesn't beat them to it.*

I didn't see Thad or my father again until the next morning. A chambermaid awakened me at six with a tray of pastries and the message that we must leave for Calais on the seven-o'clock train. I asked her to press my wrinkled gray traveling suit. By the time she returned and laid it on the bed, I'd bathed and was packed and ready to go. *At least I can feel composed and confident.*

The ride to the railway station was strained and quiet. Sober and subdued, Thad stared as his hands. Reggie and my father sat across from us, speaking in short, abrupt missives. The agent would travel with us until we were safely aboard the ferry to England. I had a myriad of questions to ask both my father and Thaddeus, but pride and Reggie's presence kept me silent.

When we boarded the train, I waited until my father and Reggie chose seats halfway up the day car, then pulled Thad toward the last row of seats. *The last thing I want is for Daddy and his friend close enough to overhear our conversations or to keep watch should Thad try to hold my hand.* I knew I was behaving like a child, and it had been some time since I felt so much like one. *Here I've lived in London's glittery fast track, I've*

seen wounded soldiers die, I've saved the lives of injured chil-
dren—all as an adult—and, now, now, my dear old dad treats
me like a twelve-year-old! Parents! Sometimes they make no sense.
Thank God, Mama will be able to talk reason into him when we
get home.

I slid into the window seat; Thad followed. "What happened
between you and the ambassador last night?" I knew it couldn't
be too bad, or the ambassador wouldn't have allowed Thad to
leave France.

"He left me with a lot to think about."

"What do you mean?"

"The ambassador had on his desk every article I've ever pub-
lished. It was like my entire life was on display and I was standing before, what my mother used to call, 'the bar of God.' " He
snorted, "If there is such a thing."

Thad stared down at his hands for some time before he spoke
again. "I had to tell him all I knew about the Communist movement in New York and Paris. Technically, I could be charged,
and probably convicted, of treason under the Espionage Act. My
penalty could be as much as $10,000 in fines and twenty years
in prison, or both."

"Is the ambassador going to prosecute?"

He shrugged. "When he makes his report, he'll recommend
one way or the other."

"Did you tell him that you no longer hold to those beliefs?"
My toes set to tapping.

"Of course, but even as I said it, I thought of how convenient
my change of heart must sound to him under the circumstances.
I doubt he believed me." Thad stared past me, out the window.
"This is really serious, CeeCee. Your father promised to do
everything he can for me."

Good old dad! He always comes through in the end.

"Your father says that my biggest hope of beating this thing
is the possibility that it will be overlooked in the excitement of
the signing of the treaty."

"Great! Your fate lies in the hands of a bureaucratic error?"

Thad chuckled aloud. "For the first time since last night, I
think there might be hope."

"Thad, be serious!" I folded my arms across my chest and pouted.

"I am being serious. After working at army headquarters, I understand the government's penchant for making blunders. There were times we'd receive the papers for dead soldiers who had never existed." He laughed again. "The army had no record of the men ever being in the army in the first place, let alone in France. What a mess!"

"How did we ever win the war?"

"Good question, my dear. Fortunately, the competent officers outnumbered the inept—a fact I tend to forget at times."

I captured one of his hands with mine. "So, what happens next?"

"The investigation will continue at the London office, thanks to your father. They took my claims seriously that my life would be in danger if I stayed in Paris. They'll be sending my personal belongings in a diplomatic pouch in a few days." He shrugged. "I don't have much. Fortunately for me, there's nothing in my garret that would incriminate me further. I was careful about that."

He squeezed my hand. "Oh, CeeCee, you are all I have left right now. I'm so afraid I might lose you too."

I leaned my head back against the seat and turned my face toward his. "That won't happen; I promise you."

"But your father—"

"Leave my father to Mama and me." I attempted to smile reassuringly. "He'll listen to reason."

"I don't know— No regrets about yesterday?"

"No regrets." I ached to kiss away the worry lines creasing his forehead, but things were different in the pale morning light. We both felt the restrictions that had been lacking the day before. I sighed at the loss. Paris was behind us, and an uncertain future lay ahead. "Regardless of what happens, I do love you. And I'll stand beside you."

"I love you too, Chloe Celeste—for always, no matter what happens." Thad pressed my hand to his lips.

I looked up to find my father standing in the aisle beside our seat. The scowl on his forehead matched the fire in his eyes.

Behind him, Reggie pretended to be interested in the sheaf of papers he carried.

Thad followed my gaze toward Daddy and dropped my hand instantly. My father grunted his displeasure. "Terribly free with my daughter's person, aren't you?"

Thad reddened. "Sorry, sir."

Daddy continued to glare. "When we leave the train, I need to stop at the local police station before boarding the ferry. I was going to suggest that you two go straight to the boat without me, but maybe that's not a good idea."

"Daddy, it's not as if we might elope between the station and the dock!" I slunk back against my seat, again feeling like a twelve-year-old, and set my toes to tapping once more. *I am so embarrassed. I wish I'd stayed in Chamonix. At least there I was treated like a responsible adult!*

"CeeCee!" Thad hissed. "Don't talk to your father that way!"

Wonderful! Now I have two men scolding me! Just what I need. The reflection in the train window of my angry, pinched face was hardly becoming, but I didn't care. I wished they'd both go away.

"Sir, I apologize for any actions of mine that appeared unseemly. You can trust me to deliver your daughter safe and sound to the ferry."

I shot Thad a hateful glare. *How can he kowtow to the enemy? Enemy?* The idea startled me. I'd never thought of my father as an enemy. My mother, maybe, but never my father.

I maintained my foul mood throughout the rest of the train ride. When we reached the train station, I set out for the ferry dock at a pace that challenged Thad and his long legs to match. Glancing over my shoulder, I was surprised to see Reggie fifty yards behind, tailing us. *So Daddy really doesn't trust us enough to let us walk between the train and the dock without chaperonage! I don't believe it!*

Eyeing the overcast sky, I remembered my earlier crossing and cringed. *Please, no storms today. I have enough troubles without adding nausea to the list.* For a moment, I wondered if the same officer who'd kept me from leaving the cabin during the storm would be on duty and remember me. *Who cares? All I*

*want to do is find a seat by myself and make Thad, Daddy, and
Reggie disappear.*

My mood didn't improve once we docked in Dover. That's when
I learned Reggie hadn't been following me but had been following Thad. For on the other side, an embassy security car awaited
our arrival. Helplessly, I watched two embassy officials take
him into custody. I wanted to run to him, throw my arms about
him, and apologize for wasting our last hours together by pout-
ing.

"Daddy!" I turned to find my father standing directly behind
me. "Do something. Stop them."

"I've done all I can do. Thaddeus will be under house arrest,
as a favor to me, until the State Department decides his fate."

"What do you mean, 'as a favor to you'? Are you that desperate to keep the two of us apart?" I spat the words in his face.

A wave of sadness swept across my father's face. "I mean, as
a favor to me, the ambassador has agreed to the house arrest
for the time being, instead of jail."

"Oh." I reddened and dropped my head.

"Let's get through customs and meet your mother. I'm sure
she's been waiting for hours, knowing her. Probably didn't sleep
last night, knowing you were coming home."

I allowed him to lead me to the customs desk. When he showed
his embassy badge, the agent waved us through English customs without a second glance. My distress over Thad's arrest
faded when we entered the large waiting area and I first saw
my mother. One glance, and I ran into her waiting arms. Tears
fell as I buried my face in her shoulder.

"I missed you so much," I cried.

Mama held me in her arms. "Oh, CeeCee, I'm so glad you are
back safely! Come on, let's get you home." She released me, then
kissed my father. "Everything all right?" I saw a warning look
pass between the two of them. "Ralph is waiting outside with
the car."

"Ralph?" I frowned. "Who is Ralph?"

"Our embassy chauffeur."

I brightened. "Is Thad with him?"

My father pursed his lips and shook his head. "No, they took him back to London in another car."

"Oh—"

Again, my parents exchanged worried glances. "Must we wait for any luggage?" Mama asked, her voice too bright, her smile too broad.

"Daddy, will I be able to see Thad again, I mean, in the next day or so?"

My father took my mother's arm and directed us toward the exit. "I don't know. I'll talk with the ambassador and see if he'll give the two of you a few minutes together."

"Thank you." I fell into silence during the walk to the waiting government car. Once inside the spacious Packard, I remained silent as my parents discussed the latest on my stepsister and brother and the fate of their disputed treasure.

My father removed the chocolate brown velvet jewelry case from his pocket and handed it to Mama. "The ambassador suggested I turn over the gold bars to the French government and not mention this. Something about its being a family heirloom."

"That was nice of him." Mama opened the case and gasped. "How beautiful."

"I had the feeling that he hated the thought of relinquishing any of the children's wealth to the French or Communist governments."

I stared out the window as they continued their discussion. "So everything's settled as far as the children are concerned?"

My father cleared his throat. "Everything except Thaddeus's problem."

An unbidden sob escaped from me. My mother patted my leg. "Perhaps we should talk about this later."

"Why?" The question burst from my throat with a force that startled even me. "Do you think you can protect me from knowing the truth? I'm no longer a little girl to coddle and smother!"

"CeeCee, no one's trying to—"

"Everyone treats Thad's and my relationship as if it were a childish crush that will fade away in a week or two. It won't! I can promise you that, it won't." Mama reached for my hand. I snatched it away. "I love him. His pain is my pain; his troubles are mine!"

"Honey, I know you think that you—"

"Don't, Mother!" I snapped, fire shooting from my eyes. "You don't know anything about me or my feelings! You haven't seen me for more than four months. And you know nothing about Thaddeus."

"Chloe Celeste!" The fire in my father's eyes matched mine. "I won't have you—"

"Don't, Cyrus." She placed her hand on his. "She's right. We bade a teenage girl farewell, and she has returned to us with the mind and emotions of a woman. I am sorry for condescending to you as I did."

My anger disarmed, I sputtered, trying to save face. "It's difficult for me to have been treated as an adult at the orphanage and to have made adult decisions, then to return home to little-girl status in your and Daddy's eyes."

She nodded slowly. "I'm sure it is, darling. Give us time to adjust, all right?"

"She's still a minor," Daddy muttered under his breath. Mama patted his hand to silence him.

"And as an adult, you must realize that Thad's legal problems won't disappear overnight."

"I never said they would," I defended. "You act like you think we're going to run off and get married." Each time I used the word *married*, a gentle thrill passed through me. *Would such an idea be so bad? If he should ask me, of course.*

Mama smiled. In her eyes, I could see a sad, faraway look. "I would hope you are both too wise to make such an unfortunate choice."

"I do love him!"

"I'm sure you do, but at this point, all you'd have going for you is your love."

"Our love is strong enough to see—"

"Strong enough to weather a possible prison sentence?"

"I'd wait for him."

My father heaved a massive sigh. "The boy has nothing going for him right now—no job, no education, no financial support of any kind."

"I-I-I can find work. The doctors at the clinic say I have superior talents as a nurse."

Mama's smile faded. "But you are not a licensed nurse at this point. After a two-year nursing course—"

"And what about your basic philosophical beliefs?" my father interjected. "Jamie told us that you began to believe in Christ while at Chamonix. Thad—"

"I can change that. Thad's a reasonable man."

My parents looked at one another and smiled sadly. Mama shook her gloved finger in the air. "One of the first lessons you will learn as a young wife is to never try to change your husband. It doesn't work."

I folded my arms and sank back into the car's leather seat. "That may be true for you and Daddy, but it will be different with Thad and me."

Daddy leaned forward. "Look at it this way. Thad needs time to find himself. In time, he'd resent you for not giving him time to discover what he wants from life."

"And what about God's leading in your life?" Mama always could deliver the *coup de grâce*.

I flung my hands into the air. "Fine! What choice do I have, anyway? I'm considered a child until my twenty-first birthday, so a child I shall be." I returned to my pout, grudgingly admitting to myself that my behavior fit my statement far too well. My snit intensified when I arrived home and found Phoebe installed in my bedroom and her clothing filling half of my wardrobe. By the petulant pout on Rusty's face when he met me at the front door, I knew he was equally as inconvenienced and displeased by the arrival of Nikolai in his orderly little world.

"Mama said it is temporary," Rusty grumbled.

"Right." I slipped my arm around my brother, who'd grown a good inch and a half during my absence. "And when we get back to New York?"

Rusty dug his toe in the deep blue carpet at the top of the staircase. "Daddy says he's going to buy land and build a place along the Jersey shore now that the war is over."

When the front door opened and we heard Nikolai and Phoebe enter the house, we stepped back. "I don't like Nikolai at all. I don't care if he is my brother."

"You know what?" I whispered. "I don't like him either."

"Good!"

"But for Mama and Daddy's sake, we've got to get along, you know."

Rusty's pout deepened. "I know!"

"Maybe, in time, we may come to like him."

"I doubt it."

"Perhaps Nikolai acts so mean because he's scared."

Rusty cocked his head. "Scared?"

"Yeah, like you. You're scared Daddy and Mama will love him more, and Nikolai could be scared no one will love him."

He snorted. "He'll be right if he continues to act like he does."

That evening, while Phoebe took her bath, I sat at my desk and wrote in my diary. *Dear Emily, What is wrong with me? In Chamonix and in Paris, I felt so adultlike—confident about myself and where I was going. Now, the minute I get home, I'm thinking and acting like a spoiled schoolgirl.* I nibbled on my pencil for a moment, then continued. *I can't seem to stop myself. I find myself saying things I don't mean and in a tone of voice I abhor. What's wrong with me?*

Frustrated with the unwelcome convolutions in my life, I stood and walked over to the window, looking down at the quiet square in front of our town house. An old man with a cane hobbled along the sidewalk. A way behind him, a middle-aged couple, arm in arm, strolled casually along. I thought of Thad, scared and alone, uncertain if his future included a prison term.

Dear God, this isn't fair. None of it. Thad was only following his conscience, doing what he believed to be right. Besides, he is now disillusioned with Communism—that should count for something!

I picked up my Bible and opened to a verse in Psalm 25 that I had heard my father quote to Reggie during the ride to the train station in Paris. "Remember not the sins of my youth, nor my transgressions: according to thy mercy remember thou me."

Oh, please, Lord, make the ambassador see that Thad's indiscretion has more to do with his age than with treason against his country.

The next several days, I prayed that prayer. The following

week, my father arranged for me to visit Thad at the embassy. I started dressing for the afternoon reunion before seven in the morning. I must have tried on fifteen dresses before I chose the lavender-and-gray floral chiffon dress with a soft capelike bodice and tiny pearl buttons. Carefully piling my hair on top of my head, I pinned a natural-straw picture hat in place, adding a jaunty lavender velvet ribbon around the crown at the last minute.

Riding along the busy London streets in the back seat of the embassy car, I wondered if things might have changed between us during Thad's incarceration. Would he be bitter? Angry? Would he still love me?

Daddy met me at the curb, dismissed the driver, and escorted me into the American Embassy. The office staff greeted me warmly, remembering me from the week my family had lived in the guest quarters upon arriving in England. I detected glances of sympathy from them as my father led me into a receiving parlor to await Thad's arrival.

For five minutes, I paced in front of the floor-to-ceiling windows. When I heard the massive oak doors swing open, I whirled about to see Thad and my father standing in the entry.

"CeeCee." Thad's voice broke. "You came!"

I flew across the room to Thad but stopped short of his arms when, over Thad's shoulder, my father's and my eyes met. Instead, I grasped Thad's hands in mine.

"It's so good to see you. Are they treating you all right? I missed you."

He gave me a wan smile. His eyes looked tired, wary. "I missed you too."

Daddy cleared his throat. "If you two will excuse me, I, er, need to speak with the ambassador for a few minutes." He backed out of the room, closing the doors behind him.

Surprised by my father's exit, I continued holding Thad's hands for a few seconds, then glanced shyly up into his face. He looked at me with similar apprehension. At the same instant, we released each other's hands and fell into each other's arms. As my head flew back, I grabbed for my hat.

"You and your hats," he laughed and tossed it onto a gleaming mahogany desktop, then gathered me into his arms again. "I've missed you so much." He swept me off my feet and twirled me around in his arms.

I squealed with laughter and pretended to beat on his chest. "Put me down, you Neanderthal! Let me go."

He buried his face in my neck. "I'm never going to let you go! Never, ever, ever."

"You're crazy."

Throwing his head back, he shouted, "Crazy with love for you."

"Sh-sh-sh!" I touched my fingers to his lips. He caught them between his lips, nibbling on them gently. "Someone will hear you."

"So?"

"So, it would be embarrassing."

His face darkened. "Do I embarrass you?"

"Thaddeus Adams! How dare you ask such a question? Of course not." I placed a firm kiss on his lips and led him to the Victorian sofa on the opposite side of the room. "Now, tell me what is happening. Has anything been decided?"

"Actually, yes. Good news too. The ambassador has decided to send me home with a reprimand and a promise that I will, as he put it, 'keep my nose clean.' "

"What?" I had to restrain myself from leaping into his arms.

"That's right. He suggests that I enroll in a four-year college to study journalism."

"Where will you get the money to start college? It costs money."

"That's the best part. While stationed at headquarters in Paris during the war, one of my superior officers, Major General Oliver Tate, was impressed with my writing ability. And he offered to pay for further training if I so desired. At the time, I wasn't interested, but now—"

"Praise God, I can hardly believe it. I was so afraid for you, for us." I sniffed back a sudden wash of tears. He retrieved a handkerchief from his pocket and dabbed at my eyes.

"It's all right. Everything is going to be all right." His face beamed with happiness. "I'm supposed to sail for home on Thursday."

"Thursday? But that's two days away!"

"I know. The first thing I want to do is to mend fences with my father." He paused, studying my face for my reaction. "Then, I thought I'd apply at New York University. It is supposed to have a great journalism program."

"New York?" My eyes widened with delight. "Oh, Thad, it would be so nice to be together again."

He nodded enthusiastically. "All along, our timing has been terrible. I figure we need time together to give our love a chance to grow."

I threw myself into his arms. "Oh, yes, yes, yes."

He untangled himself from my arms and captured my face in his hands. "And if things work out, say, after a year or two, will you marry me?"

"Oh yes!"

As we gazed into each other's eyes, we could hear the voices of my father and the ambassador in the hallway. After a quick kiss to seal our agreement, we drew apart. The doors swung open. I reached up to tidy my hair while Thad strode over to the nearest window.

Awkwardly, I said goodbye to Thad, promising to write as soon as he sent me his address. He took my hand and bowed politely, then acknowledged the two men and left the room. My hands shook as I gathered my hat from the table and adjusted it on my head, all the while avoiding my father's and the ambassador's eyes.

Daddy rode home with me from the embassy. He was the first to speak. "The ambassador is impressed with Thaddeus. He has decided to overlook the boy's indiscretion and send him home, but you probably already know that."

"Yes. Thad said he'd be sailing on Thursday."

"He's on probation, of course."

"Probation?"

My father nodded. "Any further subversive activities or even a traffic violation will bring the United States Justice Department down on his head.

"Did he tell you he plans to attend college?"

"Yes." I smiled. My eyes grew misty. "Oh, Daddy, I appreciate so much all you've done for Thad. He's worth it, honest."

My father patted my hand. "I hope so. I truly hope so."

"What do you mean?"

"He seems like a fine young man—confused but fine. Give him a few years—"

"A few years?"

Daddy explained, "He's young. Like it or not, he's much younger than you spiritually and emotionally. He has no idea what he wants or where he's going."

"Oh, Daddy."

"I know you don't like to hear it, but it's true."

I sighed deeply and turned toward the window. "When can I leave for New York?"

My father didn't answer immediately. "I'm sure you'll want to stay in London until after Jamie and Auriel's wedding in August."

"August? That's two months away," I wailed.

"Two months is a short-enough time for your big brother, don't you think?"

"In the meantime?"

"In the meantime, why don't you apply to a couple schools of nursing in the States? Mama said you'd decided that's what you wanted, right?"

Cautiously, I nodded. Nurse Bouchard had told me before I left Chamonix that an accredited nursing program would take two years to complete. I had promised her only that I would think about it.

We didn't speak of Thaddeus or the nursing program again that evening. I could see that Mama's eyes danced with curiosity, but I needed time to think before I shared my thoughts with her, since I already knew her position on the situation. Besides, I had no doubt that Daddy would inform her of every detail before the evening ended.

After supper, I begged exhaustion and headed upstairs for a long, hot bubble bath. The Lord and I had a lot to discuss.

Wedding Bells and Fond Farewells

Deep, rich mahogany; polished brass; and stained glass provided a counterpoint to the bouquets of summer flowers in the parlor and in the three bedrooms of our suite on the SS *Constitution*. I helped myself to a bunch of concord grapes from the gigantic basket of fruit, compliments of the ship's captain. Everything was perfect, almost perfect enough to make me forget I was once again baby-sitting my stepsister, Phoebe, and my rebellious stepbrother, Nikolai—this time on a voyage across the Atlantic to our Grandfather and Grandmother Chamberlain's house in Baltimore, Maryland. One other factor marred the perfection of the voyage—my impatience to see Thaddeus again.

The days had been busy since he'd sailed for New York. When I had seen him off at the docks, I felt as if my heart were being torn from me. I berated myself for being so dramatic but couldn't deny the pain I felt. Mama must have understood, for on the ride home, she afforded me the silence I needed to nurse my hurts.

Letters from Thad began arriving two weeks after he had left. I cried when he described his bitter reunion with his father. *I don't understand it; they're both wonderful people. Why can't they see it as I do?*

When I wrote to Ashley of my pending return to the States, she went insane with delight. Every letter from her proposed exciting things we would do together. Mama was less than pleased to send me alone to New York, especially because of my cousin. The fact that I was older and wiser than I'd been during my cousin's previous capers didn't seem to impress her any.

Preparations for Jamie's wedding, the arrival of Auriel's uncle from South Dakota, and touring London with Phoebe and Nikolai filled my days to overflowing. I tried to contact my friend Charlotte but discovered she'd left for the country. The maid who answered the telephone remembered me and confided that Charlotte had finally conceived and couldn't be more delighted to be carrying the heir to her husband's title.

The tensions between Phoebe and me smoothed out as we became better acquainted. Under her veneer of aristocratic arrogance, I was delighted to find a tender shyness. However, Rusty didn't fare so well with Nikolai. I spent more and more time helping my little brother deal with the adjustment he'd been forced to make.

When it was decided that Phoebe and Nikolai should not risk returning to France for the wedding but remain in London, both Rusty and I were secretly pleased to have our parents all to ourselves for a few days.

After the wedding, I wrote in my diary, *Returning to Chamonix will be a memory I will treasure always. Auriel's white organza gown with the ribbon trim accentuated her delicate features. The wildflower bouquet she carried couldn't completely hide the tremble in her hands. And my brother Jamie, ah, has any groom ever looked so happy and so much in love?*

Saying my final goodbyes to the children at the orphanage—especially to Mimi—was difficult. The most poignant moment was when I played one last violin-and-piano duet with Sarge. As I prepared to leave, the soldier kissed my cheek. "Remember me, CeeCee, when you give your first concert at Carnegie Hall."

I laughed. "I'll dedicate the performance to you, but only if you name your eight-fingered concerto after me."

"It's a deal, kid." He grinned.

Once back in London, I counted the hours until I boarded the SS *Constitution* for New York. Yet, I must confess, my heart twisted as I stood at the rail, waving goodbye to my parents, who stood on the pier. *What if something happens, and I never get to see them again? What would I do? Where would I go? Oh, God, please protect them. Bring them home safely to me.*

The familiar words "Trust in the Lord with all thine heart; and lean not unto thine own understanding" drifted through my mind as the ship edged away from the dock. My last glimpse of my parents would stay with me the entire journey. They stood on the dock, sixty feet below, my mother with her face buried in my father's shoulder, my father waving gamely up at me.

As the ship's horn drowned out the cheers and shouts of the celebrating travelers, a tremor of uncertainty shot through me. I turned my attention to Phoebe and Nikolai. The plan had sounded so easy when we had discussed it in the safety of our town house, but now very real doubts flooded my mind. *I've gone and done it again. What if*— I forced the portent of fear from my mind and hurried to our suite. Phoebe followed, complaining of a headache.

While I supervised the maid unpacking our clothing, I suggested Phoebe take an herbal bath in the luxurious tub in our private bathroom. I was secretly glad when, once Nikolai had claimed the smallest bedroom in our suite as his own, he disappeared. I'd been praying for weeks to learn to like the boy, whom I knew I must claim as my brother. Seeing the excitement in his eyes as we boarded the ship softened my feelings somewhat. I was certain he'd inspect every inch of the ship before dinner.

How different this voyage was from my first. On the first, I was the ingenue, the darling of the first-class society; and my mother spent her time worrying about me. This time, I played the role of the mother, trying to keep Nikolai from inciting the crew to mutiny and to keep leering lotharios from toying with my stepsister's affections.

A long week later, I was relieved to see the New York skyline come into view. From the top of the gangplank, I spotted Thad first, then my blond cousin. While Thad looked the same, on closer inspection, I saw that Ashley had shorn her long locks for a short, modern bob. By the way she hung onto Thad's arm, I knew she and I would need to have a long, serious talk before the day ended. Aunt Drucilla and Uncle Ian were waiting for us also.

When Thad swept me into his arms and kissed me, Uncle Ian's eyebrows shot up, Aunt Drucilla gasped, and Ashley stared in disbelief. *Maybe the talk with Ashley won't be necessary after all.*

"Thad, not here," I whispered, as he crushed me into his arms.

"If not here, where? And when?" He nuzzled my neck. "I've missed you so much."

"I missed you too." I squirmed free of his grasp, blushing and self-consciously adjusting my cloche.

"Aunt Drucilla, let me introduce my stepsister, Phoebe Magdonovich, and her brother, Nikolai. My aunt, Mrs. McCall." After I had introduced everyone, we climbed into my uncle's Packard and headed for their home. Ashley's good humor returned quickly. She wanted to know all about Jamie's wedding, our voyage, and our escape from the Communists. When Thad interjected his part of the adventure, my relatives exchanged knowing glances but said nothing. I wondered how much Mama had written and how much came as a surprise.

"We'll sightsee for a few days; then I'll take Phoebe and Nikolai to my grandparents in Maryland, where we'll spend the rest of the summer until my parents' return."

"Oh, pooh!" Ashley pouted. "I thought you were going to be here in the city with me!"

"We really would enjoy having you stay with us for a time, my dear," Aunt Drucilla added. "That's all Ashley's been talking about since you wrote of your visit."

"Well—" I hesitated, glancing wistfully at Thad. "—we'll see how it goes at my Grandmother Chamberlain's place."

"Thaddeus." My uncle turned to him and grinned. "It looks like you have more influence on my niece than we do. Perhaps you can convince her to return quickly to New York."

Thad grinned back. "I'll certainly try my best, sir."

I was grateful that my aunt invited Thad to dine with us that evening, even though he and I had little time alone together. They did allow me to escort him to the front door, where he stole a little kiss before he left and promised to meet me at the train when I returned to New York.

That night, Ashley, Phoebe, and I talked until well after midnight. Or, I should say, Ashley talked while Phoebe listened, wide-eyed and envious, and I watched. As Ashley regaled us with her latest exploits into the exciting world of romance, I could see the longing in my stepsister's eyes. I studied her soft ash brown hair, her deep green eyes, her mysterious smile. *Don't worry, sweetheart. When my cousin gets done with you, the eligible New York bachelors will be circling you too.*

Upon reaching Grandmother and Grandfather Chamberlain's estate in Baltimore, I was relieved to turn my charges over to my grandmother's eager and efficient ministrations. My grandfather treated Nikolai with the same affection he showered on Rusty, his natural heir. Though Nikolai struggled to remain aloof and untouched by the family, I could occasionally catch glimpses of the scared little boy beneath the arrogance.

By the time I boarded the train for New York ten days later, Phoebe could have passed as a modern young American woman of breeding, and Nikolai was well on his way to what I called humanization. Waving goodbye to them all at the station, I must confess that I felt a twinge of jealousy, sensing that my Grandmother Chamberlain was glad to finally have my stepsister and brother to herself for a time. I'd never gotten to know my father's parents well because of the distance between California and Maryland. *And, now, Phoebe will become the granddaughter they always wanted me to be.* I sighed and found an empty seat in the first-class day coach.

Several hours later, as the train chugged into Grand Central Station, I spied Thad scanning the cars as they passed. I waved frantically until he spotted me. Impatiently, I pushed my way through the passengers preparing to deboard. The conductor had barely had time to put the steps into place when I leapt from the train into Thad's waiting arms. Oblivious to the people around us, he whirled me about in circles.

I laughed and squealed. "I've been gone less than two weeks."

"It seems like forever." He set me down and grabbed my satchel. "Any other luggage?"

"Yes, but it will be delivered directly to Aunt Drucilla's."

"Speaking of the clan, where are they? I expected they'd all be here to meet you."

I blushed. "I didn't tell them which train I'd be taking."

He grinned and slipped his arm around my waist. "Good."

"Thaddeus, behave," I whispered, wriggling out of his grasp. "This is New York City, not Paris."

"You're right. I apologize for my forwardness, Mademoiselle. Your arm, please?" I slipped my gloved hand into the crook of his elbow. "And, now, would it be permissible for us to take a brief detour to a small coffee house before delivering you safely to the bosom of your loving family?"

"Oh, Thad!" I slapped his arm with my free hand. "You are so dramatic."

As we strolled along the avenue, I told him about my week and a half with the Chamberlain branch of the family before asking about his father.

"I'd rather not talk about that." His face darkened. "As far as my father is concerned, I died on the battlefields of Europe."

"Oh, Thaddeus, I doubt that."

"Trust me. He will never forgive me for being what he calls a traitor to my country."

"Give him time. God has a way of softening the most hardened hearts."

"God?" He looked at me with uncharacteristic scorn. I paused in surprise, my breath catching in my throat. Thad continued, "I hoped you'd outgrown those fairy tales."

"For a time, I doubted. But too many things have happened for me to ignore the very real presence of God in my life."

Before I could continue, he broke in. "I always thought you were too analytical and practical to fall for such old wives' tales."

"Thad, aren't you jumping to hasty conclusions here? You haven't even heard me out."

"I've heard it all, believe me."

I clicked my tongue. "That's a nice open mind for you!"

"Hey, I'm sorry. I wanted today to be perfect for us."

"But, Thad, you don't realize how important this is to me."

"Aw, come on," he coaxed, "let's talk about you and me and the things that really matter."

Really matter? Oh, Thad, don't you realize that my belief in God is a big part of who I am? Overwhelmed in my sudden despair, it was several minutes before I realized he'd moved on to cheerier topics.

"This week, I called upon Mr. Tate and told him of my hopes of attending college. He always told me I was the son he'd never had. CeeCee, are you listening?"

"Hmm? Um, yes."

"He's agreed to pay my way to the University of Chicago, his alma mater, for four years. He's even supplying me with a stipend for board and room. The way I figure it, you and I could get married as early as Christmas, if that's all right with you."

"Married this December?" My mouth went dry.

A frown darkened his brow. "That was what we talked about before I left England, wasn't it?"

"Yes, I guess so."

"You guess so? You don't know?" He stared in disbelief. "Didn't we vow our love forever?"

"I'm sorry, Thad. This comes as a total surprise. I never imagined there would be a way for us to marry before I finished my nurses' training."

"Nurses' training? I don't remember your mentioning anything about nurses' training."

I looked at him in dismay. "I told you that I applied to a number of schools of nursing for this fall. As it turns out, I have received a number of acceptances."

"But I thought— I thought that was just something to keep you busy until we could get married. I never imagined—"

"You never imagined that, perhaps, I had dreams and goals as well as you?"

"I didn't say that. But I'll be making a good salary as a writer. My wife will never have to work to help support me."

Support you? I clutched his arm, unnerved by his words. *How could we have misunderstood one another so completely?* When I had told him of the excitement I felt at Chamonix, caring for the needs of the children and the patients, hadn't he heard? Aware that God had used me in such positive ways, I'd never be the same again.

"Besides, you'll be home caring for our babies. In fact, I can see where your nursing skills will be quite valuable in the home."

"How nice of you to say so." I found myself glowering at Thad. "Well, as you said earlier, we have lots to discuss before we make any announcements regarding our future together."

"Why do I not like the sound of that statement?" He stared down at me, but I averted my eyes.

Aunt Drucilla met us at the front door of their brownstone town house. "Goodness, CeeCee, why didn't you tell us when you were coming in? We would have met you at the station." When she spotted Thad by my side, she clamped her lips shut.

"I'm sorry, Auntie." I kissed her cheek. "But Thaddeus asked if he could meet me this time. I hope you're not angry."

"My, no. I only hope your mother won't be angry that we didn't supply you with the proper chaperonage."

I laughed. "Let's just make it our little secret, shall we?"

"Mummy, who's there?"

I looked past my aunt to my cousin bounding down the fight of stairs. "Oh, goody! You're here in time. I was hoping you'd be. And you too, Thad."

Aunt Drucilla stepped back to invite us inside. Thad placed my satchel on the marble-tiled floor as Ashley tripped over to me and kissed my cheek. "Now, you'll be able to go out this evening with Charles and me. Mummy was reluctant to let me go out alone with him, his being ten years older than I." She cast a coy, but scolding look at her mother. "I guess she thinks he's toying with my affections."

I smiled at Thad. *If there's any toying going on—*

"You'll want to dress for dinner, Thad, that is, if you have the appropriate attire." She giggled, innocent of her unintentional slur.

Thad responded graciously. "I promise not to embarrass you, Miss Ashley."

She giggled again. "Oh, Thaddeus, you are such a joker. We have reservations downtown at eight. So you'll want to be here by seven-thirty at the latest."

Thad took my hand and tipped his head. "Until this evening?"

I smiled in spite of a strange sadness growing inside me. "Until tonight. And—thank you, for everything."

He caught and held my gaze for an instant, then bowed again and left.

Ashley broke into her incessant chatter as she led me up the stairs to her room. "I know you have a wardrobe full of gorgeous gowns from which to choose. I took the liberty of having Kate, our maid, unpack while you were gone. I hope you don't mind."

I cast a look over my shoulder to find Aunt Drucilla thoughtfully studying me.

"So what is all this nonsense of your going into nurses' training this fall? I thought you hated being around sick people!" Before I could reply, my cousin had forgotten her original question and was telling me about the wonders of her newest conquest, Charles Everett Billingsly III. I laughed, relieved that at least some things, my cousin included, hadn't changed.

"I met him at the Franklins' Fourth of July bash at Coney Island. You remember the Franklins, don't you?" She waved her hand dramatically. "Sure you do. They are mentioned in the society pages almost daily. Anyway, Charles is a rising star in the brokerage firm of Franklin, Myers, Guttenburg, and Strauss—a financial genius, to be sure." She flung herself impulsively onto her bed. "Isn't life utterly fabulous?" She rolled to her stomach and supported her chin with her hand. "Men, men, and more men! So tell me about all the marvelous chaps you met while in England and France, you lucky little minx."

I laughed and perched on the foot of her bed, the warmth of familiar old times together washing over me. I wanted to tell her about Paul and Sarge—and, of course, Thad and our day in Paris.

"So what is this with you and Thaddeus? He looks pretty taken with you." Her guileless smile convinced me she held no resentment toward me. "Is it serious?"

I shrugged. "I hope so." Before our talk on the way home from the railway station, I would have been more positive.

"Do you love him?"

I nodded. "I think so."

"You think so? You don't know?"

"Well—" I leaned back against the brass footboard. "—there are some complications."

"Does he love you?"

"Yes, he says he does."

She threw her hands into the air. "Then what complications

could you possibly have?" She sighed dramatically. "Love conquers all, you know—well, all except money, perhaps."

"I wish it were as simple as that."

"Well, it's true. Take it from one who's been in love hundreds of times."

Smiling, I closed my eyes to my cousin's naiveté and tossed a small embroidered bed pillow at her. "Oh, Ashley, you're such a silly goose."

She caught the pillow midair. "What? What did I say?"

"Nothing that surprises me. Where are we going tonight?" I was concerned about the cost to Thad; we hadn't yet discussed his finances.

"If you're worrying about money, Charles is covering everything. All you and Thad have to do is come with us, have a good time, and satisfy my mother's Victorian preferences."

"Your mother? Victorian?" I'd never connected the Aunt Drucilla I knew with anything Victorian.

"Yes, I don't know what's gotten into her. If Auntie Chloe were here, I'd blame her, but your mother has been in London for months." Ashley climbed off the bed and sauntered over to her dressing table. She picked up a crystal decanter of French perfume and spritzed herself. "Actually, if she knew—" My cousin whirled about to face me, her eyes dancing with excitement. "Charles has asked me to marry him. Not officially, of course. We want to save the engagement announcement until the upper crust of New York society is back from the shore."

"Engaged?" Thinking of Thad's proposal earlier, I gulped.

"Isn't it just too, too lovely?" She ran to me. "You won't tell anyone, will you? Not even Thad. Promise?"

"I promise; no one will learn of your engagement from me."

She giggled and gave me a squeeze. "You are such a dear friend. You will be my maid-of-honor, of course. And I promise not to make you wear some horrid pink or orange dress, honest."

I laughed at my cousin's enthusiasm. She'd changed so little during the last few months, and I'd changed so much. "Would it be too much to ask if I took a long, hot bath and a nap before this evening? I feel a headache coming on, and I don't want to ruin our evening."

"Of course not." She leapt to her feet. "You must try my new gardenia bath oils. Bubbles are fine, but bath oils leave you feeling so silky smooth." She flung her head back and caressed her arms. "Charles loves the aroma of gardenia on my skin."

By the time I closed the bathroom door and slid into the tub of steaming bath water, my head did ache. As the aroma of gardenia filled my nostrils and soothed my nerves, I forced the memory of my disturbing afternoon with Thad from my mind. I promised myself there would be plenty of time to iron out the little wrinkles in our relationship.

The knocking at the door startled me out of my reverie. "Hey, did you fall asleep in there or something?

"I'll be out in a minute, Ashley," I called, reluctantly stepping out onto the thirsty bathmat beside the tub.

"When you talked about taking a bath and a nap, I didn't realize you meant to do both activities at the same time," she teased when I returned to her room. "I hope you don't mind, but I took the liberty of having the maid press your midnight blue chiffon. I thought it would be the perfect foil for the red satin chemise I'm wearing. You know, fire and drama. Passion and sophistication."

I lifted my eyebrow. "And which, my dear, will you be?"

"Drama, silly. You are such a tease." She giggled, gathering a pink satin robe and matching slippers into her hands. "With Charles being so much older than I, I can risk wearing more dramatic evening attire. And I love it!"

I waited until she closed the door behind her to stretch out on the down-filled mattress for the promised nap. Once Ashley returned from her bath, all thoughts of sleep or privacy vanished. Like a girl of twelve playing dress-up in my mother's clothing, I threw myself into the excitement of dressing for the evening. I'd styled the last tendril about my face when Ashley turned my face toward hers and rubbed a dab of rouge on each of my cheeks.

"No!" I wailed, rubbing what I could from my skin. "I look like a hussy from the Bowery."

"Nonsense. You look glamorous. Old-fashioned, but glamorous." She painted her lips ruby red. "Have you ever considered getting a bob?"

Ashley straightened and tugged at the neckline of her red chemise. "Let me take you to see Marie. She's a magician with scissors."

"Uh, we'll see. Let me think about it." I stared at the fountain of curls piled on my head and tried to imagine my hair shorn into a wavy bob.

I pursed my lips at the stranger in the mirror. "Something's still missing."

"I've got it!" Ashley ran across her room to the wardrobe and returned with a silver bandeau. Before I could respond, she adjusted the headband around my curls. Grudgingly, I had to admit, my cousin's instincts were right.

I arose from the dressing table and dropped the soft folds of the slippery chiffon knee-length dress. Glittering metallic lace inserts sewn to the matching silk lining sparkled through the chiffon. I examined the scalloped hemline in the mirror. "Are you sure this isn't too short?"

"Nonsense. The dress is too, too divine."

"I wish this were a trifle higher," I muttered, tugging at the fashionably scooped neckline. I slipped into a pair of silver glacé shoes with sharp pointed toes and French curved heels, then studied the effect in the mirror. Ashley stepped into the reflection. Again, I had to admit it, she was right. My outfit was a perfect foil for her red satin chemise.

She chattered excitedly as we finished dressing. "Charles will probably buy my diamond at Tiffany's. He has such exquisite taste." Her face darkened for a second. "If only he didn't get so upset over little things." She brightened. "But I'll change that after we're married."

I smiled as my mother's words flashed through my mind. The smile faded when I remembered Thad's tirade against God earlier in the day. When we heard the doorbell ring, Ashley and I slipped on our opera-length gloves, snatched our beaded purses from the bed, and ran to the door of her bedroom. I could hear Thad's voice, my Aunt Drucilla's, and a stranger's voice, which I assumed belonged to the glorious Charles.

"One, two, three, four, five." She took a deep breath. "There! I'm ready." And together, we glided down the stairs to meet our escorts.

From the moment we were introduced, I knew Charles would never be one of my favorite people. *Be fair*, I told myself. *You've not given the poor guy a chance.* Determined to enjoy my evening with Thaddeus, I pushed my negative thoughts aside and basked in the glow of approval from Thad's eyes as my cousin and her fiancé led us to a sporty little Stutz waiting by the curb. Thad and I squeezed into the back seat designed by and for elves. And while I wouldn't call it comfortable, I enjoyed being so close to him that the bay rum with which he'd shaved made me feel lightheaded.

My giddiness dissolved when Charles leered over his shoulder at me, then looked at Thad. "Sorry, old sport, for the inconvenience. I have dinner reservations at La Maison's, an elegant European restaurant catering to a select clientele. And, lest there be any question, the evening's on me." He glanced over at my cousin. "Ashley and I are celebrating, you see."

Thad raised his eyebrows and looked at me. I shrugged innocently. At the restaurant, we dined in style as the waiters and Alfonse, the maitre d', bowed and scraped to please Charles Everett Billingsly III and his bulging money belt. "Sorry about the lack of champagne, folks. This ridiculous ban on alcohol!"

Thad opened his mouth to reply. "That's perfectly—"

"But, never fear. New York's night life doesn't begin and end with stuffy establishments like this one." Charles turned his gaze on Ashley. "Does it, my little puddin' patch?"

My cousin giggled and shook her head demurely from side to side.

He waved his hand in the air. "Alfonse! We're ready to leave. Just put everything on my bill."

"Of course, Mr. Billingsly. As you wish, sir." The middle-aged Alfonse, with his pencil-thin mustache and greedy little eyes, bowed.

"And give yourself a hefty tip, you hear?"

The maitre d' brightened. "Very well, sir."

Once outside, I asked, "Where are we going?"

"You'll see, beautiful." Charles winked and helped me into the car. "You'll see."

A few blocks away, Charles parked his car. Thad and I walked arm in arm behind my cousin and her fiancé up the street past a number of darkened businesses sprinkled among a row of private residences. Charles paused beneath a burned-out street lamp and glanced about nervously. "Come quickly." He waved us toward a wrought-iron gate guarding a small flight of steps down to a green painted door.

"I don't like this," I whispered to Thad.

"Me either."

At the door, Charles knocked three times. A slot in the door opened, and an eye peered out at us.

"Johnny's back in town," Charles whispered.

A voice behind the door asked, "Where's he staying?"

Charles shot a glance up and down the street. "At the Ritz, where else?"

I heard a click. The door opened enough for the four of us to enter, single file, then slammed closed behind us, engulfing us in total darkness. I grabbed Thad's arm. "It's OK," he whispered. "I'm here with you."

I tried to quiet my pounding heart and the eerie feeling that, while I had no idea where I was, I would prefer to be elsewhere.

"I don't like this," Thad whispered. "If I didn't know better—"

A second door swung open.

"Follow me," our guide growled. We entered a dark, stuffy room, the air acrid with odors of cigarette smoke, sweating bodies, and stale alcohol. Flappers and their sheiks danced in the center of the crowded room to the popular tune "A Pretty Girl Is Like a Melody," crooned by a dark-haired female on stage at the far end of the room. A five-piece band backed her up in an effort to cover the sound of laughter and the tinkling of ice in the glasses of what I was certain was bootleg hooch. We picked our way through to one of the few empty tables.

"Isn't this exciting?" Ashley shouted in my ear as our escorts seated us. I glanced at the seedy characters at the table beside ours and at the amber-colored liquid in each of their glasses.

Oh no. This time you've really done it, Ashley. Thad's hands still rested on the back of my chair when I stood up.

"Thad, we've got to get out of here, right now. Do you know what this is?"

"Sorry, CeeCee." He leaned closer. "I can't hear you."

"Do you know where we are?" I leaned across the table. "Ashley, Thad and I can't stay here. I'm sorry. We'll catch a cab home."

"Oh, CeeCee, don't be a prude!" Ashley pouted. "We just want to have a little fun."

"Afraid you might loosen that Victorian corset of yours?" Charles smirked. "Afraid you might become a modern woman?"

I glared, lifting one eyebrow meaningfully. "My corset is no concern of yours, Mr. Billingsly." I turned to Thad, who'd missed hearing our little exchange. "Please take me home."

"Come on, CeeCee." My cousin put on her most pitiful gaze. "Tonight's supposed to be special, remember? Please stay."

"I'm sorry, Ashley, but the sooner I get out of here, the better I'm going to feel!"

"Well, now you've gone and spoiled everything!" She rose to her feet and swung her shoulders in frustration. "You're becoming just like your mother! I suppose we'll have to leave too!"

"You do whatever you want, but I'm leaving." I placed my arm in Thad's.

Charles leaned against the back of Ashley's chair and cast an insolent sneer at Thad. "Do you always jump when she tells you to?"

"As the lady says, we're leaving." He turned to me. "Let's get out of here. I need some fresh air."

"You can't go home." Ashley leapt to her feet. "You'll put Mummy in a tizzy."

"Fine. We'll take a walk through Central Park." Thad put his arm around my shoulder and led me away from the table. "We'll meet you outside your home at ten. Don't be late."

We made our way through the club and then the darkened hallway. When the outside door swung open and we stepped out into another world, relief swept over me.

"Whew!" Thad took my arm and led me toward the intersection, where we'd have a better chance of locating a taxi. "I'm glad to be out of there. I've heard about those places, but I've never been in one."

I glanced back over my shoulder at the innocuous-looking door and building. "So that's what they call a speak-easy."

Thad leaned his head toward mine and half-sang and half-hummed the words to the song we'd left behind.

I rested my head on his shoulder. "Thank you for getting me out of there."

"I should thank you, my dear. If that place had been raided while we were there, I'd probably be sent directly to prison. I'm on probation, remember?"

"Remember?" I chuckled. "That was my first thought. So, that place is a shining example of what the news editorialists call 'our century coming of age.'"

Cold Light of Day

Charles's yellow Stutz drove up to the curb in front of my aunt's house at eleven that evening, pausing only long enough to deposit Ashley on the sidewalk. Like a lost kitten caught in a rain shower, she stood on the sidewalk and watched the car roar off into the night. Thad and I had spent the previous hour perched on the steps of a brownstone two houses down from the Chamberlain town house. Though we had much to talk about, I was relieved to know Ashley was home and safe.

"Ashley," I hissed, rushing to her side as she began to climb the steps into the house. "We're right here. We've been waiting for you."

She turned to me, relief flooding her face. "Oh, I'm so glad you waited for me. I was afraid I'd have to go in to face the storm alone."

Thad strode out of the shadows. "What happened to Charles?"

Even in the soft light of the gas street lamp, I could tell that Ashley had been crying. "I, uh, made him upset at me. Excuse me, but I can't talk right now. CeeCee, can we go inside right away?"

"Of course." I wrapped my arms about her and led her up the steps. Glancing over my shoulder at Thaddeus standing on the sidewalk, I called, "I'll see you tomorrow, OK?"

"Sure. Is Ashley going to be all right?"

I shrugged. "I'm sure she'll be fine. All she needs is a little female consoling."

He waited until I rang the bell and Aunt Drucilla's butler

opened the front door. After Ashley had entered the house, I turned. "Good night, sweetheart."

Thad waved, blew me a kiss, and left.

The door had barely closed behind us when Aunt Drucilla's head peered over the staircase railing. "Is that you girls? Ashley?"

"Yes, Mummy," Ashley sniffed.

"Are the boys with you?"

"No, Mummy. We said good night on the stoop."

"Ashley, are you all right? You sound like you're coming down with a cold."

Ashley darted a quick glance of panic at me.

"I told you that dress was too light for the season."

"You were right, Mummy. I think I am getting a cold."

"Don't worry, Aunt Drucilla. Leave her to me." I peered up the stairway, blocking my aunt's view of her daughter. "I'll fix Ashley a cup of my mother's sure-cure herbal tea, then see that she gets a hot bath and to bed as quickly as possible."

"Ah yes. I remember your mama's herbal remedies. If I weren't so tired, I'd come down and have a cup myself."

Ashley's eyes filled with terror. "No, she can't see me like this!" she hissed.

"You just get your sleep." I waved her toward her room. "If you'd still like some of Mama's tea in the morning, I promise to fix you a cup."

"Oh, you are such a dear, CeeCee, just like your mama." She straightened. "Then if there's nothing else I can do—"

"Good night, Aunt Drucilla."

Behind me Ashley called, "Good night, Mummy."

"That was close." I turned to find a weeping Ashley. I placed my arm about her and led her to the kitchen.

"Oh, CeeCee, I've really done it this time."

"Oh no. Don't tell me. The police raided the speak-easy!"

"What? Oh, oh no. If only it were that simple."

I drew out a chair from the table. "Well, make yourself comfortable while I heat a kettle of water. You can tell me all about it. Whatever it is, it can't be that bad."

"Yes, it can. It's so bad, I can't talk about it." She buried her head in her arms.

"That's all right too." I picked up the kettle from the stove and took it to the sink. "I'm sorry we had to leave you two, but Thad had to get out of there. I told you about his problem in France and the ambassador's warning. If he'd been found in an illegal drinking establishment, he could have been prosecuted and sent to prison for twenty years or more."

She didn't respond.

"But understand one thing, Ashley, if you ever want us to go out again with you and Charles, make certain he knows—"

A sob escaped from my cousin. I set the teakettle down on the burner and rushed to her side.

"Ashley! I didn't mean to upset you!"

She continued to weep, first gently, then in long, agonizing sobs. I stood over her, helplessly massaging her shoulders, caressing her short blond hair, and uttering useless little clichés that were meant to comfort.

The teakettle whistled before my cousin's sobs subsided. Even as I steeped the tea, she remained with her face buried in her arms. Sliding the cup full of steaming liquid toward her, I coaxed, "Come on, Ashley. Drink a little tea. It really will make you feel better—whether you have a cold or not."

She lifted her head from the table, her eyes red and puffy. I handed her a linen napkin from the stack of freshly laundered and pressed table napkins lying on the corner of the breakfront.

"Thank you." She hiccoughed and blew her nose.

"Are you going to be all right?" I folded my arms across my chest and rubbed my arms nervously.

"No," she replied. "I'll never be all right, ever again."

Ah, I thought, *this is the dramatic Ashley I know.* I poured myself a cup of tea, then circled the table and sat down across from her. "Do you think you can talk about it now?"

She shook her head and blew her nose a second time. "Charles is so angry with me. He threatened to break off our engagement."

Good! I can't think of anything I'd like better. One evening with him was enough to last a lifetime. "I'm sure he wasn't serious. All couples have little tiffs now and then."

"No, it's not like that. He was serious, believe me. If I don't agree to—"

"To do what?"

"Don't you understand? I'm pregnant!" she gasped. Her words hung in the air several seconds before I could respond.

"You're what?" My teacup clattered against the china saucer.

"You heard me."

"What are you going to do?"

Agonizing terror filled her eyes. "What can I do? Charles has a friend who's a medical student at N.Y.U. who will—" Her voice drifted off into a sob.

Instantly, my mind filled in the words she couldn't bring herself to utter. "No! I've seen the results of bungled abortions at my mother's clinic. You could die." I leapt to my feet and rounded the table, kneeling by her side. "Oh, Ashley, please don't let him talk you into doing this."

"I don't know. I'm not ready to be a mother. Charles so wanted a spring wedding and honeymoon on the continent."

"Ashley! For pity's sake, who cares about a spring wedding? Either you marry this jerk, or you send him packing and, and—" My words faltered even as I spoke. Either way, my cousin's life was in ruins. I gathered her into my arms. *Oh, God, how can such a thing happen? I don't know what to say. Please give me some sort of wisdom.*

She lowered her head to my shoulder. Even as I stroked her hair and neck, comforting her as my mother had done with me so many times during my childhood, I knew it would take far more than a kiss and a pat on the head to heal my cousin's anguish. Ashley wasn't an eight-year-old child, and this wasn't a bruised knee or a spat between two third-graders.

I brushed my mother's predictions from my mind. *"I told you something like this would happen; Ashley has always been a willful child. Sooner or later, her recklessness had to catch up with her."*

My only thoughts were for the fragile young woman weeping in my arms. Yet, as quickly as I imagined my mother's distress over my cousin's actions, Mama was the person I most wished were here. She'd know what to do; she'd know what to say.

"Come on. Let's go upstairs." I grabbed a second napkin and

dabbed at her eyes. "We can talk about this more tomorrow or later tonight, if you like. Right now, you need a hot bath to relax you."

She nodded and hiccoughed. Like a child of five or six, she allowed me to lead her out of the kitchen and up the stairs to her room.

After her bath, Ashley slept throughout the rest of the night. As for me, well—I'm glad one of us slept anyway. By dawn, I knew I had to convince her to get help from her parents, regardless of the consequences. The battle I imagined fighting never materialized, for the next morning, Aunt Drucilla overheard my cousin experience her first bout with morning sickness and immediately surmised the cause. The rest of the day was one of tears and recriminations.

I hid out in the library until Thad arrived that afternoon and met him at the door with my purse, sweater, and hat in hand. "Come on. We need to get out of here for a few hours. The roof is ready to rise." I grabbed his arm and whirled him about.

As the door slammed behind us, Aunt Drucilla called, "Ian, is that you?"

"Huh? What?"

"Come on. You don't want to go in there right now, trust me."

"I don't?" Awkwardly, he allowed me to lead him back down the front steps. "Where are we going?"

"Anywhere but here." Once safely away from the house, I explained the situation to him. "And that cad, Charles, actually suggested that Ashley get a back-alley abortion!"

He answered in a monosyllabic grunt.

"Is all you have to say 'umh'?"

"What do you want me to say?"

"I don't know. Maybe, 'poor Ashley' or 'that's too bad' or—I don't know!" I flailed my arms in the air.

"OK. Poor Ashley. That's too bad."

"Oh my, I can see you're stirred with emotion here."

"Look. I've known your cousin for at least three years now, and, frankly, she's been playing with danger the entire time. If it hadn't been Charles, it would have been the next guy or the next." He looked at me, surprised at the irritation he could see in my face. "Hey, it could have been me, if I'd wanted—"

I stopped short, my hands firmly planted on my hips, my jaw jutted forward. "Are you saying that my cousin is promiscuous?"

"No, not promiscuous, just foolish, or maybe naive."

"Thaddeus! Of all the—" I whirled about and marched back up the street toward my relatives' brownstone, sputtering all the while. "How like a male! Last time I knew, making babies took two!"

"Hey, what did I say?"

I glanced over my shoulder to make certain he would hear. "You said, 'Goodbye, CeeCee!' "

"That's not fair!" He started after me.

"Leave me alone, or I'll call a policeman!" My face reddened. *That was cruel, under the circumstances.* I hadn't meant to say that.

"Fine! Alone you shall be!"

"Fine!"

"Fine!"

I turned back in time to see Thad disappear around the corner in the direction of the subway station.

If I had to determine at what point my life took a decided change, I would say it was at that bizarre, unreasonable moment. I wandered the few blocks to Central Park, bought a bread stick from an Italian bread cart, found a park bench on the edge of the park, and shared my supper with the pigeons.

By the time I returned to my aunt's house, my anger at Thad had forced me to an important decision regarding my life. *Men! I am going to enter the nurses' training at the Manhattan School of Nursing. Thad can go to his university in Chicago if he desires—or anywhere else, for that matter.*

At the brownstone, other monumental decisions were being made—by Uncle Ian and by his reluctant guest, Charles Everett Billingsly III.

Less than a month later, wearing a Sybil LeBeq original, I stood beside my teary cousin as she became Mrs. Charles Everett Billingsly III. Only a handful of family members occupied the pews of the little red-brick church that the growing city had forgotten. Grandma and Grandpa McCall, Uncle Ian and Aunt Drucilla, the groom's immediate family—hardly the grand event Ashley had imagined so many times during our late-night chats. Even as the minister pronounced them husband and wife, I searched the audience for Thaddeus, whom I hadn't seen since that fateful afternoon. *Well, it just goes to show how careful a woman needs to be about choosing a husband,* I consoled myself.

A week later, after wiring my parents of my school choice and not having heard anything from Thad, I enrolled in the two-year nursing program. The first few weeks of the program moved slowly through the rules of basic hospital care that I'd already learned from the nurses at Chamonix. I wished the time would go faster so I could push Thad from my mind. Uncle Ian and Aunt Drucilla, caught up in their own disappointment, never spoke of his sudden absence.

Aching to curl up in Mama's arms and let her soothe away my hurts, I marked the days on my calendar until my parents would be returning from England. To keep busy, I arranged to have our town house opened and cleaned. I also arranged to have Maria, the caretaker my parents had hired before leaving for England, return Sundance and Meeker to the house.

After classes one Thursday, I stopped off at the place to see how much had been done and let myself in through the front door with my latchkey. Having told Aunt Drucilla where I'd be, I didn't worry about getting back to her place before supper. I had opened the door an inch when I heard Sundance's familiar bark. The golden retriever bounded around the corner of the staircase, his long, gangly legs scrambling for secure footing on the Persian rug runner.

"Sundance!" I cried.

The dog skidded to a stop in surprise; then, as recognition filled his eyes, he leapt on me, eager to give me a damp welcome with his lolling tongue.

"Hey, watch it." I laughed and rubbed his head and neck. "I missed you too." Abandoning my stack of textbooks on the marble-tile floor, I dropped to my knees and buried my face in his ruff.

"Oh, Miss, you startled me."

I glanced up at the little Italian woman I'd barely gotten to know some months previously.

"Maria, it's good to see you again. Is Meeker somewhere around?"

The bright-eyed woman grinned and pointed up the stairs. "Her royal highness is hiding in the attic, I believe. She won't come down for meals. No, I have to carry her food up three flights of stairs!" The affection in her tone belied the complaint.

I laughed and stood to my feet, much to Sundance's frustration. "Some things never change."

"I hope you'll excuse me, but I have some errands to run, restocking the larder before your parents arrive, you know."

"Oh, don't let me hold you up. I can let myself out if you're not back before I leave."

She pinned her small black cloche to her tightly wound ebony chignon. "Then, if you'll excuse me."

I waved absently and wandered into the parlor, then on to the library, where a sense of warmth and comfort flooded through me. *How strange. It looks and feels like we never left this place. I never thought I'd think of this place as home.*

Sundance followed me through the dining room and the kitchen, then out into the postage-stamp yard and garden. While he reestablished his legitimate boundaries in the neighborhood, I examined each of my mother's rosebushes. *Looks like Mama has her work cut out for her this fall. She'll have this place in shape in no time.*

Back inside the house, I toured the upstairs rooms—the guest room, my parents' room, Rusty's, and last, mine. The bed had been stripped of linen to air. The sketches Thad had given me still hung on the wall beside my bed. I ran my fingers over the row of diaries lining my bookshelf, each representing a year in my life. My fingers brushed past my favorite storybooks of childhood, from Mother Goose rhymes to *Little Women*.

My hand rested on a narrow bamboo box, wedged between *Around the World in Eighty Days* and my books of poetry by Emily Dickinson. *Au Sam's fan.* Slowly, I opened the box and removed the exquisite white-silk fan. The threads of the embroidered flowers of red, gold, and blue still held their vibrancy. I fanned myself slowly, mourning the loss of my gentle friend and confidant, whom I'd missed so many times in the past several months.

Remembering the turquoise brocade Mandarin dress she'd purchased for my eventual wedding day, I ran to my wardrobe and removed it from its box. The fabric glistened as I examined it in the late-afternoon light. Whether it was Ashley's precipitous marriage or the disappointment I felt over the loss of Thad's and my relationship, I knew I had to try it on again. Shedding my everyday clothing, I dropped the silky fabric over my head and fastened the matching fabric-covered buttons in the tiny loops. *Hm, wasn't this dress a little longer before? Surely Mama didn't have time to take it in before we left for Europe.*

After a long look in the mirror, I began removing the pins from my hair, then fluffed my long red curls as they cascaded onto my shoulders. "What do you think, Sundance?"

The dog, who'd sprawled out on the carpet by my feet to nap, opened one eye appreciatively. Suddenly, he leapt to his feet, barked, and bounded from the room. *Maria's back already?*

An instant later, a shot of gray fur flew past me, into the hall, and up the second flight of stairs into the attic. "Meeker!" She'd been hiding all the while under my bed.

I started up the stairs after her, the close-fitting dress impeding my movements. By the time I reached the third floor, the cat had sequestered herself at the farthest point under the eaves. I crouched down to coax her from her hiding place. "You little scamp! Come on out here. You know me."

Hearing footsteps on the stairs, I called, "Maria, I'm trying to catch that cat of mine. Imagine her not knowing me." I stood and turned. "I've only been gone for— Thad! What are you doing here?"

"I-I, uh, your housekeeper said y-y-you were u-u-up here."

I eyed him curiously, trying to decipher the strange expression on his face.

"I-I, uh, stopped at your aunt's house, and she told me—where did you get that dress?"

"This?" I glanced down at the garment. The gold-and-silver

scroll work trimming the Mandarin collar and closure glistened in the sunlight seeping in through the dust-covered window. "Au Sam left it to me when she died. It's a Mandarin wed—" I stopped, my words frozen on my lips. We both reddened.

"It's beautiful. You're beautiful. I-I-I—"

"I was trying to catch Meeker. She won't let me hold her. Imagine, and my cat too." I brushed past Thad into the hallway. "I guess I'll have to let her get used to me in her own time. So, what are you doing here? You missed Ashley's wedding."

"I was out of town, but I sent a note with a small present, explaining my absence."

I led the way down the stairs to the second floor, then on to the main floor of the house. From the entry, I called to Maria, "Do we have any tea or hot chocolate to serve Mr. Adams?"

"Yes, Miss." Maria appeared around the dining-room door and bobbed a curtsy. "Part of the groceries I just purchased. Oh, Miss, that dress is breathtaking!"

"Thank you. It was a gift from a dear friend. Thad, which would you like? Tea or cocoa?"

He squirmed impatiently. "Tea would be fine."

I slid the parlor doors open. "Mr. Adams and I will be in the parlor." After crossing the room to the white-marble fireplace, I lighted the two brass lamps over the mantle. Sundance sprawled out on the carpet in front of the hearth. "So, you've been traveling?"

"I was in Chicago, visiting Mr. Tate. He's made the arrangements for me to attend the university there." Thad shifted nervously from one foot to the other. "I wanted to talk things over with you."

I waited for him to explain his absence further.

"You are unbelievably beautiful. I hope you won't wear that dress too often—for others, I mean."

"Excuse me?"

He shook his head as if trying to restructure his thoughts. "Look, CeeCee, I've been doing a lot of thinking, about us, I mean." He strode over to a window and drew back one of the heavy brocade drapery panels and gazed out onto the quiet street in front of the house.

"And?"

"And—" He shook his head, casting about for words. "And, why is it always the wrong time for us? I don't know of two people who love each other as much as I love you but have worse timing—except perhaps in Shakespeare's *Romeo and Juliet*."

"And they committed suicide," I answered laconically.

He laughed and turned to face me. "You can always make me laugh. That's one of the things I love about you."

My face softened at the look of love and admiration reflected in his gaze. "Is that the only—"

"You know better than that." Three long strides, and he stood before me, close enough to reach out and touch but far enough away to cause me to hesitate. "You yourself said that we have some strong basic differences between us—our own personal goals, my ability to support a wife and family, and more important, this God-thing. Your father was right."

"My father?"

He ignored my response. "As I see it, until we can work these out, we can't consider a future together."

I felt my heart constrict, and a lump of foreboding formed in my throat. "Thad," I rasped, "what are you saying?"

"I'm saying we can't allow our feelings for one another to control our better judgment."

I struggled to voice my thoughts. "Is that it? You say goodbye and walk out of my life forever?"

A sob escaped his throat as he grasped my hands. "Oh no! I can't just let you go. You mean far too much to me."

I swallowed hard, forcing myself to remain rigid to his touch. "You yourself said we can't go back to just being friends, remember?"

"That's right, but—"

"And we obviously can't go forward—"

"No, but—"

"And no relationship ever stands still. You know that." I knew that my eyes mirrored the same desperate look I read in his.

He drew my rigid body into his arms, massaging my neck in frustration. "Oh, CeeCee girl, what are we going to do?"

I set my teeth against the wave of tears building inside of

me. *I can't cry. I can't let him see me cry.*

Over his shoulder, I saw Maria peer through the doorway, then back away. I drew away from his arms. "It's all right, Maria. Come right on in. Mr. Adams just informed me that he's leaving for Chicago to attend school there."

"Oh, how very nice." She curtsied. "I have a cousin in Chicago, Vincent Batto. He works at the stockyards."

"Really. If I run into him, I'll tell him that I met you. Of course, Chicago is a large city, you know." Thad smiled and seated himself on the nearest sofa. I chose to sit on the sofa across from him. Maria placed the tray on the sofa table between us.

"I arranged a plate of shortbread, Miss. Will there be anything else?"

"How thoughtful. Thank you. But I think we can manage from here." I waited until she left, then offered Thad a cookie.

"No, thank you. I don't want cookies or tea." A sharp edge entered his voice.

"What do you want, Thaddeus? Do you know?"

He sank back against the sofa and folded his hands across his lap. "I know what I don't want, and that is to lose you forever."

The painful honesty in his eyes melted my defenses. "Nor I you," I whispered. "But what can we do? I'm here, attending classes in New York. You'll be in Illinois, a thousand miles away. Two years, four years, how can we possibly maintain any kind of relationship under these circumstances?"

He studied his hands for a moment. "I don't know. I just don't know." He looked up, his eyes filled with longing. "I know I can't expect you to wait for me to get my life together. It wouldn't be fair."

"To either of us."

"I know. I know. But I don't want to give up without a fight."

"What do you mean?"

Thad stood up and came to sit beside me. "Do you really love me as much as you say you do?" His demand for an honest answer unnerved me momentarily. Taking my hand in his, he began tracing the veins with his finger.

Instinctively, I knew this was no time for playing coy little sweetheart games. Unable to speak aloud through my emotion-constricted throat, I breathed, "Yes."

"Oh, CeeCee!" He pulled me into his arms and gave me a hug, then released me to arm's length. "You had me scared there for a moment. I love you so much that I'm willing to defy the law of averages."

"What do you mean?"

"Look, you and I have survived the test of time, incredible distances, a world war, the influenza, and your cousin, Ashley. Can't we at least give our friendship a try for the next few years, until I finish college? Who knows, we might fool even ourselves."

I thought about his proposal for some time. "No strings? We're both free to form other relationships, should they come along? And no recriminations?"

"Absolutely."

I shook my head and clicked my tongue. "It will never work. I think we're setting ourselves up for major pain."

"Look at it this way; we've been each other's best friend for three years now, right?"

I nodded.

"Personally, even if you fell in love with and married the son of the United States ambassador to Sweden, I'd still want to keep you as one of my dearest friends. Forty years from now, I'd travel halfway around the world to hear you play Chopin on your fiddle."

I growled, "It's not a fiddle; it's a violin."

He laughed. "And I'd travel the rest of the way around the globe to hear you remind me of that fact."

I closed my eyes, feeling the futility of his experiment. "And just how do you plan to keep our love for one another from becoming more, uh, well, you know."

"Physical?"

I nodded. "We can't pretend that the physical attraction we feel for one another doesn't exist. And if I don't miss my guess, it will grow stronger if fed."

"That's the difficult part." He paused for a moment, his hands still holding mine. "If we wrote regularly but only saw one another once or twice a year—"

I wrinkled my forehead with doubt.

"We can't violate moral standards by way of the U.S. mails, can we?"

"I don't know—" I glanced down at our linked hands. He eased his away from mine.

"I didn't say it would be easy," he defended, "just worth it!"

"Perhaps," I said tentatively. "But only if we each vow to be totally honest with one another about any liaisons we might be forming with others."

He nodded eagerly and started to speak, but I pressed my finger against his lips.

"And that we reevaluate the arrangement each year, say, at Christmas."

He kissed my finger tenderly.

"And no more of that!"

"What?"

"You know what—kissing me and holding me. It isn't fair to either of us."

Reluctantly, he agreed.

We talked for several minutes, both of us aware of a strange uneasiness between us. He asked about my classes. I asked about the university he'd attend in Chicago. It wasn't until I glanced toward the window and saw the street light blink on that I realized how late it had become.

As I slowly rose to my feet, Sundance stood and shook himself. "I've got to go. Aunt Drucilla will be worried."

"Wait. You haven't agreed to—"

"I fear I'm going to be sorry for doing this." I closed my eyes and sighed. "All right, friends, only friends."

"Right! And you won't be sorry, I promise."

I shook my head. "Don't make promises you might not be able to keep."

"Let me walk you home." He stood and straightened his jacket. The pot of tea sat cold and untouched on the sofa table. "Did I tell you that I'm leaving for Chicago tomorrow morning?"

I smiled and nodded. "Three times."

"Oh yeah. I guess I did."

I started briskly toward the foyer, where I caught a glimpse of myself in the gilt-framed mirror. "Oh my, I forgot I still had on Au Sam's dress. Give me a minute to change, OK?"

Sundance bounded after me up the stairs. I changed into my regular clothes and hurried back to the foyer. After telling Maria I was leaving, I patted Sundance on the head and promised to return the next day to spend some time with him. "In a few days, Rusty will be here for you." I patted his head playfully. "Take care of Meeker for me, you hear?"

The dog panted, his tongue lolling, his eyes sparkling.

Thad laughed at me. "He can't understand a word you're saying."

"Oh yes, he does. Don't you, boy?" The dog seemed to grin more broadly. "See? I told you so."

Thad opened the door, and we stepped out onto the darkened stoop. We strolled the five blocks home to Aunt Drucilla's place with my hand in the crook of his arm.

"I'll write every week," he vowed, pausing under every other street light.

And each time, I reminded, "Don't make promises you might not be able to keep."

When we reached the steps of my aunt's home, I paused and turned to him, tears forming in my eyes. "Please, let's say goodbye right here on the steps. I-I-I don't want an audience."

Holding my hands, he studied my face for many seconds without saying a word. I did the same, feeling as if I needed to memorize every line, every feature of his face.

"Godspeed, my love. I'll be praying for you." He remained silent. I stepped onto the first step, bringing us closer to the same height. "I hope we're doing the right thing."

"Me too." He let go of one of my hands and caressed the side of my face. "I love you, Chloe Celeste Chamberlain."

"And I, you."

"The four years will go fast—you'll see." Both of us knew that wasn't true. "I know I promised, but— One goodbye kiss?" In spite of the warning bells ringing in my head, I met him halfway. His arms encircled me, crushing me against him until I didn't know which I feared more, not being able to catch my breath or his releasing me. When the porch light flashed on, we broke apart.

Uncle Ian opened the door and picked up the evening paper from the stoop. "Sorry. I didn't know you two were out here. The air's getting a bit nippy. Perhaps you should come inside."

"Sorry, sir." Thad explained, "I was just saying goodbye to CeeCee. I leave for school in the morning."

My uncle waved, a jovial smile pasted on his face. "Good! Glad to hear you're going to further your education. That's important nowadays." A long pause followed. "Well, I'll leave you two alone to say goodbye."

"Thank you, Uncle Ian," I called as he closed the door. "I'll be right in."

Thad kissed me lightly one more time, turned, and walked down the avenue, stopping under each street lamp to throw me kisses. As he disappeared around the street corner, I reluctantly climbed the steps to the door. *Four months till Christmas. It's going to be a long four months, let alone four years, Mr. Adams, no matter what you say to the contrary.*

As Time Goes By

Dear Emily, My four-year voluntary prison term began this morning. Since I had a class at the time Thad's train left New York, I couldn't see him off at the railway station. But I remember looking up at the classroom clock and whispering a prayer for his safety at the time his train chugged out of Grand Central Station.

Every morning before I dressed for classes and every evening before turning off the lights to go to sleep, I counted the days until Christmas on the calendar in Aunt Drucilla's guest room.

By the time my parents and Rusty arrived from England at the end of September and I moved into my own room back home, Thad and I had established our once-a-week letter-writing routine. I would have willingly written to him every day, but we'd decided it would be wise to limit the frequency of our communication. So I reduced my frustration by writing long missives to Emily.

Mama and I talked late into the night her first night home. She held her tongue when I first told her about Thad's and my four-year arrangement, but I could see the concern in her eyes. "Mama, say something. Do you think we did the right thing, under the circumstances?"

"This isn't about what I think," she explained, "but what you think."

"But you're not pleased. I can tell."

"Honey, this is between you and Thaddeus. However, I can tell you, four years is a long time to be engaged."

"We're not engaged!"

"You have a commitment, don't you?"

I nodded.

"Then you're simply playing word games with yourself, aren't you?"

I hated to admit it, yet the *x*'s accumulating on my calendar and the eagerness with which I awaited each of Thad's letters indicated she might be right.

My stepsister and stepbrother returned from Grandmother and Grandfather Chamberlain's place in Maryland, with Americanized wardrobes and pampered attitudes, creating a new strain on each of us. My mother and Rusty suffered more than Daddy, whose work schedule kept him commuting between Washington, D.C., and New York, and me, whose classes and shifts at the hospital with which the school of nursing had affiliated filled most of my waking hours. It didn't take Mama long to enroll Nikolai and Rusty in school and to convince Phoebe to enroll in a general-studies program at a Manhattan college. This freed her to return to the great love of her life, volunteering her time at the women's clinic on the lower East Side, where she'd worked before going to Europe.

Add to my schedule daily violin practice, weekly lessons at the conservatory, outings with my suddenly domesticated cousin, plus weekend church services—and the last quarter of the year flew by more quickly than I would have imagined possible. Before I knew it, I stood beside the rails at Grand Central Station, awaiting Thad's arrival on Christmas Eve.

The train arrived on schedule. We greeted one another with ill-concealed impatience but maintained proper decorum until Thad cranked the engine and climbed into the Packard on the passenger side and closed the door. Suddenly, we were alone, sitting next to one another. I couldn't take my eyes off him. *This is an illusion, a dream. It has to be.* I touched his wrist with my gloved hand. *No, he's really here, and so am I.*

His hair was longer than I remembered, thick and wavy. His large dark eyes sparkled with merriment. I slipped off my glove and touched his square jaw, then brushed my fingertips across his wide mouth. True happiness wreathed his face.

"Welcome back," I whispered. He drew me into his arms as if

I were delicate crystal. I felt small and protected against his rough wool jacket. We kissed as if it were a shared breath of life. For the first time in months, I felt alive again.

But after the initial excitement, the week he spent with me in New York began roughly. During the first few days, we were like two gears, set to grind instead of mesh. But we managed to smooth out our communication problems in time for us to enjoy several truly happy days before Thad had to return to the university. Then the long separation began.

I threw myself into the new semester at school. To fill another evening with activity and to have a little time together, my mother and I joined the choir at the small church my family and I attended. Thursday-night choir rehearsal became a pleasant oasis for both of us. Almost as much as the opportunity to sing together, I treasured our stop after rehearsal for hot chocolate at a tiny Swedish restaurant around the corner from the church. On frigid New York winter evenings, we'd linger over the hot and delightfully decadent drink, chatting and giggling like schoolgirls.

In my plans, I hadn't anticipated meeting a tall, sandy-haired baritone named Raymond, who could make me laugh with the arch of one eyebrow and who could, with one pithy phrase, open my mind to fresh and intriguing concepts of law, theology, and music. His rugged good looks and strong, mellow baritone voice that blended so well with my own soprano voice piqued my fascination more than I cared to admit.

One snowy February evening after rehearsal, Mama and I minced our way over the slippery sidewalk to our little rendezvous. Once inside the restaurant, we slid into our favorite booth and ordered two hot chocolates and two squares of gingerbread.

"It's lucky we don't have choir rehearsal twice a week; I'd have to buy a new wardrobe." Mama patted her stomach.

"I hope the gingerbread is as good as the apple cobbler last week."

"If Cy and the others knew how good the Christiansons' pastry was, the church choir would grow by four."

The waiter placed the steaming cups and the whip-cream-topped cake in front of each of us. "Umm. That looks delicious. What do you say we keep this beautiful secret between us?" I cooed, licking a dab of cream from the tip of my finger.

"What secret?"

Mama and I glanced up in surprise to find Raymond standing beside the table, grinning down at us. "Sorry. I didn't mean to eavesdrop, but I saw the two of you sitting in here on my way to catch the subway and decided a cup of hot chocolate was too tempting to resist."

"Join us." Mama gestured toward my side of the booth.

Trying to decide if I felt happy or sad over his arrival, I made room for him to sit down. My mother motioned to the waiter. "Another cocoa and gingerbread." To Raymond, she asked, "Do you have to travel far to come to Thursday-night practice?"

"Not really—two stations." He gave his address—five blocks from our town house. The waiter set the second order in front of Raymond.

"You know, CeeCee and I would be happy to chauffeur you to rehearsal each week in the Packard, if you don't mind riding with a woman driver, that is." My mother smiled sweetly, avoiding my startled gaze. I sensed her scheme immediately.

"Oh, that would be so nice of you. As to women drivers, I am sure you are quite capable, Mrs. Chamberlain." The young man filled his fork with gingerbread.

She grinned coyly. "I was speaking of my daughter. She usually drives for us."

"Really?" He blinked in surprise. "A Packard is a mighty powerful vehicle for such a delicate, young, uh, er— Are you sure I can't pay you a little something for your trouble?"

"Nonsense." She waved away his offer. "CeeCee and I would appreciate the company, and it would save you the cost of the subway. Why, just this evening, as I prepared to leave the house for rehearsal, Cyrus was objecting to CeeCee's and my driving alone on these darkened city streets."

I stared into my mug, idly stirring the dark brown liquid. *Mother! Since when have you become squeamish about being out late at night without the benefit of male companionship? Daddy protests every Thursday evening, partly out of concern and partly out of guilt for not attending with us. Wait until he hears this one.*

Raymond was the first of many unsuspecting young men my family arranged to have pass through my life during the next ten months. Because Thad's agreement with his benefactor stipulated that Thad work at the man's newspaper during the summer months, and my program at the school of nursing required that I take classes throughout the summer, we knew that limiting our visits to Christmas was unavoidable. My family took his absence as a sign of instability in our relationship.

After my twentieth birthday, it seemed as if Mama, Aunt Drucilla, Ashley, Grandma McCall, and Grandma Chamberlain joined in a conspiracy to get Chloe Celeste Chamberlain "married off." Even Granddaddy Spencer sent one poor bachelor all the way from Shinglehouse, Pennsylvania, to meet his "gorgeous granddaughter," under the guise of delivering my birthday present—a silver-framed photograph of my deceased grandmother and him. I treasured the picture and, if the truth be known, I also treasured his concern for my future, however misdirected it might have been. The arrival of Ashley and Charles's baby, Lucinda Julietta, didn't ease the pressure from my family or ease my own inner conflicts.

I kept my part of Thad's and my agreement by telling him about each of these escorts. In his letters, he never let on how he felt about any of the young men I described. I know how I felt, however, when Thad told me about a friendship with a pert little blond music major named Lucille, who sat across from him each afternoon in the university library. But in my next letter, I responded simply, "that's nice," when in truth I wanted to scratch out the woman's baby-blue eyes.

Along with the insecurities of conducting a long-distance "friendship," as we insisted on calling it, were the spiritual insecurities I experienced daily. The turmoil inside of me faded only when I stopped fighting. I remember the evening clearly when I finally agreed to give Thad's and my love over to God. I was driving home after a late shift at the hospital, angry at my family's apparent resistance to my continued interest in Thad.

When Thad had first left for Chicago, I had ranted at God over the unfairness of our circumstances, even while knowing that my real problem had nothing to do with our ages or the miles separating us. Thad's spiritual condition separated us more than miles or our ages ever could. It was as if I were grasping the ends of two ropes that were being pulled in opposite directions. And painful though it was, I didn't want to let go of either. That night, alone in the car, the Holy Spirit spoke to me through the words I'd read that morning during my private devotions.

"Delight thyself also in the Lord; and he shall give thee the desires of thine heart. Commit thy way unto to the Lord; trust also in him; and he shall bring it to pass. And he shall bring forth thy righteousness as the light, and thy judgment as the noonday. Rest in the Lord and wait patiently for him" (Psalm 37:4-7).

Delight in the Lord, desires of thine heart, commit, trust, rest, and *wait.* The words tumbled through my mind to the rhythmic rumble of the Packard's tires on the deserted cobblestone avenue.

Delight in the Lord. I recalled the experience I'd had standing at the top of the gorge near Chamonix, praising God and shouting for all the world to give Him praise. It had been months since I'd experienced such joy and delight in Him. *Sorry, Lord. I know I'm the one who lost it, not You.*

Desire of thine heart. That surely describes Thad, doesn't it? Is this a guarantee that You will fulfill my desire to one day marry him? I waited for an answer, but none came.

Taking a deep breath of disappointment, I continued through the list. *Commit. Oh, this one's hard to do! Are You saying I need to commit Thad's and my relationship to You to handle?* Tears stung my eyes as I realized it wasn't the relationship that needed committing to Him as much as me. I needed to recommit my life and my future to my Saviour. *All right, I give. I've allowed my busy schedule and what I want to come between us, Lord. I'm so sorry. Thank You for showing me how far apart we've grown.* The words were difficult to think, let alone say. *Father, please take Thad's and my love and do with it as You please. I accept Your wisdom and trust the love You have for me to work everything out to bring honor to Your holy name.*

Like the cool Atlantic surf, the words *trust*, *rest*, and *wait* washed over me, refreshing my mind and assuring me that the same God I'd taken as my Friend in Chamonix had everything under control. With my prayers answered and my soul at peace, I knew that Thad's and my futures—whether together or separate—were secure.

The rest of the summer passed quickly. I found new energy with which to perform my tasks and to study. My joy returned, making life for me and those around me much more pleasant.

The first week in September of 1920, I returned to Bide-a-wee for my first visit since the fateful exile during the influenza epidemic. Pausing in the doorway of the kitchen—Au Sam's kitchen—I gazed about the room. Her copper teakettle—I'd almost forgotten. Across the room, on the back of the pantry door, her blue-and-white-checked apron hung from the brass hook.

Mama, Phoebe, and the two boys had spent the summer on the Cape, while Daddy and I had kept the town house running. Now, in September, Maria and I had taken the train to the Cape to help my mother and Phoebe close up the cottage for the summer. Walking along the beach again, I realized how much I missed the tranquillity of the ocean. Memories of running with Thad across the sand, of climbing on the rocks, of racing the surf filled me with conflicting emotions of missing him and still feeling close to him. These feelings made me wish I'd accompanied my father to the cottage on the weekends throughout the summer. *Someday, I want to live by the water again, permanently.*

On the morning I would be returning to the city with my family, I drove into town to see Thad's father. While the man seemed genuinely pleased to see me, he refused to listen to news about his son.

"Son? I have no son!" No amount of my arguing would change his mind.

Exasperated, I stopped trying. "Well, at least I know from whom Thad got his stubbornness."

A small smile curved the bearded grocer's lips, and a momentary sparkle appeared in his eyes. When I bade him goodbye, I couldn't resist the urge to give him a hug. I knew that since his wife had died in the epidemic, he had probably received very few. There were tears in his eyes when I opened the car door, turned, and waved. As I drove to the intersection and turned the corner toward Bid-a-wee, I could see him standing in the doorway of his store, returning my wave.

In my next letter to Thad, I told him of my visit to see his father and of the man's obvious loneliness. I didn't mention, however, his obstinate refusal to acknowledge his son. Thad said as much about his father as he had about my decision to leave our love in God's hands—he said nothing. That's when I realized that the only link left between Thad and his father was me.

I remembered the story Mama often told of her persistent efforts to repair the severed relationship with her father, Granddaddy Spencer. She believed the constant link with her sister Hattie was what eventually softened my grandfather's heart.

And suddenly, I knew what I would do. I would write to both Thad and his father, keeping each of them informed about the other. I also would occasionally share with both of them the spiritual blessings I was experiencing.

When the first letter from Mr. Adams arrived, I knew that my instincts had been correct. Reading between the lines, I could tell that the man was hungry for news about his only son but couldn't swallow his pride to admit it.

With untempered eagerness, I watched the cool days and cold nights turn the leaves of the trees along the avenue to bronze, then drop them at my feet. I first sensed a coolness in Thad's letters around the beginning of November. His eagerness for the coming Christmas holiday didn't seem to match mine. I had noted that Lucille's name no longer appeared, which I took as good news. Frankly, it galled me to read about how the woman hung onto every word Thad uttered.

During the next six weeks, I scrutinized every word he wrote, trying to analyze the change in his attitude. *Is it me? Is he tired of our long-distance relationship? Or is he simply overtired from his heavy load of classes this semester?* My feminine intuition flew a battery of warning flags when, in his last letter before semester-test week, he wrote, "I'm looking forward to the upcoming break from studying. I'll be arriving at five-thirty on the evening of the twenty-third. After an entire year apart, you and I have a lot to talk about."

If it hadn't been for my determination not to lose hold of the promises I'd made to God and that He'd made to me, I don't know how I would have made it through my final exams. Knowing I had less than six months before I'd graduate with my degree in nursing helped also.

I wished I could talk with my mother about my concerns. But always, the knowledge that she and Daddy were not completely happy about Thad held me back.

At home, I was determined to bring magic to the holidays.

I became a Christmas elf, draping garlands of evergreens over doors and fireplace mantels, which filled the house with their aroma. I placed a tall white candle in each front window and supervised the positioning of a fifteen-foot blue spruce in front of the parlor's triple windows.

Rusty, Phoebe, Nikolai, and I decorated the boughs with ribbon candy, candy canes, and crystal baubles. At the tips of the branches, delicate white candles glowed.

On the 22nd of December, with semester finals over and my last shift at the hospital completed until after the new year, I invited Phoebe and Ashley to go shopping with me for an outfit I could wear when I went to meet Thad's train. I'd had so little time for frivolous pursuits like shopping excursions, I decided I deserved the break.

What a mistake! Both women had definite ideas on the appropriate look for such an occasion, each far different from my own. Phoebe's tastes ran toward flowered dresses with fussy lace collars, while Ashley recommended the look of the young New York sophisticate. I laughed to myself when I pictured their reaction if I were to wear the turquoise wedding dress Au Sam had left me. *Thad would like it*, I mused. The frigid temperatures sweeping down from the Arctic did more to prevent me from carrying out such a whim than did the inappropriateness of the garment.

I'd given up hope of finding anything suitable when a salesclerk who'd been listening to our banter brought out an emerald green wool dress with matching coat.

"Ooh, CeeCee, it's perfect for you," Ashley squealed. "What an incredible color! Look what it does to the color of your eyes!"

"It is dramatic," Phoebe admitted.

"All it needs is a contrasting scarf." Ashley dashed across the dress shop to the display of scarves and mufflers.

"And maybe a brooch on the lapel of the coat," Phoebe added. I respected my stepsister's excellent taste in jewelry. "I'm sure Mama has something that would suffice."

"I found it! I found it!" A long silk scarf fluttered in Ashley's hand as she ran toward us. At first, I narrowed my eyes at the scarf's vibrant array of colors, but when she draped it on the emerald green coat, I had to admit that my cousin's eye for fashion had been right again. While we admired Ashley's choice of scarves, the clerk disappeared and returned with a pair of matching gloves. "Now, what about a hat?"

"It needs to be a small one," Ashley announced. "We want him to see as much of that fabulous hair as possible." To me, she whispered, "I'm so glad that you resisted the pressure to bob your hair. I wish I hadn't bobbed mine. I'd like to grow mine long again, but Charles won't let me."

"Won't let you?" I asked incredulously.

She nodded. "He's afraid I'll begin to look too matronly."

"You? Look matronly?" I coughed, choking on the very thought. "Not a chance!"

She ran her hands self-consciously along her trim form. Only a slight bulge remained as evidence of motherhood. "The baby and all, you know, wreaks havoc on a woman's figure."

Matronly! Hmmph! I'd like to see what his body would look like after giving birth to an eight-pound-eleven-ounce baby girl. My lips tightened involuntarily. Charles's arrogant demeanor reminded me of another family member I didn't much like—my Uncle Phillip, a San Francisco lawyer.

Her remark, "He won't let me," plagued me the rest of the afternoon and into the evening. When Mama stopped by my room to wish me good night, I told her about it.

"I don't know what I'd do if I were married to a man like that," I confessed. "I had thought no male could break my cousin's spirit. This one's well on his way to doing that, if you ask me."

"I'm sorry to hear that." My mother wrinkled her brow.

"I wanted to say, 'Whose hair is it, anyway?' "

Mama chuckled. "I'll bet you did. However, you were wise to remain silent. You can't improve Ashley's marital situation."

"I know, but—"

"She'd resent your attempts, no matter how good your intentions."

"I suppose you're right." I pursed my lips. "He's such a, a jerk."

She laughed. "Aren't you glad that you're not married to him?"

"If Thad ever acts like that, I'll— Hey, how do you like the suit? Honestly!" I gestured toward the open doors of the wardrobe.

I couldn't interpret the strange expression on her face. "It looks lovely on you, darling." She paused to moisten her lips. "The shade of green reminds me of a dress James had made for me before we went on our honeymoon to Denver."

"Really?" The comparison of my mother and real father's life together to Thad's and mine warmed me. "What was your dress like?"

A distant look swept across her face as she settled herself on the end of my bed. "Let's see. It was an emerald green satin gown, with ecru lace on the bodice. In order to fasten the long row of fabric-covered buttons, I first had to first lace myself into a whalebone corset."

"You?"

Mama chuckled and nodded. "What we women do for our men."

"Well, I would never—"

"Careful, sweetheart, in making those kinds of predictions. At your age, I would never have imagined myself wearing my skirts halfway up my calf either, but, as you know, my blue-chiffon dinner dress—"

"Mama! That hemline barely clears your ankles!"

"I feel conspicuous in it," she huffed.

I laughed. "If you want short, you should go downtown on Saturday night and see the shimmy girls strutting about on the arms of their sheiks."

"No thank you. I'll take your word for it, if you don't mind."

I laughed, then sobered, studying for a moment the wedding-ring design on the quilt covering my bed. "I've been wondering. How would you and Daddy feel if Thad and I announced our engagement on Christmas morning?" I hurried on without glancing over at her, fearing her initial reaction. "In June, I'll be twenty-one and will graduate with my RN degree. Then I'll be capable of getting a job and supporting myself anywhere in the country."

A small wall clock across the room ticked away the seconds while I continued tracing my finger over the rings on the quilt, awaiting her reply. Finally, I could stand the suspense no longer. "Well, what do you think?"

She took a deep breath. "You know that your father and I have nothing against Thaddeus himself. He's a fine young man—nothing like Ashley's Charles, thank the good Lord. Having said that, we are very concerned by the spiritual gulf that remains between the two of you."

"But, I don't think—"

"Wait. Listen to me. Just last night, we were talking about the beautiful growth we've both witnessed in your spiritual life these last few months." Mama paused before continuing. "When God commands us to not be unequally yoked together, He does so for a reason. The effect a husband and a wife have on each other's thinking is unbelievable. Look at the changes in your cousin since her marriage, for example."

I opened my mouth to reply.

"I know you think that's different—Ashley's different from you, and Charles isn't Thad. However, until you're married, for better, for worse, you can't imagine how the intimacy of that bond will influence your thinking."

I clamped my mouth shut. She leaned forward and placed her hand on mine. "Daddy and I love you very much. And—" She measured her words carefully. "—should the two of you decide to go against our counsel, we will continue to love you, and we will love Thaddeus as the son he will become. Is that what you want to hear?"

Tears surfaced as our eyes met. "Thank you, Mama."

"But," she continued, "you need also to realize that all the parental love in the world will not change the results of your choice. Until you and Thaddeus are united spiritually, the emotional, physical, and intellectual aspects of your marriage will be incomplete. This will bring discord and sadness into your home."

I wanted to argue that, while her observations might be true for some couples, Thad and I had a special relationship. But I knew better. Over the years, I'd learned that when my parents and God came to an agreement on something, they were usually right. "Thad's a good man, Mama—a kind, considerate human being."

Without speaking, she nodded and squeezed my hand.

The next day, I donned my new dress and coat, swept my hair up into dramatic waves on each side of my face, and pinned it into a chignon. I left a couple of long tendrils to soften the overall effect. After pinning the tiny hat into place, I stepped back to study the results. *Hmm, not bad. Not bad indeed.*

On the drive to the station, I drummed my fingers impatiently on the steering wheel, every few minutes checking the gold brooch-style watch I'd borrowed from my mother. *Thanks to this traffic, I'll be late, and he'll hop a train back to Chicago before I can get there.*

I fussed the entire journey. The fact that I parked the car and strolled through the station to the waiting platform a full thirty minutes before his train was scheduled to arrive didn't ease my mind. *Calm yourself, CeeCee*, I scolded. *Remember, grace and loveliness emanate from a tranquil mind.*

As the train from Chicago to New York hissed to a stop in front of me, I adjusted the silk scarf and nervously touched the back of my hair, checking for straying locks. I walked along the passenger cars, searching for his face in one of the windows but didn't see him until he stepped down onto the platform. "Thad. Thad! Over here," I squealed as I hurried toward him, calling his name.

When I ran into his arms, I felt him hesitate an instant before he wrapped them around me.

"Oh, Thad, it's so good to see you again. I've been counting the hours for months now." Just as he had the previous December, Thad led me through the station to the waiting automobile, where he tossed his valise into the back seat and helped me into the driver's seat, cranked the engine, then hopped into the front seat on the passenger's side.

"So, how was you trip? You look tired. Have you been eating right?" I asked as I studied his face.

"Perhaps I am a little tired. It is a long ride, as you know."

As I directed the car through the late-afternoon maze of horse-drawn wagons, delivery tucks, taxis, pedestrians, and bicyclists, the coolness I'd detected in his letters took on a new reality. When I asked him about his final tests and the trip east, he responded with only brief replies. Only later did I realize that he had not even commented on my new outfit.

The chill that began during the ride from the station remained between us throughout the evening with the family and the next day. It wasn't until Christmas Eve, after we had returned from the candlelight service at the church and the rest of the clan had retired for the night, that we were once again alone, except for Sundance, who kept teasing to be petted. When the dog knocked off one of the crystal baubles from the tree, I dragged him from the room and closed the door.

Flames danced in the fireplace as the two of us blew out the small white candles on the tree. The room darkened, easing the awkwardness lingering between us. Reluctantly, I blew out the last candle, knowing the time had come for a confrontation. I gestured toward the sofa.

"Our apple cider is getting cold."

We seated ourselves on the sofa. The smile on Thad's face couldn't obscure the sadness in his eyes or the strip of sofa upholstery visible between us.

"All right, I know you've been wanting to tell me something since the moment I met you at the station. What is it? Another woman?"

"Not exactly."

I swallowed hard. "What do you mean, 'not exactly'? This is a yes-or-no question, not multiple choice. Either there is or there isn't another woman."

"Oh, CeeCee, must you be so blunt?" Thad continued to watch the flames dance in the fireplace.

"Well?"

He sighed. "There is, yet there isn't."

"Would you please explain yourself?"

"The only reason I'm dating Lucille is your strange fixation with religion. I can live with the ritual of attending church on Christmas Eve, as we did tonight; it's merely part of the spirit of Christmas." He studied his hands. "But, on a day-to-day basis, to be forced to listen to naive, irresponsible babble about some Deity no one can see, hear, touch, or taste? I—"

"Naive? Irresponsible?" I gripped the arm of the sofa, attempting to stay calm.

"Look, I've always admired your intelligence. I admit that your ability to express abstract concepts has, at times, been intimidating. But, with all the evidence current in every scholarly journal, newspaper, and magazine discussing the irrelevance of your kind of God, I can't understand your stubborn persistence." An edge entered his voice. "I couldn't cohabit with anyone holding such blind, rigid beliefs. One thing I can say for Lucille, she reflects the beliefs of whomever she's around." He sighed.

"A cute little chameleon."

"CeeCee, don't!" Turning to face me, his eyes begged for understanding. "She loves me; and in time, maybe I can come to love her too. Did I tell you that her father is a philosophy professor at the university?" His tone turned cynical. "I'm afraid she didn't inherit his intellectual ability, though she is quite talented musically. She plays the piano and sings, of course."

Music major? I felt as if he'd slapped me across the face. He continued talking as if nothing were wrong.

"But as my roommate says so often, 'You don't choose a wife for her intelligence, anyway.' "

I tightened and relaxed the muscle in my cheek several times before I spoke. "And just what are the qualities your roommate expects to find in the wife he chooses?"

Thad blushed, uncomfortably tugging at his collar. "It doesn't matter. I don't agree with him, of course."

I uttered a polite little laugh. "It matters to me, since he has so measurably influenced your thinking."

"I-I, uh, well, what he believes is important in a wife are her appearance, a compliant spirit, good family breeding, and, well—"

"And?"

"A body structure that makes childbearing easier."

"A broodmare?" Flames, hotter and more deadly than those in the fireplace, darted from my eyes. He cringed slightly. "Does this roommate of yours recommend prying open the young lady's mouth to check her teeth?"

"Chloe Celeste Chamberlain! That was an indelicate remark."

"I'm sorry if I offended your sensibilities, but you have to admit, your list paralleled the qualities one looks for when purchasing a horse."

"If you can't be serious, perhaps I should—" He arose to his feet.

"Perhaps you should." Angry at the tears flooding my eyes, I folded my arms and sank back into the sofa.

Thad walked to the parlor door and slid it open. "I-I-I'm sorry. Even after all that's been said, I do love you. If only you could get rid of this one flaw—"

I stood and faced him. "I was thinking the same thing about you." My mood softened. "If only you could grasp the fantastic difference it makes to live a God-centered life."

Though our feet remained rooted to the carpet where each of us stood, I could see the gulf between us widen. "Oh, Thad, I—"

"We will continue to be friends, as we promised, won't we?"

I ached to run to him, throw my arms around him, kiss away the barriers to our love. *If only I could. If only it were so easy.*

As we gazed at one another, it was as if he read my thoughts. For suddenly, he darted around the sofa and swept me into his arms. "Oh, CeeCee, I will never be happy thinking of you as only a friend. I love you so much. Maybe we can give it a try." He cupped my face in his hands and placed several light kisses on my lips. "Surely our love for one another is strong enough to weather these silly religious differences, isn't it?"

In his arms, the feeling of being cherished and protected washed over me. However, the passion between us grew as his kisses grew more demanding. I responded with the same fervor. It was as if we were both trying to blot out the reality we knew to be true.

My legs felt weak, and I swayed against him. I tried to silence my mother's warnings niggling my mind as he eased me onto the sofa, his lips still pressed against mine. Desire like I'd never before experienced flooded through me.

Oh, dear God, please forgive me. I can't— Please, forgive me.

Without warning, a huge weight landed on top of us both. "What in the—" Thad sprang off me, terror filling his face.

I shot up to a more ladylike position. "Sundance!" I shouted. "Get out of here!"

The golden retriever ignored my command, slurping his tongue along the side of my face and nuzzling his head onto my lap.

"Oh, Sundance." I buried my face in his ruff and wept. I didn't hear Thad tiptoe from the room.

Getting on With
My Life

Christmas, 1920—not one of my favorite memories. The tension between Thad and me permeated the entire day. In addition, Phoebe and Nikolai languished in their rooms, suffering from homesickness for Russia and their parents; Charles behaved toward Ashley like an insensitive cad; and baby Lucy was teething. All in all, I felt relief when the day passed.

Early the next morning, I took Thad to meet his train. He'd made a weak excuse to my parents about needing to get back early to visit his benefactor for a few days but fooled no one by his story. He'd been scheduled to stay through New Year's Day. My family, including Phoebe, Nikolai, and Rusty, followed us into the foyer to say goodbye. Daddy helped me with my coat, then kissed my cheek.

"Courage, sweetheart," he whispered.

I blinked back the sudden flood of tears filling my eyes. At the station, when it was time for Thad to board the train, he brushed his lips past my cheek. "Thank your parents again for having me here during the holidays."

Nodding mechanically, I studied a crack between the platform boards by my feet. "I'll do that."

"Good luck as you finish your studies."

"You too."

"You will write, as you promised?"

"Give me some time."

"OK." He shifted his weight from one foot to the other.

The conductor shouted, "All aboard."

197

"Guess I'd better get on board."

"Guess so."

I didn't lift my eyes to see him walk away. Instead, I walked determinedly into the station, letting the doors swing closed behind me. Once at the car, I cranked the engine and drove north, out of the city, to an abandoned stretch of beach in Brooklyn. I sat watching the cold December clouds roll across the sky until my fingers grew stiff from the chill and the joints in my knees ached. The lonesome warning blast of a foghorn interrupted my melancholy reverie, and I glanced down at my watch. The thought struck me that somewhere in the last two hours I'd lost my entire world.

In all the time that had passed since Thad bade me goodbye, I hadn't cried—not one tear. I wanted to. I'd chosen the empty beach for that very reason. For some reason, I had no tears to shed—for me, for Thad, for us. After staring, unseeing, at the bleak gray world beyond the windshield, I rested my forehead against the steering wheel and closed my eyes. *Dear God, You promised You'd give me strength to do what is right. Well, I did it, even though I didn't want to. So where's the peace that I'm supposed to feel?*

I waited for a thunderclap or a celestial applause to let me know that my sacrifice had been appreciated. None came. I waited for a wave of peace to flood through me, but an agony and an emptiness more profound than I'd ever imagined possible filled my soul. My life stretched out before me, as bleak and as cold as the ocean surf pounding in my ears. Remembering Job's words, "Though he slay me, yet will I trust in him," I put the car into gear and drove home.

My last semester in nurses' training and my music lessons filled my every waking moment. When I had any spare time, I volunteered for extra shifts at the hospital. I received a short letter from Thad on the average of once a month. No mention was ever made of Lucille. I tried to tell myself I wished he'd stop writing, but I hungered for each letter weeks before it arrived.

On the weekend of my graduation exercises, I received three letters—one from Thad, one from my Granddaddy Spencer in

Pennsylvania, and one from my mother's friend, Indian Pete. Uncle Pete, as we children had called him when he used to visit us in San Francisco, was a lawyer. He and his wife, Auntie Faith, lived in southern Oregon.

It was Uncle Pete's letter that suddenly turned my world upside down. After the preliminary congratulatory remarks, he wrote, "I can't believe that the little girl with long red ringlets whom I used to bounce on my knee has grown into such a beautiful and accomplished young woman. Your mother told me about your courageous adventure in France. It sounds as if you've inherited more than just your mother's good looks."

I chuckled to myself. As a child, I had always imagined that Uncle Pete had a slight crush on Mama. I continued reading. "Last month, the nurse who served the town and the local Klamath Indian population died, and we are left with no one who has any medical training whatsoever. The nearest hospital is in Jacksonville, eighty miles away. A circuit-riding doctor visits the reservation once every quarter, but he's so sodden with whiskey, his breath could ignite a bonfire." I didn't like the premonitions I was getting as I read. "I don't know what your plans may be, but I have a proposition I wish you'd consider, which will take incredible courage and dedication on your part." My stomach lurched. "Your Aunt Faith and I will pay your ticket west, if you'll come to Oregon and stay at least one year. The town fathers have plans to build a clinic and advertise for our own physician."

He went on to describe the primitive conditions. *No hot running water! No bubble baths!* Even before I read the last sentence in his letter, I knew where God was leading me.

By the end of the week, I was packed and ready to leave New York. This time, when I packed to leave home, I took everything—my diaries, my books, the dress and the fan Au Sam had given me. Mama took my departure harder this time than she had when I left for Chamonix. She'd been excited about my plan to work at her clinic until I could find what I truly wanted to do. For her sake, and for Daddy's, I tried to hide the excitement I felt inside as I stood on the platform, surrounded by my family, waiting to board the train west.

"Lucy will be talking by the time you come back to us," Ashley reminded.

I kissed the baby's soft cheek and handed the child back to her mother. "I know. You'll have to send me regular letters, describing her at every stage, promise?"

In an unexpected display of emotion, Rusty threw his arms around me. "I'm going to miss you so much!"

"I'll miss you too." I tousled his hair.

Daddy insisted on praying for my safety right there in the middle of the platform. Somehow I didn't mind at all. After kissing each of my family members and promising to write, I turned to my parents and couldn't think of anything to say. When my mother's lower lip began to quiver, my eyes filled with tears.

"I love you, CeeCee. God go with you."

I nodded, unable to speak. As we kissed each other goodbye, the conductor announced the last boarding call. With tears streaming down my cheeks, I turned to my father for strength, but his face was moist with tears as well. For one last time, I buried myself in his arms, absorbing every ounce of security I could from him. "Be good, Freckles. Write as often as you can."

His face swam before my eyes. I nodded and gulped.

The train whistle blew, and I scrambled aboard. My family's goodbyes and well wishes echoed in my mind for miles after the train had chugged out of the station.

I'd promised my mother that I'd stop for a few days in Shinglehouse to see her family—which I did. Granddaddy Spencer and I took long walks along the oil pipelines. I don't know how many times I played my violin for him during those three days together. But before long, I was on my way again. I thought of Mama, a young girl of sixteen, hopping a similar train for California. I thought of my brother Jamie. How terrified he must have been, five years old and surrounded by strangers.

Thad met my train when I reached Chicago, for I'd written him immediately of my plans. As I stepped off the train, he placed an awkward kiss on my cheek. "It's so good to see you. How long can you stay?"

"Well," I said hesitantly, "overnight, if that's all right."

He took my valise from my hand. "Of course, it's all right.

I've arranged for you to stay at Lucille's parents' house. They're great people; you'll love them."

I swallowed hard. "I'm sure I will."

"Oh! Speaking of Lucille—" He turned and motioned toward a blond young woman standing by the station door. "—let me introduce you to her. She's been so anxious to meet you."

I tried not to sound sarcastic. "I'm sure she has."

After his introductions, I extended my hand. "Nice to meet you, Lucille. Thad has told me so much about you. We've been good friends for years."

"Oh?" She cast a surprised look at Thad. "He hasn't told me much about you at all."

I linked her arm in mine and entered the station, Thad trailing nervously behind us. "Isn't it convenient, then, that you and I will have this time to get acquainted?"

I glanced over my shoulder and repaid his withering glare with a naive Ashley-smile. The best part was that Lucille and I got along famously. I genuinely liked her, and we had our music in common. If she'd been dating anyone else, I would have told her of Thad's crass slur about her intelligence and of his criteria for choosing a wife.

Thad sulked throughout the taxi ride to Lucille's home and throughout the lovely dinner her parents provided. When he bade us both good night in the foyer of her home, fear and frustration filled his eyes.

The next day, when Thad arrived to take me to the train station, Lucille apologized for not being able to see me off. I assured her that it was perfectly all right, that I understood. "It's just that I've been finding this class difficult and don't dare skip even one lecture. On your way home next year, you'll stop and see us again, won't you? Maybe you could spend a few days so we can really get to know one another."

"I'd like that." I was surprised that I sincerely meant what I'd said.

Once inside the taxi on our way to the station, I began the conversation. "Lucille's a very nice young woman. You don't deserve her; she deserves more than you seem ready to give."

His mouth dropped open. "I beg your pardon."

"I said—"

"I know what you said."

"I'm only telling you how I feel, as your friend. I've seen what happens in a loveless marriage. Look at Ashley and Charles." I turned to face him. "Charles treats her as if she were a mindless child. He doesn't respect her."

"I'm not Charles."

"I didn't say you were. All I said was, make sure you truly love and respect whomever you marry before you trap her in a marriage that will be tragic for both of you."

Thad turned his face toward the window. "Are you finished?"

"Yes."

"Good." A heavy silence fell between us during the rest of the drive. It wasn't until we were standing in the waiting area of the station that either of us spoke again. "CeeCee," he began, "will you send me your address when you get settled?"

"Do you still want to continue writing, after all—"

"Of course. I meant it when I said that I didn't want that to change."

"If you're sure."

When the conductor announced the first "All aboard," I mumbled something about needing to get settled in my compartment and leaned forward to kiss him on the cheek. At the same instant, he leaned forward, with similar intention. Instead, our lips met, setting off a spark neither of us had anticipated. Hastily, I stepped back. Seeing my fear reflected in Thad's eyes, I whirled about and flew aboard the train, forgetting that he still held my valise.

Terrified that Thad might follow me on board, I ran to my compartment and slammed the door behind me. I leaned back and closed my eyes, listening as the wheels screeched and the train hissed into motion. A knock on the door terrified me.

"Who is it?" I hissed.

"The conductor." I opened the door a crack. "Your young man asked me to give you this."

I took the case and thanked him, then threw myself on the narrow berth. This time, the tears continued until I fell asleep from exhaustion. It was evening before I awoke enough to wash and purchase something to eat.

All across the prairie, during the two days I spent with Aunt Bea in Hays, over the weekend in Denver with Aunt Gladys and Uncle Phineas Putman, I thought of nothing but Thad. I tried to read my Bible but couldn't concentrate. I tried to write in my diary; no words came. The thought of food nauseated me. By the time the train headed northwest toward Oregon, sleep also eluded me. In desperation, I cried out to God, "You promised me peace! You promised."

By the time the train reached Oregon, I was exhausted. Worse yet, my nose was red and my eyes were puffy, not only from crying, but from a cold. *Great way to start your first job as a nurse—sick yourself!*

I arrived in Klamath Falls late one evening. No one was there to meet me, and no taxis waited in front of the station. Shafts of golden twilight slanted across the deserted train station.

Dressed in a blue seersucker suit and wearing stylish new high-heeled shoes with narrow toes, I stood in the middle of the platform, my two trunks and three valises surrounding me, and tried to decide what to do.

A uniformed porter put my luggage into storage so that I could explore the town. I hoped to spot Uncle Pete's law office along what appeared to be the main street. Taking a good grip on my drawstring leather purse, I stepped off the platform into the dusty street, grimacing at my impractical footwear.

Red-brick buildings and peeling framed houses lined the street. I passed storefronts with prominently displayed signs reading Closed. A moment of panic rose within me—*the entire town is closed down for the night.* In the distance I could hear a tinny player piano clanking out "Don't Sit Under the Apple Tree." *Maybe not the entire town.* I headed in the direction of the music.

A tall, rangy cowboy leaning against a veranda post touched the brim of his hat. "You look lost, little lady. Can I help?" His features obscured by the gathering shadows, he looked remarkably like Thad.

"Could you direct me to either a boardinghouse or a hotel?"

"Sure. The hotel's just up the street a piece." He eyed the

purse I clutched tightly. "I happen to be heading that way myself. Have any bags for me to carry?"

"I left them at the depot with the porter." I gestured in the direction of the station. "I'll send for them as soon as I find a place to stay."

He nodded and grinned. "The name's Blair, Calvin Blair. People 'round here call me Cal. I own a cattle ranch out of town a piece."

I hesitated, trying to decide if I should skip proper protocol and introduce myself. Before I could decide, he asked, "Are you visiting relatives? Or just passing through?"

"Actually, I am supposed to meet Mrs. Nina Cook. Peter, the lawyer, arranged for her to be here."

"Sure, everybody knows Pete and Nina." He pushed his hat on the back of his head. "If Nina said she'd be here for you, she will. As to Pete, he and the missis had to make an unexpected trip to Portland. They'll be back in a few days."

The man paused in front of the two-story building with a large sign mounted above the veranda—Hot Springs Hotel.

"This is it, ma'am." He hopped up onto the wooden veranda and held the door while I swept into the dimly lighted, deserted lobby. My nostrils closed at the stench of mildew and tobacco smoke. Multicolored Indian blankets, dingy with dust and smoke, draped the adobe walls, interspersed with mounted trophies of mountain lions, deer, and pronghorn antelope.

I stepped around one of the strategically placed brass cuspidors as I followed Cal through the lobby into a second parlor.

"Hey, Shorty, I brought you a boarder." He turned to me. "What did you say your name was?"

I cleared my throat. "Miss Chamberlain."

"A Miss Chamberlain. She's looking for Nina. Hey!" He turned with recognition. "You must be the nurse Pete's been talkin' about. You look pretty young to be a nurse, I'd say."

I straightened my shoulders and opened my mouth to reply, when a whiskered old man clomped through the doorway. Behind him, the smoke was so thick I could barely make out the forms of four men seated around a poker table, playing cards.

"Shorty, this is Miss Chamberlain. See that she gets your

best room, you hear?"

"Yes, sir, Mr. Blair." The man named Shorty touched the brim of his hat in respect.

Calvin Blair smiled down at me. "If you're a bit hungry, I'd be glad to escort you to the town's one and only eatery, Jane's Place."

"That's very kind of you, Mr. Blair, but I ate on the train," I demurred. "What I really need is to get some sleep."

"Sure, I understand. I feel the same way every time I return home from San Francisco."

Behind him, the hotel door swung open. A woman's voice called out, "Hey, have any of you fellas spotted a young woman wandering about town?"

"Nina!" Calvin Blair whirled about. "We were just talking about you. This is—"

"I know who this is. Miss Chloe Celeste Chamberlain, from New York City, that's who. Why do you think I've been meeting every train that has pulled into town during the last few days? I would have met this one on time, too, if it hadn't been for a blown tire on the outskirts of town." A short, stocky woman, dressed in men's denim pants and a red-plaid work shirt, held out her hand. "How are you doing, honey? Glad you arrived here safely."

As I shook the woman's hand, she continued, "Don't mind this old cowboy." She poked Calvin Blair playfully in the ribs. "Cal thinks he's the town's most eligible bachelor. Trouble is, he's right!"

Her eyes narrowed as she scanned me from my hair to my high-heeled shoes. "You look a mite fragile for reservation living. What's an elegant young lady like you doing out here, anyway?"

I straightened, feeling defensive. "I'm much stronger than I look."

She pursed her lips. "You'll need to be, if you're going to last through the winter." Noticing Cal still hovering nearby, the woman gestured. "Shoo! Get on out of here. Miss Chamberlain needs to rest after her long journey. You can get acquainted tomorrow."

The cowboy sauntered out the hotel door, his hands tucked in his back pockets. Nina grabbed the room key from Shorty's hand. "Get on over to the station for the lady's luggage." The man obeyed immediately. She placed the key in my hand. "Your room is at the top of the stairs. We'll head out to my place on the reservation tomorrow morning after breakfast."

I said good night and headed up the stairs.

"The bathroom's down the hall," Shorty called. "Toilet's next to it. You'll find a chamber pot under the bed for in the middle of the night."

I called a cheery "thank you" in spite of my embarrassment.

The room at the top of the stairs, the best room in the house, turned out to be a tiny cubicle with bare wooden floors and a military-style cot piled high with quilts. I closed the door and walked the six feet to the window and looked down on the dusty street. Three tipsy cowboys staggered down the center of the street, clinging to one another and singing "Coming Through the Rye."

When my luggage arrived, I thanked the man and tried to hand him a tip.

"No, ma'am," he said, "just part of our service."

The next morning I was up with the first crow of the town's roosters. By the time Nina and I had finished breakfast at Jane's Place, I'd decided to tuck away the memory of Thad and embrace my future.

Nina's high-step Oldsmobile chugged out of town in an cloud of dust. We followed a dirt road that stretched across a flat plain. Suddenly, she turned to me. "It was a man, wasn't it?"

"Excuse me?" I looked at her incredulously.

"A man, that's why you came here—same as me."

She continued speaking, despite my attempt to reply to her question. "I was born and raised in Lexington, Kentucky. My parents sent me to finishing school in Boston, where I met and married Horace Cook, an irresponsible, good-looking gambler. He dragged me to a town called Winnemucca, Nevada, where he got into a brawl and killed a man." She shook her head. "I moved north after the judge sentenced him to hanging. Taught school on the reservation for thirty-five years."

Nina pointed out her side window. "See that ranch house in

the distance? Cal Blair's place. Cal's a good man, and he owns the biggest and the best ranch in these parts." She glanced at me with a meaningful nod. "He took a shine to you yesterday. You could do a lot worse."

"You're crazy."

She threw her head back and laughed. "My eyesight might not be what it once was, but I can see the love light in a man's eyes, gal."

I heaved a sigh. *It's starting again. First Mama, now Nina.* "I am not interested in men, I assure you. I am here to do a job, that's all."

Nina snorted. "A good-looking woman like you is made to be loved and protected. Alone in these parts, you have to be tough. And you're not tough."

I clamped my mouth closed and stared out at the semiarid land stretching from the horizon to a cluster of ragged hills. A few miles later we left the main dirt road for a desert track that wove its way over dry creek beds and around buttes toward the hills. The closer we got to the hills, the higher they grew.

At the top of a mesa, Nina stopped the car and pointed to the valley below. "That's the reservation." Shifting the car into gear once more, Nina drove down the narrow, rutted track to the village and parked in front of a small wooden shack. "There is the clinic. You might like to take a look inside before we go meet Chief Echo Hawk."

It took less than two minutes to tour the building and inspect the meager stock of medical supplies. "Where is the rest of the equipment stored?"

"This is it, honey. Your biggest problem will be patching up drunks after Saturday-night brawls. Alcohol will destroy the Indian culture yet."

I met the balding middle-aged chief; then we continued on to Nina's three-room cabin. As I stepped into the large room that served as the woman's kitchen, dining room, and parlor, I inhaled sharply. It was obvious that the room was her pride and joy. Sunlight streamed through the sparkling windowpanes, free of draperies, and across the highly polished floor.

An oak trestle table, equally polished, filled the center of the room. A small sofa, a rocker, and a winged-back chair clustered around the massive stone fireplace. Graceful oak end tables stood beside each of the chairs. Two silver-framed photos, one of a man sporting a handlebar mustache and the other of a bride and groom, decorated the mantel, along with a row of leather-bound books. Cast-iron pots and frying pans, interspersed with copper utensils, hung on the wall beside the cookstove.

"Come this way." She gestured toward the second door along the wall opposite the fireplace. "I hope you'll like your room."

I smiled. "I know I will."

The room I would occupy during my stay was as charming as the rest of the cabin. A brass bed filled much of the tiny room. At the foot of the bed was a carved oak wardrobe. A rocker sat next to a small chest of drawers under the window. The window was decorated with a red-and-white gingham curtain, tied back with red ribbons. A rag rug covered a portion of the glistening hardwood floor. Whether it was the bright, cheery colors or the sunlight flooding the room, I didn't know. But I did know I was going to very happy here.

I turned to compliment her on the lovely decor, when she asked with uncharacteristic shyness, "Do you like it?"

"Oh yes. I love it."

The lines in her forehead disappeared as she broke into a wide grin. "I think you and I are going to get along just fine."

"I think so too."

My work at the clinic started early the next morning when a young woman brought a small boy to be treated for ratbite.

I treated injuries, colds, sprains, and what I suspected to be intestinal worms until the sun was low in the sky, and Nina dragged me from the clinic, saying, "Tomorrow will be another day. You can't cure all the troubles of the world in one day."

On Sunday, Uncle Pete and Aunt Faith arrived at the reservation to take me on a picnic. When I invited Nina to join us, she demurred, saying, "You should spend time with your friends without me tagging along."

No amount of insisting would make her change her mind.

Uncle Pete delighted me by telling stories about my mother

and my real father. I'd never fully appreciated my mother's brav-
ery until I heard the stories from his lips. Midafternoon, they
returned me to Nina's care and drove back to town.

Before they left, Uncle Pete said, "By the way, Cal Blair sends
his regards."

Nina grinned, first at me, then at Faith and Pete.

As I trudged back inside the cabin, I had no way of knowing
this was but the beginning of a determined campaign Calvin
Blair was about to launch. During the rest of the summer and
on into the autumn, Mr. Blair appeared at the reservation several times a week, sometimes delivering mail, sometimes bringing medical supplies donated by the Christian Ladies Guild of
Medford, a town west of Klamath Falls.

When Thad's letters began to arrive, Cal's visits increased. I
wondered how he managed to run his cattle ranch and spend so
much time at the reservation. And while I resented the efforts
on Nina's part to throw the two of us together, I did find the
man's attention flattering and his sense of humor engaging.

I couldn't say the same for the circuit-riding doctor, Dr.
Jenkins. The night after his first visit, I told my mother about
him in a letter home. "Using the title 'doctor' for this rum-toting
man is a travesty of the term. I've never before met an individual less deserving of the honor." I paused, recalling how many
times in one day I had to correct his errors or ward off his inde-
cent proposals toward me and toward the young Indian women.
"These poor people deserve better. Where are the Jamies and
the Pauls of the profession? Obviously not in Klamath County,
Oregon."

A big surprise came a week before Thanksgiving—a letter
from Lucille, of all people. After her salutation and a page of
chatter about her classes, the weather, and the latest Holly-
wood movie, she wrote, "Thad and I are no longer seeing each
other. Last summer, while covering a tent revival for his newspaper, he found God—if you can believe it. Needless to say, I
couldn't abide all the spiritual hocus-pocus and decided to call
it quits."

I stared at the sheet of linen paper scented with lavender for
several seconds. *Thad hasn't said one word in his letters, not*

one word. I continued reading. "He has transferred to a small Christian college in the area and plans to become a preacher, of all things! Can you picture Thaddeus Adams preaching the destruction of the world?"

No, I had to admit I couldn't. On rereading all of Thad's recent letters, I found no mention, not even an inference, of his conversion. *Why hasn't he told me? I would have thought he'd— Obviously, his romantic inclinations toward me no longer exist. That's the only thing that makes any sense.*

During the next few days, I moved mechanically through my chores at the clinic. On Thanksgiving Day, Cal showed up at the door with a feast for a crowd. I had to admit that as I gazed at the faces of the chief and his wife, at Nina, Cal, the members of the tribal council and their wives, all assembled around Nina's table, it was a Thanksgiving I'd never forget.

The week before Christmas, the first snow fell. Other storms from the north followed, whipping across the flat lands and filling the passes. On Christmas Eve, Nina stared out of the parlor window. "It's going to be a long, cold winter, I'm afraid. We aren't getting out of here before spring."

Her prediction was right. On the first of March, I was making a list of needed supplies when suddenly, Cal burst through the door of the clinic and dropped a heavy saddlebag full of letters on my examination table.

"Thought I'd bring you some reading." He grinned. "That young man of yours sure writes a lot."

I blushed uncomfortably. "He's not my young man. Thad's just a friend."

The rancher brightened. "One would never know it by the numbers of letters he sends. Looks like he's moved too—different postmark."

I planted my hands on my hips and snarled, "And what else have you deduced from my personal correspondence?"

He looked at me in surprise. "Sorry, I didn't know you'd be touchy about what's there for all the world to see."

I pressed the palm of my hand against my forehead. "I'm sorry, Cal. My outburst was uncalled for."

"Shucks." He grinned. "You're just reacting to your first case of cabin fever. You'll feel better once the weather breaks and the snow melts."

That evening, I curled up on the sofa in front of a roaring fire and read the news from home. My eyes misted when Nina handed me a cup of hot chocolate.

"To take off the chill," she said.

Later that evening, I had the urge to examine my treasures from home, including the turquoise satin dress. Nina oohed appreciatively when I modeled it for her. I told her the story of the fan and about the gentle little woman who'd shared so much of herself. "I miss her so much," I admitted.

"Praise God, you had her as long as you did."

I'd long since learned that Nina praised God for everything—rain, sleet, snow, hail, sunshine. You name it, she praised Him for it. I was amused by the woman's ability to scold and praise simultaneously. Regardless of the circumstances, I never saw Nina discouraged or depressed. Even when the pipe that brought spring water into the cabin broke, she hauled on her coat, grabbed a wrench, and headed for the door, saying, "Praise God, He's determined to keep me young."

Without warning, spring burst on the hills surrounding the reservation. One day the world was white with snow; the next, a yellow green. The fields were dotted with wildflowers of yellow and orange, red and purple. To get away from the confines of the cabin and the village, I took my Bible and climbed the butte overlooking the town each morning. I came to enjoy these moments of tranquility and study. Sometimes I would make up tunes for my favorite psalms. Other times I would take along my violin and play concertos to the wind.

Before long, summer scrambled up the hillsides. And somewhere along the way, I turned twenty-two and agreed to stay on at the reservation for a second year. I also decided it was time to come face to face with my maturity.

I don't look like a spinster, I thought as I gazed at my reflection in the framed mirror. *Is that a wrinkle?* I frowned, touching the crease arching each side of my lips. *My face is more angular, my cheekbones, more prominent. My daily hike to the butte has eliminated any excess weight on my stomach and thighs.*

In spite of enjoying Cal's visits, I didn't feel the need for romantic companionship and regularly told him so. I was grateful he chose to keep our time together light and impersonal, for I appreciated his friendship.

On the other hand, during the early spring, Thad had begun to mention his conversion and change of focus. From then on, our correspondence evolved into a friendship that was stronger and sweeter than I could ever have dreamed possible. Romance with Cal or with Thad would change both relationships—possibly ruining everything. I wouldn't take the chance. When I read Saint Paul's comments on the glories of remaining single, I decided that perhaps God had made me the kind of woman who should remain single. Perhaps I could serve Him better, more fully.

Cal no longer mentioned the steady stream of letters from the college in the Midwest when he dropped by to see me. And I didn't feel it necessary to mention Cal's name in the letters I mailed to Thad, though I did mention the rancher in my mother's letters. I also told her about the changes taking place in Thad's life.

As the month of June faded into July, Thad's mention of God's guidance in his life became more and more frequent, giving me more reason to praise God. His big surprise came when he wrote, "I chose to stay on at the college to take course work that will enable me to graduate with my class in the spring. Because my newspaper job was terminated (Mr. Tate wasn't too happy with some life-changing decisions I'd made), I've been scrubbing pots and pans in the school kitchen to help pay my tuition. Also, Dad's been sending me pocket money following my visit last Christmas."

My eyes widened in surprise. *Mr. Adams didn't say anything about a visit from Thad. What is going on?*

Unwelcome Surprises

"I said I'd take you to town today, and I will!" Nina shouted over the cough of the car engine. "Besides, the weather's perfect, a late Indian-summer day. Not a cloud in the sky."

Stubborn! Stubborn! Stubborn! I'd never met anyone quite like Nina. Yet, in the months I'd boarded with her, I'd grown to love her dearly. Her spiritual insights and intellectual acumen often left me speechless.

"We could wait a few days until your shoulder begins to heal. It doesn't have to be today, you know." But as I glanced up at the cloudless sky, I had to agree with her; it was a beautiful day. I shrugged and climbed into the passenger seat. The woman winced as she shifted the car into gear. Two days earlier, Nina had pulled a tendon in her left shoulder while stacking a cord of firewood. I had scolded her and treated the injury with one of my mother's old-time mustard plasters. Obviously the arm still pained her, but that didn't slow her down.

The Oldsmobile took the washboard road at a speed meant for cars competing in the Swiss Alpine Auto Races. Once or twice I saw her wince when guiding the car around the sharp turns leading to the top of the mesa.

"Look," I shouted, "I've been driving automobiles since 1917. Why don't you let me take the wheel?"

"Nope!" She shook her head emphatically. "No one drives Archimedes but me!"

The car crested the mesa, traversed the flat tabletop of sandstone, then started down the other side. "It takes skill and cun-

213

ning to outwit this mountain." She laughed and stepped down on the accelerator. "And this girl's got it!"

The vehicle careened down the side of the mesa, dust and gravel shooting in every direction in the wake of the charging automobile. A jack rabbit froze in the middle of the road ahead of us.

"Rabbit stew," she shouted above the racket. To my relief, the creature sprang to safety at the last second. "Play chicken with me, will you?" Nina challenged.

We sailed around another S-curve, and I breathed a prayer of gratitude. The golden high desert spread out before us. A few minor turns, and we'd be in the clear. *We're going to make it safely, Lord.* My prayer of thanksgiving was interrupted with a loud bang and hard jolting as Archimedes lurched off the road. As we bumped to a stop against a rock, water and steam began to spout from the radiator.

In the silent seconds that followed, the world seemed refreshingly peaceful. Then Nina pounded her fist on the steering wheel, opened her door, and climbed out of the vehicle. I heard her desert boot kick the rear tire, not once, but twice. Before I could open my door to join her, Nina stuck her head inside the open window.

"Which do we repair first, the radiator or the rear tire?" I threw my head back and laughed in frustration. "I vote for the tire, since the radiator will need to cool before we can replace the water. You did bring extra water, didn't you?"

"Of course!" She opened the trunk. "I always keep a spare container in here."

Relieved, I tugged at the collar of my dress. *For October, the sun is sure putting out a lot of energy.*

Behind me, I heard Nina clear her throat, so I turned to see what else was wrong. She held a deflated canvas desert bag in her hands. "Looks like I made a little mistake—I didn't check the bag for leaks."

I groaned and swiped at a trickle of sweat coursing down my cheek. "Well, take out your spare, and I'll see what we can do about the flat."

"No spare."

"No what?" I couldn't believe it. "You drove out across this forsaken patch of sagebrush without either water or a spare tire?" My voice was getting shrill. "Great! What are we going to do now?"

"I guess we patch the existing tire."

I cast one of my Meeker stares at the woman. "You do have a tire-repair kit in there, don't you?"

It was a hot, exhausting job. We'd barely patched the one tire and replaced it when a loud hiss erupted from the opposite rear tire.

"Oh no," I groaned. "Oh, well, considering how the day has been going, why should I be surprised?"

"I'm hungry. Let's take a break before we fix the second one," Nina suggested, reaching into the back seat of the car for the picnic basket.

"Only decent suggestion you've made all day," I mumbled.

She pulled her head and the basket out of the car. "What did you say? I'm sorry, I couldn't hear you."

"Nothing important, just grousing."

She nodded and strode over to a large rock. "This should make a good table."

"For rattlers and scorpions!" I curled my lip in frustration. *The car seat would be more comfortable.* I stomped over to the rock and plopped myself down, leaving no doubt as to my foul mood.

We shared the picnic lunch I'd packed, then wrestled the second tire from its rim. By the time we'd patched the tire, pumped it up, and replaced it on the rim, the sun had passed its zenith and had slid toward the hills. A gray-green lizard scurried away as I rounded the front of the vehicle.

Dirty, thirsty, and disgusted, I glared at the radiator. Nina approached from the opposite side. "At least it's ready to go, once we fill the radiator with water. Maybe there's a spring nearby."

"Right!"

After Nina had spent some time under the hood, wiggling wires and tightening caps, she called, "Were there any apples left in the basket?" She straightened, banging her head on the hood. "Ouch!" She rubbed the injury. "That hurt."

I wanted to say "good" but snickered instead. My snicker developed into giggles; my giggles, into belly laughs.

"Laugh, you nincompoop!" Her growl was echoed by a louder growl from her stomach. Instantly her scowl dissolved into a grin as I leaned against the car, doubled over with laughter. "Stop it! Stop laughing this instant."

"I wish I could," I gasped as tears rolled down my cheeks.

"It's not that funny!"

"I know," I wailed. "That's what's so funny!"

"Hmmph! I'll look for the apples myself." She left me standing beside the car, holding my sides in pain while she rummaged through the basket for more food.

By taking a number of long breaths, I finally managed to control my laughter.

Nina handed me an apple, then sat down on the running board and chomped into the second one.

"Sure gets dark fast." I bit into the fruit.

"No twilight on the desert."

Finished with the apple, I tossed the core into the sagebrush and hoisted myself onto the front fender. From there, I watched long, dark shadows fill the canyons and draws behind us until an eerie howl broke the desert silence.

"A coyote," Nina said, her voice flat and tired. She rubbed her injured shoulder and glanced over at me. "I'm sorry. I should have let you drive. We'll be stranded here for a while."

"It's OK. Someone will come looking for us tomorrow morning when the clinic doesn't open on time."

She shook her head slowly. "No, they won't. Because I thought you needed a short vacation, I told the chief we probably wouldn't return until tomorrow night."

I stared at her in disbelief. "Then no one will look for us until Wednesday? And we're out here with just a little canteen of water?"

"I'm afraid so." She massaged her injured shoulder. Both of us knew the hazard of running out of water in the desert. "Maybe I should try to start the car again."

"There's no water in the radiator."

"What about the water in the canteen?"

"It's not enough to fill the radiator; besides, we will need it for our own survival."

Nina sagged wearily against the steering wheel.

"Dear God." My words echoed in the night air. "What are we going to do?"

"Though I walk through the valley of the shadow of death, I will fear no evil. . . ." Nina's calm response contrasted with my heightened anxiety.

"For thou art with me." Our words blended together in unison. "Thy rod and thy staff, they comfort me. . . ." As I recited the familiar psalm, I watched the last rays of light fade from the sky. Behind me, the mesa loomed menacingly above us. "Thou preparest a table before me." My stomach growled at the mention of a table and food. The apple had only whetted my appetite, not satisfied it. I rubbed my stomach and said to Nina, "It's going to be a long night."

"Look at those stars!"

The sky was ablaze with pinpoints of light. "So beautiful!" I sighed and lowered my gaze to the desert floor. "Not a man-made light anywhere.

"Wait!" I pointed toward the west. "Is it my imagination, or do I see a light bobbing over there? Look! Someone's coming."

"Probably your imagination," Nina responded.

"There *is* a light; someone is coming."

Slowly she turned her gaze in the direction I was pointing. An instant later, she sprang to her feet. "By gum, there sure is. Looks like a horse and rider. My guess is that it's Cal Blair. But what would he be doing out here at this hour?"

I whooped with joy and ran around to the driver's side to sound the car horn. A series of ooga-oogas echoed off the mesa. As the light drew nearer, I patted my tangled curls into place and straightened the neckline of my dress.

"Need some help, ladies?" a welcome voice called out of the darkness.

When Cal dismounted, I ran to him and gave him a quick hug. "How did you find us? I thought we were stuck out here all night."

He gave a self-conscious little laugh and patted my shoulder. "Nina told me the two of you were heading into Klamath Falls this morning. When I didn't see you drive past the ranch, I started to worry, because I knew how determined Nina has been to get you away from the reservation for a few hours."

"It's about time you got here." Nina climbed out of the car. "What took you so long? We had to change and repair two flat tires all by ourselves."

He laughed and tied his horse to a gnarled juniper.

"So, did you bring some water?" she asked.

"Of course." He slung a water bag over his shoulder, ambled to the front of the car, and peered under the hood. "Starting out across the desert without water! Tsk! Nina Cook, you should be ashamed of yourself!" He grinned at me and winked. "You! Make yourself useful. Hold this lantern so I can see what I'm doing."

I licked my parched, dry lips as he poured the precious water into the radiator. And I admitted to myself, *It's good to have a man around, at least at a time like this.*

He cranked the engine to life. "Hop in, ladies. I'll drive."

Nina and I squeezed together in the front passenger seat. Cal climbed into the driver's seat and jammed the engine into first gear. Slowly, the car rolled forward through the loose gravel and sand, at a much slower pace than we'd traveled hours earlier. "It's closer to my place than back to the reservation. You'll be able to get a hot bath and a good meal before you continue your journey into town."

"A hot bath?" I spoke the words with reverence.

Nina cast a curious glance at me, then at Cal. "My shoulder is painin' me mighty bad."

"Then it's settled." We inched our way toward the ranch, making several stops to add water to the radiator. As dawn broke over the mountains, we drove under the wooden arch at the boundary of the Blair ranch. Before Cal could ease the car to a stop in front of the low-slung ranch house, the radiator erupted another cloud of water and steam.

"So much for our town trip." Nina shrugged.

"I can tow the car into town behind my Packard and have Fred work on it," he suggested.

Nina just grunted.

"While I stable Lucky, why don't you two whip up a batch of fried cakes. You'll find everything you need in the pantry." The interior of the ranch house, while furnished with every convenience, overpowered me with its bold masculinity. From the trophies mounted on the walls to the massive dark oak furniture and the stone fireplace that ran the length of one entire wall, the place reflected the personality of Mr. Calvin Blair. *No trace of a woman's presence here*, I thought.

Immediately after breakfast, Nina complained of extreme pain in her shoulder and begged off from helping with the cleanup. "What I need is a long, hot bath."

As she padded from the room, I glanced at Cal, color rising up my face. "Sorry. Not too subtle on her part."

He shrugged and without comment gathered up the soiled plates. For several minutes, we did the dishes in amicable silence.

My hands deep in suds, the rugged cowboy waited with dish towel in hand for more dishes to dry. When I handed him a fistful of silverware, our fingers touched. Gently, he placed his other hand atop mine. "CeeCee, I've been thinking a lot about us. We get along very well together."

I stared at my small hand trapped between his large, calloused hands. "I think that eventually, if things continue to develop between us, we may get married. So I have a suggestion."

I gulped. "Yes?"

"I would like to officially begin courting you." He studied my face. "I'm in love with you. For a thirty-four-year-old cowpuncher, that's not easy to say. I've never needed anyone in my life before, since I left home fifteen years ago." He took a long, hard breath.

I studied the veins in the man's hardened, muscular hands and wrists. "Cal, I, uh—"

"Wait!" He touched a finger to my lips. "I know about the guy back east." Again he paused for a moment before continuing. "All I want to know is whether there is a chance that, in time, you could come to love me."

My eyes filled with tears. "I-I don't know what to say, Cal.

You're a wonderfully kind and gentle man, and I admire you greatly—" As my words drifted into nothing, he released my hand and began drying the silverware I'd handed him. *At least Cal believes in God and attends church each week. And he wants me—more than I can say for Thad.* It irked me that in all his letters telling me about how he had found God, Thad had never once indicated that he'd like to renew our romance.

"No, wait! Please, hear me out." I placed my hand on Cal's muscular forearm. "In the last year, I've come to accept the fact that God seems to have plans for my life that don't include marriage. Considering your—" I cleared my throat. "—suggestion, I need time to discover what He does have in mind for me. Having said that, I'm willing to give us a try, if you're willing to be patient with me."

In one swift motion, Cal gathered me into his arms. "That's all I need to hear, that you are willing to give me a chance. Oh, CeeCee, I'll do anything I can to help you learn to love me."

I hope so, Cal. Dear God, let it be so.

Holding me with one arm, he tilted my chin upward. I found myself staring into his warm brown eyes. He leaned forward until our lips were but a breath apart. "May I? May I kiss you?"

I closed my eyes and waited. Tentative at first, his lips touched mine, slowly increasing the pressure. I waited for a response, any response, but I felt nothing—not a spark, not a tremor. I could have been kissing Rusty good night. Disappointed, I stepped back. Though disappointment registered in his eyes as well, he tenderly stroked my cheek. "Don't worry, darling, it will come. It will come."

I nodded and turned away.

"I wish I didn't have to tell you this, but the latest mail pouch is on the desk in the study. You have your usual sheaf of letters." The heaviness in his voice told me I'd find one from Thad in the stack. "I'll finish up here while you read your mail."

I tried to look casual as I hurried from the room. As I shuffled through the stack, I identified Thad's bold scrawl immediately. I also found a letter from my mother and one from Ashley. Curling up in the leather wingback chair beside the fireplace, I opened Thad's letter first.

"Dearest CeeCee," he began, "I've been thinking about you and praying for you a lot lately. You have me worried. In your last letter, you said you believe God's plans for you don't include marriage.

"I can't accept that, dear friend. You're too warm and loving a person to spend the rest of your life alone." Tears rushed to my eyes. *Of all times to receive such a letter. Are you releasing me from our commitment? Are you telling me to find another man?*

I thought of Cal and the sadness in his eyes when I failed to respond to his kiss. *He's so personable, well read, and kind. He was right; we do get along well together.*

God, are You using Thad, of all people, to tell me something? Are You telling me that I'm supposed to let go of the past and get on with my life? Is that what You're saying?

I lingered over the rest of the letter, searching for additional clues, but found none. I read Ashley's letter next, saving Mama's for last. My cousin's big news was her second pregnancy. "The baby should be born sometime around your birthday. Charles wants a boy, but if it's a girl, he's agreed to name her Celeste, after you."

Unconsciously, I placed my hand on my abdomen. *Another baby? Life's not fair.* Brushing the thought from my mind, I tore open my mother's envelope. *No bad news, please!*

I scanned the first paragraph. "Dearest CeeCee, Good news! The company has made your father senior vice-president in charge of the West Coast branch. By the time you receive this letter, we'll be packed and on the train, heading for San Francisco." I let out a squeal just as Cal walked past the open doorway.

He stuck his head in the room. "Is something wrong?"

"Oh no. In fact, everything's wonderful." I skimmed through the next few lines. "My parents are moving back to San Francisco and want me to celebrate Christmas with them. Isn't that fabulous?"

"I can tell that you think so." He strode over to the fireplace.

"Oh, I can hardly believe it. Wait! You should come home with me to meet my family."

Panic flashed across his face. I laughed. "They'll love you, I promise. Besides, it would give us time to get to see one another in a different environment. What do you say?"

"Well," he drawled, "I suppose my foreman could handle things here for a couple of weeks. Would we drive down to the bay?" The moment he asked the question, we both recognized the impropriety of the two of us traveling alone over such a distance. His face flamed. "Probably not. I-I-I didn't mean to imply that you and I might—"

Blushing myself, I stopped him before he dug himself in any deeper. "It's all right. I didn't think—" I stared back down at the letter. "Wait a minute. Mama's unwittingly solved our problem. She's invited Uncle Pete and Aunt Faith also; we can travel with them."

We talked for a few minutes longer about our Christmas plans before Cal showed me to the guest room, where I could rest while Nina's car was being towed to town. "Just make yourself at home. It may not be fancy, but it's clean."

Tired as I was, I couldn't relax. Thoughts of the day's strange events played monkey-in-the-middle, and I was the monkey. I was relieved to get back to the reservation and the predictable routine at the clinic.

During a pause in the flow of patients, I wrote a letter to my mother, mailing it to my Uncle Joe's ranch. I knew that would be one of the first places she'd visit once she arrived back in California. In it, I told her about Cal's proposition. "He's such a wonderful man that I know, in time, I'll learn to care for him deeply. He kissed me. It's been so long since I've been kissed, I think I have to learn how to feel again. I hope you don't mind, but I invited him to come home with me."

I went on to tell her about Thad's letter. "I'm so confused. I don't know what he's trying to tell me. How ironic! Here we are, both mature enough to know what we want and both desiring guidance from God, and so many miles between us." Idly, I brushed a stray curl from my forehead. "Thaddeus once said our love was ill-fated from the beginning. He compared us to Shakespeare's Romeo and Juliet. At the time, I laughed at him, but I guess he was right."

I closed my eyes and rubbed the back of my neck, easing the

tension that threatened to erupt into a major headache. "I know I need to be practical and mature about our relationship. Maybe it's time to let go."

Mama's reply arrived two weeks later, in a ten-page letter. She told about her and Daddy's escapades moving into their new house. "I wish we'd never sold our old home. This one's bigger, but it's too brash and showy for my taste.

"Phoebe is seeing a young college professor. She met him at your Uncle Phillip's and Aunt Jenny's welcome-back party for us. The girl's absolutely radiant!"

How nice. She continued with her news. "Rusty plans to attend a college north of the city once he graduates in the spring." *My little brother thinking about college? Impossible!* "Nikolai continues to be a problem. Every other day, he threatens to leave for good. How does he think he'd manage on his own?" *Poor Mama, having to put up with such a sullen and bitter young man.*

"I have a surprise for you when you get here. Speaking of surprises, your news about Mr. Blair came as a total shock. Of course, you can bring him home for the holidays. In this house, there's no shortage of guest rooms—eleven bedrooms and seven baths! Isn't that ridiculous?"

Eleven bedrooms? I'd become so accustomed to Nina's humble three-room cabin that I couldn't fathom having that many rooms. "We agreed to lease the place, completely furnished, from the company's retiring vice-president and his wife until we could find something more suitable to our taste. They're building a 'small' ten-room retirement home up north in the wine country."

Next, she described the marvelous renovations Aunt Jenny had made in the women's clinic in Chinatown. "By soliciting contributions from San Francisco's wealthy businesspeople, she's opened two branch clinics, one in Oakland and the other in the Italian/Jewish neighborhood of the city. Your aunt has done what I never could; she's made the clinic financially stable. Even Uncle Phillip seems pleased with her success."

Hooray for Aunt Jenny! Ha! I'll bet Uncle Phillip is surprised. I remembered the scene he had created at my mother's dinner party on the evening before we left for New York.

"Last night, she offered me a partnership, and I'm seriously considering it." *Oh, Mama, do it.*

"As you know, I left my heart with the clinic when we moved east. Your father thinks I should take her up on the offer." *Of course, you should. Listen to him.*

I thought about how, as a child, I had resented my mother's involvement in the clinic. *Now, I understand, Mama. I left a big piece of myself in Chamonix. And I suppose, when I leave Oreg— Wait! If I marry Cal, southern Oregon will be my home!* The thought disturbed me. I considered Oregon, like Chamonix, a sojourn, an interlude in my life, never a permanent residence.

That evening, Cal arrived at Nina's around seven to escort me to a holiday program at the reservation school. The program was the fourth event to which Cal had officially escorted me. He brought me gift, a box of walnut fudge made by Hester, his widowed housekeeper. I tried to gently tell him that he needn't bring gifts every time, but he reminded, "That's what you do when you are courting, isn't it?"

Cal hosted the Thanksgiving Day celebration at his ranch that year. When I arrived with Nina, the chief, and his wife, Cal insisted I play the role of hostess. That evening, as we said good night on the veranda, he drew me into the shadows, out of the view of his other departing guests. And for only the second time since I had agreed to give our relationship a try, he kissed me, not with a tentative, schoolboy kiss, but a real kiss.

On the drive home, while Nina and the others chatted about the day, I gazed out the window at the moon shadows redefining the landscape. Cal's kiss disturbed me. *Maybe I've buried my emotions so deep, for so long, that my body will need to be retrained to respond. Maybe I just need to relax. Maybe my memory is faulty, the idlings of a spinster. After all, Thad is the only other man I've ever kissed, and we were only kids. Maybe it was Paris, a city known for its romance. If Cal and I could visit a place as romantic as Paris together— Yes, that's it! A romantic tour of San Francisco should trigger an appropriate response on my part.*

During the days before we left for California, Cal arranged with Uncle Pete to drive his own car to San Francisco. The fourteen-hour drive passed amiably, with Pete sitting in the front seat with Cal, discussing national politics, while Faith and I sat in back, talking local Indian politics. Occasionally the two conversations merged.

"I'm still not convinced that United States citizenship will change the conditions of the American Indian!" Cal defended.

"What? Are you saying that the Indian was good enough to die for America in the war but not to vote?" Uncle Pete insisted.

"It has nothing to do with being good enough. It all goes back to the Dawes Act of eighty-seven, the government's efforts to 'Americanize' the Indians," Cal defended.

Faith leaned over the back of seat. "That's right! Take away the individual tribe's rituals and culture, and in two generations, we, as a people, will be extinct."

"That's nonsense!" Pete argued. "Citizenship will give the tribes due process under the law. They'll be able to defend their rights."

Faith's voice rose, which for Faith meant a notch above a whisper. "Peter, what good will it be to defend our rights in court if we, as a tribe, as a culture, no longer exist?"

Faith and Pete's passion on the subject of Indian rights intensified. It was obvious that this wasn't the first time the two of them had debated the issue, and with feeling. Yet, as I listened to their exchange, the deep respect they had for one another was evident in every word and gesture.

I caught Cal's attention in the mirror. He grinned and rolled his eyes. I leaned back in the seat, closed my eyes, and smiled to myself. *I could be listening to Mama and Daddy "discussing" the illegalities of the United Mine Workers' strike or the steel strike or the Palmer raids directed against alleged Communists.* The fact that I couldn't picture Cal and me in the scene frustrated me. *Time, give it time,* I reminded myself. *God promises to work out His will in His time, not in mine.*

Faith awakened me when we arrived at the ferry terminal. "Isn't it beautiful?" she said, gazing at the city lights across the bay.

"From here, it looks magical."

Mama's directions to the house brought us straight to the massive wrought-iron gates at the edge of the estate. Sundance announced our arrival. One look at the barking, leaping dog, and Uncle Pete and Cal agreed that I should be the one to open the gate. The dog sniffed at me, uncertain for a moment, then broke into a barking frenzy. When I finally could get back into the car, Sundance trotted alongside my window, barking and slobbering on the side of the vehicle as the car wound its way up the redbrick driveway.

By the time we stopped in front of the sprawling stucco mansion with its soaring arches and wrought-iron railed balconies, a hoard of family members were pouring through the open carved oak doors. Uncles, aunts, cousins, siblings, and parents surrounded the slightly unnerved Calvin Blair.

When I introduced him to my mother, I sensed a slight reserve in her. I chuckled to myself. *Kind of the way she greeted Thad the first time she met him, if I remember right.*

Uncle Phillip eyed Cal's western garb with distaste while Aunt Jenny shook his hand. *Never judge a book by its cover, Uncle dear. This rancher has more in the bank than you'd ever guess.* Cal hit it off immediately with Uncle Joe, who owned a horse ranch across the bay from San Francisco. "Don't worry about remembering our names," my Uncle Joe reassured Cal. "Sometimes I can't remember them all myself."

Rusty behaved like a big brother, scrutinizing Cal's every move. And I had to admit, by the amount he'd grown since I had seen him last, it was appropriate. Phoebe blushed prettily, and, in turn, introduced her young professor. My younger female cousins blushed and giggled while the males, along with my stepbrother, Nikolai, showed little interest in the proceedings.

"Meeker, where's Meeker?" I turned toward my mother. "You did bring Meeker west with you, didn't you?"

"I don't know why we did. Once she discovered her new hunting grounds, she disappeared into the bushes. She's been spotted early in the mornings, eating from her dish on the back veranda, so I know she hasn't run away."

We moved inside into the spacious parlor. There, we spent

the rest of the evening swapping childhood tales and catching up on family news. After my aunts, uncles, and cousins left for home, my sister and brothers bade me good night. While Mama guided her guests to their rooms, Daddy took me on a tour of the first floor of the three-story house. I oohed and aahed at the appropriate moments until I stepped into the library.

The thirty-by-forty-foot room took my breath away. The walls were lined with two-story-high bookcases of carved rosewood. A spiral staircase and an iron catwalk made the second story of leather-bound volumes accessible to the reader.

In addition to a massive oak desk and two accompanying easy chairs, there were three seating areas—one by the fireplace, one around a long library table, and the third clustered around a seven-foot ebony grand piano. Surprisingly, the furniture arrangement established a friendly, almost cozy feeling to the room, despite its size.

I tipped my head back to admire the carved ceiling and the panel of opalescent glass in the center. "This is my favorite room. During the day," my father explained, "the skylight floods the room with diffused light."

"It's—it's marvelous." I wandered across the room and seated myself at the piano, running my fingers over the keys. "I'm going to like this."

Daddy strolled over to the piano and placed his hands on my shoulders. "Did you bring your violin?"

I looked up at him and smiled. "What do you think?"

"Good." He smiled and patted my shoulder. "Mama was hoping you would."

"So, what's this great surprise?" I stopped playing. "Do I have to wait until Christmas morning to open it?"

When he didn't answer immediately, I glanced over my shoulder. My father stood silently, with a look of dread on his face. "What's wrong?"

"I think you'd better ask your mother."

I swung around to face him. "Why? What's the matter?"

He sighed before beginning. "Your surprise is arriving tomorrow afternoon. Oh, dear, I really think you should wait to hear this from your mother."

"Daddy, if something's wrong, I deserve to know now."

"Your Granddaddy Spencer is arriving in Oakland on the afternoon train. The cold winters of Pennsylvania have bothered his arthritis a lot these last few years. He's going to help your Uncle Joe run the ranch."

"What a wonderful surprise! Why didn't you want to tell me?"

"Well, you know your grandfather. When he gets a bee in his bonnet about something, nothing can stop him—" His voice trailed off.

I eyed him suspiciously. "Why am I getting the feeling that you haven't told me the entire story?"

My father gave a nervous little laugh. "First, you've got to remember, none of this is your mother's fault."

"None of what? Will you please get to the point?"

"Well, after your mother wrote to Granddaddy Spencer about Thad and about Cal, your grandfather decided to take matters into his own hands."

A wave of fear welled up within me. Fighting the urge to bolt from the room, I somehow managed to ask in a quiet, controlled tone, "What did he do?"

"When he got your mother's last letter regarding your possible engagement to Mr. Blair, your grandfather telephoned your mother. Unfortunately, Rusty answered because she was at the clinic with your Aunt Jenny."

"Yes? Go on."

He licked his lips a couple of times, then continued. "To come to the point, your grandfather asked for and received Thad's address."

My breath caught in my throat.

"Three days ago, we received a telegram from your grandfather, telling us that he and Thaddeus were on their way to California."

"What?" I screeched. For a moment, I thought I might faint.

"I have no idea what your grandfather said or did to convince the young man to make the trip, but convince him, he did."

"This is terrible!" I leapt from the piano bench and paced across the room. "What will Cal think? And what about Thad? What could he be thinking, showing up uninvited?"

As the implications of the turn of events became clear, I could see the walls of my carefully constructed world tumbling around me. *Just as I've come to accept things as they are, just as I can see a future for Cal and me!* I paced back and forth across the library, shouting, "No, he can't do this. No, not now! He has no right!"

"I'm sure the old man thought he was—"

I whirled about, tears streaking down my cheeks. "I'm not talking about Granddaddy Spencer! It's Thad!" I wailed. My father gathered me into his arms. "Please, Daddy, do something. You've got to do something."

"I don't know what I can do at this point, CeeCee."

I sobbed out my pain onto his shoulder. The aroma of my father's bay rum aftershave only intensified my agony by reminding me of Thad.

Suddenly the library's double door flew open, and Mama burst into the room. "What's going on down here? I could hear CeeCee's voice all the way upstairs on the third floor. I have no doubt but that our guests heard you as well." She cast a warning look at me.

Daddy sheltered me from her wrath. "I had to tell her about your father."

"Oh—"

I wrenched myself from my father's arms. "Mother, how could you let this happen?"

My father grasped my arm. "It isn't your mother's fault."

I glared at my father. "No one told her to tell the world my private business!" Sobbing, I ran from the room.

In God's Good Time

That night was the longest night of my life! I almost wore a path in the blue-and-gold Persian carpet, pacing the golden yellow wallpapered room Mama assigned to me. My attempt to appreciate the delicate Chinese porcelain vases on the dresser failed. I threw myself on the bed without bothering to undress or to remove the golden brocade bedspread. But within minutes, I was on my feet again, pacing in my despair.

Mama kept vigil with me until midnight. But when she saw that her efforts to calm me were futile, she went to bed. Soon after she left, I grabbed my coat and tiptoed out of the house onto the front veranda. Moonlight flooded the area, creating a landscape of grays and blacks. Hearing the front door close, Sundance bounded out of the shadows, delighted to find a friend awake at that hour.

Sundance and I walked around to the back of the house, where I discovered a carefully designed garden laced with meandering brick walkways. Finding a Spanish gazebo, I seated myself on one of the masonry benches, with Sundance at my feet. I gazed at the city lights stretching eastward, glittering like diamond chips on black velvet. *Thad! Tomorrow I'll see Thad. How could You let this happen, God? Is this a test? Maybe years from now, when I'm pregnant with Cal's and my third child, maybe then I could run into Thaddeus and not hurt. But now, can't You see? It's too soon, Lord.*

And poor Cal, thinking he's coming down here to meet the family. It's hardly fair to him to have this happen! He's been more than patient with me. And now, I'm putting him through this? Aren't You the One who led me to him in the first place? I leaned back and closed my eyes, trying to remember an appropriate Bible text that spoke to my situation. In spite of my predicament, I had to laugh when all I could remember was the Old Testament story of Jacob and Rachel and Leah. *Somehow, I don't see Thad or Cal agreeing to Jacob's solution to his problem, Lord. Do You have any other suggestions?*

The soft light of a December morning in San Francisco stirred me awake. I was surprised I'd fallen asleep at all. When I stood and stretched, Sundance scrambled to his feet. On the way back to the veranda at the rear of the house, I spotted Meeker. At first, the cat threatened to run from me. It took patient coaxing before she'd let me pet her.

"Beautiful animal."

I glanced in the direction of the voice. Faith stood in the doorway, sipping a cup of hot tea.

"Good morning. You're up early. Did you sleep well?"

"Yes, thank you. I'm an early riser." The woman seated herself on a nearby glider swing. "Once the sun comes up, my brain clicks on, and I've got to get active."

I continued petting Meeker until the cat decided she'd had enough and wriggled free to soak up the morning sun on the Mexican tiles. I joined Faith on the glider. "My mother tells me that sound travels well in this mausoleum."

She grinned. "Surprisingly so."

"I-I'm sorry."

"Don't worry. We heard only voices. None of us have any idea what was being said."

"Including Cal?"

"Him too."

"Then you don't know about the hurricane that is about to be unleashed on this household?"

Her eyes narrowed. "No, I guess I don't."

I told her about my grandfather and his well-intentioned meddling in my life. "Faith, I refuse to allow him or anyone else to influence my life at this point. I've made up my mind. I'm going to marry Cal, no matter what happens!" At my loud voice,

Meeker bolted under the nearest shrub.

Faith's hand flew up in self-defense. "Wait a minute. I'm not the enemy. Forgive me for saying so, but you are becoming surprisingly agitated over the arrival of a man whom you say you no longer love."

"I-I-I don't love him. Sure, Thad and I are good friends and will continue to be, but I need a mature man like Calvin—someone steady and faithful, someone on whom I can depend." I searched her face for validation.

"I'm not the one to convince. You are."

I rose to my feet and dusted my hands. "Then, it's settled! Thad and my family will have to accept my decision, right?"

"Right." She took a sip of the hot liquid. Something in the smile teasing the corners of her mouth caused me to doubt her affirmation.

"I think I'll take Cal to Fisherman's Wharf today. Would you and Uncle Pete like to come along?"

"Don't worry about us. Peter and I have business to attend to at the Bureau of Indian Affairs. Also, he's promised me a shopping trip while we're here. We'll be making a trip east in a few months, and I want to purchase a few new dresses for the trip."

"What fun!"

"Hey." We both looked up to see Cal stroll out of the house, clutching a hot mug in his hands. "Is this a private party, or can anyone join?"

"Of course you can, darling." I slipped my arm about his waist, forcing him to wrap one of his arms around me. Rising on my tiptoes, I kissed him full on the mouth.

He blinked in surprise. "If I'd known such a warm greeting awaited me, I would have awakened two hours sooner."

"So—" I cast him a flirtatious grin. "—what do you want to see today, in the most romantic city in the country?"

"My, my. I don't know what to say." He studied me longer than I would have preferred. "Perhaps, if this morning is any example of what I can expect, I shall place myself entirely in your hands."

"Good, then let's go find out what Helga, my mother's fabulous new German cook, is whipping up for breakfast."

After a quick breakfast, we walked a few blocks to the cable-car stop. Our feet had barely cleared the cobblestone street when the grip man clanged the bell and engaged the cable.

Determined to make the day as memorable as possible, I played the indefatigable tour guide. "Did you know that every grip man develops his own pattern for ringing the bell? The businessmen of the city hold a contest each year to choose the champion bell ringer."

Cal laughed politely. The cable car made its way down Russian Hill past the edge of Chinatown. "If you'd like, we can visit Mama and Aunt Jenny's women's clinic tomorrow. It isn't open right now."

"I'd like that."

The bell clanged again, clearing an intersection of morning traffic. When a group of pedestrians waved, the grip man clanged out his one-note tune on the bell for their enjoyment. "Up ahead is Nob Hill." The cable car inched its way to the crest, then stopped for passengers. "On your right, you'll see the town house where we lived before we moved to New York." I gazed at the bay window that had once been my hideaway, my safe haven, and had the unreasonable desire to flee to it once again.

"Hello?" Cal touched my coat sleeve gently.

"Huh? Oh, sorry."

"I lost you back there. Too many memories?"

I nodded. "Good ones, though. A much simpler time."

He didn't reply.

Shaking free of my melancholy, I resumed my overly sunny demeanor. "After we tour Fisherman's Wharf, would you like to visit Golden Gate Park?"

"Sure. Sounds good."

My light chatter continued until we entered the park, where we found a quiet bench on which to rest. Cal opened the bag of hot roasted peanuts he had purchased from a street vendor on the wharf. Instantly, a flock of pigeons descended at our feet.

"Don't you just love it here?" I gazed up at the giant trees, their boughs obscuring the sparkling sky. "This is where Mama came after the 1906 quake. I've often tried to imagine what it must have been like for her, stranded here with thousands of strangers, without proper shelter or food or clean drinking water."

"Must have been difficult."

"Oh, it was. I'll have her tell you about it tonight at dinner."

"Hmm."

Cal sat hunched over, his elbows on his knees, shelling peanuts and tossing them to the pigeons. "What's wrong? Are you upset about something?"

He straightened and turned toward me. "I don't know. Should I be?"

"I don't think I—"

He leaned back and stretched both arms across the back of the bench. "Come on, CeeCee, I know you better than you think. I've spent a year and a half studying your every smile, your every habit. Take this morning on the veranda—"

Color flooded my cheeks. "I'm sorry. I didn't know you'd object."

He shook his head and returned to his elbows-on-knees position. "I've always been honest with you, sometimes painfully so. I think I'm entitled to the same respect."

I inhaled sharply. "You're right. You are." I leaned my head back and gazed at the sky. "I found out last night that my Granddaddy Spencer is arriving from Pennsylvania today." I lingered on the word *today*.

"And?"

"And he took it upon himself to bring along another guest." I cleared my throat and sighed. "An old friend of mine."

"Thaddeus?"

"How did you—"

"Who else would have upset you so much?" Cal straightened and laced his fingers through mine. "Is that what kept you awake all night?"

"How did you—"

The sadness on Cal's face tore at my heart, and my eyes filled with tears. "I heard you leave the house. And I saw you walking in the moonlight with Sundance. If it hadn't been for the dog, I would have joined you." He studied our hands for a moment.

"Look, I don't know what kind of conclusions you've formed,

Cal, but, as far as I'm concerned, nothing's changed between us."

"Right."

"You don't believe me?"

"I believe that you are trying to believe it."

I placed my free hand over our joined hands. "Please, Cal, don't make more of this than it deserves. Thad will be here for a few days and gone again. You and I have our entire lives to work out."

"We'll see." He cast me a wry smile, then hauled out his pocket watch. "It's three o'clock. We'd better be heading home soon."

Reluctantly, I released his hand and rose to my feet. "I suppose so. But first, promise me that you won't make any decisions involving me without my knowledge and consent."

He stood up and bent to adjust his pant leg over his boot. "Without your knowledge, no; but I can't promise I'll wait for your consent."

"You know what I mean."

Slowly he straightened and turned to face me. Tilting my chin upward with one finger, he searched my eyes. "Will you make the same promise? No games. No stringing me along?"

I tried to look away. Tenderly, he cupped my chin with his hand and drew my gaze back to meet his. He leaned forward and touched his lips to mine, then straightened. "No games. No regrets."

"No games," I said, my voice raspy with emotion.

By the time we caught a cable car back to Fisherman's Wharf, then hopped one headed for Russian Hill, the daylight had faded. Street lights blinked on, one after another, as the trolley climbed the hill to our stop. "Tomorrow, we can drive south along the coast if you'd like. If we're lucky, we might spot migrating whales."

Cal assisted me from the vehicle without comment. "Let's wait until tomorrow morning to make our plans, all right?"

"Sure. Whatever you say."

Sundance met us at the gate. As we neared the front door, my steps slowed, and panic welled up inside of me. *I can't go in there. I just can't.* For one fleeting moment, I considered turning and running back down the brick driveway.

Sensing my distress, Cal patted my hand. "Come on. I'll be beside you as long as you want me there."

I looked up at his encouraging smile and straightened my shoulders. "All right; I think I'm ready." I gripped his arm for strength.

"Good girl."

Before our feet touched the veranda's red tile, the doors swung open. There stood Thad.

"Thaddeus, how nice to see you again." I choked back a sudden lump in my throat. "I was so surprised when my father told me that you planned to visit." As Cal and I strode toward the open door, I realized that the two men weren't looking my way—they were studying one another.

"Oh, excuse me. Thaddeus, you haven't met my fiancé, Calvin Blair. I've told him all about you." The uncertain flicker I detected in Thad's eyes at the use of the word *fiancé* pleased me. However, his smile never lessened.

"Calvin, Thaddeus Adams. Thad and I have been the best of friends for years." I tightened my grip on Cal's arm as the two men shook hands.

"Good to meet you, Mr. Adams."

"And you, Mr. Blair."

I smiled brightly and blinked innocently into Thad's eyes. "How was your journey from Chicago?"

"Educational. Your grandfather has a wealth of knowledge." Needing to escape Thad's intense gaze, I released Cal's arm and slipped past the two men toward the door. Both reacted with surprise when I said, "I know we'd both love to hear all about it, but I really should greet my favorite grandfather first."

Thad gestured toward the parlor. "He's in there with your parents."

I glided into the parlor with as much grace as I could muster in my agitated state. "Grandfather, what a pleasant surprise." I purposely avoided using the affectionate term *Granddaddy* that I reserved just for him. The men in the room rose to their feet. I headed straight for Granddaddy Spencer. "My parents didn't tell me until last night that you would be here. How delightful."

I kissed him lightly on the cheek and gave him a hug. "How could you do this to me?" I whispered in the old man's ear.

"Why, CeeCee, I didn't—" he sputtered.

I straightened and smiled. "—warn me you'd be here. How naughty of you. If I'd known you would be here, I would have brought you a surprise from Oregon."

Uncertain glances passed between my parents. My mother leapt to her feet. "Dad, you haven't yet met CeeCee's friend, Calvin Blair."

"Friend, Mama? Tsk, tsk. More like fiancé." I completed the introductions despite the awkward silence.

"My, my. Perhaps you two would like to freshen up before dinner." Mama took my arm and led me toward the hallway. She glanced over her shoulder at the surprised members of my family. "Excuse us, please. I'll be right back."

She took Cal by the other arm, smiling graciously into his wary face. "Lest my impetuous daughter failed to tell you, Mr. Blair, we eat dinner rather informally around here. Occasionally, Chloe Celeste forgets to pass on important information to others."

Like mourners following a coffin to the cemetery, we marched silently up the stairs. Once inside my room, I waited until the door closed behind my mother to speak. "I resent being treated like a child. You do not need to cover for my faux pas. It's not as if everyone in the room doesn't know what is going on here," I hissed, rolling my eyes.

"On the contrary, I resent having to cover for a daughter who was on the verge of becoming insolent to my father. This is my home, and the people in it are guests. I will not allow you to embarrass them in any way. Is that clear?"

Hands on my hips, I retorted, "I had nothing to do with this situation. If anyone should be reprimanded, it should be your father!"

For a moment, I thought Mama would slap my face. Instead, she took a long, deep breath and exhaled slowly. "I have already taken care of that."

"Well, I hope so!" I glanced toward the window, then back again. "And I do intend to marry Calvin!"

"What you do with your life is up to you and to God, not to your father and me. We'll love you, pray for you, encourage you, and—when asked—advise you; but we will not pressure you. Remember that you, not I, have to live, for better, for worse, with the man you choose to marry!"

My mother's words stunned me, sapping the resentment and anger from me. "Now, if you'll excuse me. I'll leave you to change for dinner while I attend my guests." Her spine straight, her head high, Mama strode from the room. As the door closed behind her, it was as if the door to my childhood had slammed shut as well, leaving me alone on the outside.

I took a series of deep breaths to keep from weeping. Changing into a light blue wool sheath, I checked my face for puffiness in the dressing table's three-way mirror and brushed my hair into a looser, more youthful style.

Throughout dinner and the rest of the evening, I caught myself talking too loudly, laughing too brightly, playing the role I'd watched Ashley play over the years. I thought the evening would never end. Occasionally, I caught Cal or Thad studying me.

At one point, when my Uncle Joe regaled us with a tale about my mother and him, Thad's and my eyes met and held for several seconds. I shivered involuntarily as tears sprang to my eyes. To keep from embarrassing myself by crying, I laughed and looked away, only to catch Cal avert his eyes from me.

The highlight of the evening came when my grandfather asked Thad to tell about his dramatic conversion. I sat transfixed as the onetime atheist, onetime rebel, described sitting on the front row in a citywide revival. "Bible in hand, I followed the man's message about a rich young ruler, text by text, hoping to catch him in an error. I planned to drag him and his series of meetings through the mud in my newspaper article.

"Suddenly, the preacher pointed straight at me and said, 'Son, you came here to shame and to ridicule the gospel of Jesus Christ. But God is speaking to your heart right now, at this moment, just as He did to the young ruler. Will you listen to His voice? Will you heed His call?' " Thad's voice broke. "I glanced about me, thinking he must be talking to someone in the seat behind me.

" 'No, son—' The preacher came down off the platform and pointed directly at me. '—I'm not talking to those folks; I'm talking to you.' Without warning, my eyes filled with tears. I felt a stirring deep inside me like I'd never experienced before."

Again, Thad paused to swallow. "I tried to blink back my tears, but by this time, they streamed down my cheeks. I now know it was the Holy Spirit working on my heart. I went home that night, and using the same Bible with which I'd planned to entrap the evangelist, I read myself into the family of God.

"By morning, the entire direction of my life had changed. At the end of the term, I withdrew from the university and transferred to a Bible college in the area. Praise God, the college accepted my credits from the university, and I will graduate in May with a bachelor's degree in theology."

My father was the first to speak. "What are your plans after graduation?"

Thad studied his hands before answering. "That's yet to be decided. Preaching assignments aren't made until February." He glanced meaningfully at me.

As everyone, including Cal, followed Thad's gaze, color rose in my cheeks. Fortunately, the grandfather clock at the foot of the stairs gonged nine times, thankfully drawing the attention away from me.

Uncle Joe stood up. "This evening has been a true pleasure. Thank you, Thad, for sharing your experience with us. Praise God, He's still in the business of changing hearts and lives."

Daddy seconded Uncle Joe's comments, then added, "You hardly seem like the radical young man I knew in London."

Thad grinned. "I'm not."

"Come on, sweetheart." Uncle Joe extended his hand to his wife. "We'd better be going if we plan to catch the last ferry across the bay tonight."

"Why don't you stay over tonight?" my mother coaxed. "We have plenty of room for everyone."

"Can't do it, little sis." Uncle Joe draped his arm around my mother's shoulders. "Got a ranch to run." He turned to Cal. "I'm sure you understand about that, Mr. Blair."

"Absolutely." Cal glanced first at my uncle, then at me.

Cal stood beside me as we bade my uncle's family good night. When I hugged my grandfather, he whispered, "I'm so sorry, honey, for causing you any pain. I love you."

"I know."

When our evening's guests had departed, Cal yawned. "I'm mighty tired tonight. CeeCee ran the legs off me today. Mr. and Mrs. Chamberlain, thank you for a lovely evening."

"It's been a pleasure," my mother replied.

Cal tipped his head toward Mama, then toward me. "If you ladies will excuse me, I think I'll turn in early."

At his announcement, the rest of the family dispersed in various directions as well. As I headed for the privacy of my room, Thad caught my arm and whispered in my ear, "You and I need to talk. Meet me on the back veranda at ten o'clock?"

I nodded. Out of the corner of my eye, I saw Cal pause halfway up the stairs, then resume his climb.

Thad called to my father. "Sir, would you object to my taking a look at that library of yours again? This afternoon, I found a rare book on early church history, translated from the Greek. I'd like to examine it, if I may?"

"Sure, son, help yourself. Please excuse me, though, for not joining you, but I, too, have had a long, tiring day." He extended his hand toward my mother. "Chloe, will you be joining me?"

Mama eyed Thad, then me. She had no intention of walking up those stairs and leaving Thad and me unchaperoned. "How about you, CeeCee? You must be exhausted as well."

"Oh, I am. I didn't get much sleep last night." I covered my mouth to hide my yawn. "Good night, Thaddeus. Enjoy your book."

"Good night, CeeCee." A tiny grin teased one corner of his mouth. "Sleep well."

As I ascended the stairs to my bedroom, I saw Sundance follow him into the library. Alone in my room, I waited impatiently for the hour to pass. One minute, I could hardly control my eagerness to keep the rendezvous; the next, I vowed I'd wouldn't go. After forty-five minutes, I could wait no longer.

Wrapped in a wool shawl, I tiptoed from my room and down the stairs. As I passed the closed library door, I heard Sundance give a small bark, but I hurried on through the kitchen and out the back door. Approaching the glider, I considered waiting for Thad there. *No! Too eager. The gazebo! I'll wait for Thad in the gazebo.*

Moonlight edged the garden foliage with silver as I looked out over the city. I leaned against an archway and inhaled the aroma of the sea.

"Beautiful, isn't it?"

I gasped with surprise. "You startled me. I didn't hear you coming."

Thad laughed softly. "You weren't supposed to."

The moonlight revealed every feature of his face. I looked past him. "Where's Sundance?"

"I trapped him in the library."

"Poor puppy."

"I've been aching to do that since the first day I met him. Remember?"

"I remember." I stepped back into the shadows. I didn't want my expression to show more than I was prepared to reveal. "How long have you been out here?"

"Long enough for you to walk right past me without noticing."

A cool breeze created goose bumps on my arms. I shivered and hugged myself.

"Are you cold? Maybe this wasn't such a good idea." Concerned, he placed a warm hand on my arm. I shivered again but not from the cold.

"Thad, don't."

"Don't what?"

"Please!" I gestured with my hands. "I can stay and talk with you only if you don't—if you don't touch me."

He stiffened and withdrew his hand. "Sorry. I didn't mean any disre—"

"It's not that. I just think that under the circumstances we can talk more rationally if we refrain from—"

"From what?"

Must he probe? I sighed in exasperation. "Thad, why did you come to California?"

"The real reason?"

"The real reason."

"I came to California to ask you one question."

My eyes widened. *Is he going to propose?* I swallowed hard.

"Will you be totally honest with me?"

I cast him a sheepish grin. "Is that your one question?"

"You know it isn't."

"Go ahead. Ask your question. I promise to tell the truth and nothing but the truth."

"I'm afraid to." He turned and stared out over the city for several seconds.

I walked to the bench on the other side of the gazebo and waited. The night air seemed charged with tension as Thad continued to stare at the city lights. Finally, he asked heavily, "Are you in love with Calvin Blair?"

His question hit me like a tidal wave. I'd prepared myself for all kinds of questions and arguments, but not this one. For several seconds, I couldn't speak.

He ambled over to where I sat and put one foot on the bench beside me. He leaned down, one elbow on his knee. "Yes or no?"

"It's not that simple, Thad."

"But it is. It all comes down to a simple Yes or a simple No."

"I don't know what to say."

"You promised me the truth."

I covered my mouth with one hand for a moment. "I admire Cal tremendously. He's kind and generous, extremely well read. He attends church regularly. You know how important that is to me." I swallowed hard. "Did I mention kind?"

"But do you love him?"

Oh, dear God! No, to be brutally honest, You know that I don't. I want to, but I don't. I looked to Thad for encouragement, but shadows hid his face from me. Like an earthquake rumbling from deep inside the earth, I began to tremble, then rock back and forth in agony, unable to stop. I shook my head from side to side. "Oh, Thad, you don't know what you're asking. I can't—"

"Just tell me that you love him, and I'll leave on the next train east."

A wail escaped from me. "No! No! I don't love him—at least

not in the way I loved you! Are you satisfied?" My cry seemed to echo off the gazebo pillars and roof. *Oh, dear God, what do I do now?*

"That's all I needed to know." He took my hand and drew me to my feet. Yearning for reassurance, I leaned toward him. But instead of fulfilling my need, Thad dropped my hand and walked to the far side of the gazebo.

"No, I can't. You have no idea how badly I want to hold you, my darling, and kiss away your tears, but I can't until you are free to return my affections. I respect Mr. Blair too much to take liberties with his fiancée."

I leaned my forehead against one of the arches. "You're right, of course."

Thad strode past me and paused at the gazebo entrance. "Knowing how weak my resistance to your charms can be, my love, please excuse me. I really do want to spend some time reading that book I mentioned earlier to your father. Let me know when you've, uh, cleared up your unfinished business."

I watched him stride along the pathway and disappear into the shadows of the veranda. Wandering to the archway overlooking the city, I stared up into the sky, looking past the moon toward the winter constellation of Orion. *I've never felt so miserable in my life, Father. How am I going to tell Cal? Tell the truth? That's easier said than done. I never wanted to hurt him, honest. I never wanted to hurt him.*

When I heard footsteps on the pathway, I thought Thad had returned. "Thad?" I whirled about and found myself staring into Cal's drawn face. I gasped. "Calvin, what—"

"CeeCee, I saw Thad go back into the house. I thought you might need to talk."

"It's not what you think. He didn't— I didn't—"

"I know. I'm embarrassed to say this, but I could see the two of you from my bedroom window." He pointed to the lighted third-story window. "I'm sorry, but I could hear everything."

"Everything?"

"Voices carry in the night."

"Oh, Cal, I'm so sorry."

"It's not your fault. It's no one's fault, really." Instinctively, he reached out for me, then pulled his hands back and stuffed them in his pants pockets. "Love between a man and a woman can't be forced or wished into being. Believe me, I know. And, remember, we promised one another there'd be no games and no recriminations."

"I'm so sorry."

"I'll be leaving for home in the morning."

"What about Peter and Faith? How will they get back to Oregon?"

"I've already discussed the possibility with them. They've made other arrangements." He gave a mirthless laugh. "It's not like I didn't see this coming."

"What? What do you mean?"

"The way you looked at Thad; the way he looked at you. I would have had to be blind to miss it, CeeCee."

"Oh, Cal." Tears trickled down my face.

Removing a bandanna from his hip pocket, he gently blotted them away. "Will you be returning to Oregon?"

"I-I-I don't know."

"Whatever you decide to do, my prayers are with you and Thad." He pounded the palm of his hand against the archway. "What makes it worse is, I really like the guy. It would be so much easier to hate him."

"If you want to hate someone, Cal, hate me. I deserve it."

"Never. That will never happen." He shook his head and laughed. "Hey, there's a nervous young preacher in the library on his knees. Go to him."

"How do you know—"

"I would be if I were Thad."

"But what about—"

"Me? I'll be fine. My hide's too thick to stay bruised for long."

I glanced eagerly toward the house, then back at Calvin. "If you're sure—"

"Get out of here. I want to enjoy one last look at your city before I go to bed."

I flew to the house on wings of love. The kitchen door banged against the wall, setting off startled barks from Sundance. Someone stirred on the floor above me, but I didn't care. I didn't care

if I awakened the entire household. I ran into the hallway, skidded around the corner, then threw open the library doors.

"Thad?" For a moment, I thought the room was empty. "Thad?"

"CeeCee?" I lifted my gaze in the direction of his voice.

"Thad? What are you doing up there?"

He smiled down at me. "Looking for the book on early church
history that I spotted before dinner."

"Is this what I can expect during the remaining years of our
lives?" I placed my hands on my hips. "Will I find you, in the
middle of the night, engrossed in some ancient tome?"

Thad's face darkened with questions. "I thought we
agreed—"

"To discuss our future once I was unencumbered. So discuss."

Slowly, he started to descended the spiral staircase. "You've
already talked to Mr. Blair?"

I nodded.

"And?" Thad froze, his foot suspended in the air.

"And, will you stop asking dumb questions?"

Halfway down the staircase, he leapt over the railing and
bounded across the room to where I stood.

Beaming, Thad looked down at me. "I don't know what to
say."

Standing rigid before him, I closed my eyes. "Tell me you love
me. Assure me that I've done the right thing."

"I love you, Chloe Celeste Chamberlain. I love you." The smile
on his lips spread to his eyes. "I know I will never be satisfied
with anyone else but you. God willing, I won't have to be."

I snuggled into his arms. Resting my cheek on his shirt for
several seconds, I gave a little sigh of relief.

"I love you. Did I remember to tell you that I love you?" he
whispered.

I nodded, unable to speak. Tentatively, he placed his lips on
mine. My response rocketed through me. *I guess my emotions
weren't buried as deeply as I thought.*

Thad led me to the sofa. "There were times I thought this
moment would never come."

"*You* thought. Do you know how often I prayed this might
happen? And when you didn't indicate a romantic interest in

me after your conversion, I decided that God had other plans, and I stopped asking."

"I didn't want to be because—because I was afraid you might accuse me of using religion to win your heart."

"You were willing to risk losing me to Calvin?"

"That was a mistake." He ran his free hand through his hair. "I never dreamed you and he were serious enough to be engaged."

"We weren't. I said that to anger you."

"It worked. I'd planned to storm your clinic this summer, my sheepskin in hand. But when your grandfather showed up on campus, and I learned that you were considering marrying Calvin, I—"

"Oh yes, dear, sweet Granddaddy Spencer."

"Hey, that man had to talk turkey to me before I agreed to come west. He paid for my train ticket as well."

"Bless his meddling little heart. Tell me, didn't you consider that you might be making the trip for nothing?"

"Not after I saw you again. Before that, well, let's just say that with every mile, I prayed God would give me acceptance, no matter which way things went for us." He chuckled. "But when I saw you standing at the front door, looking so defiant and petulant, I knew He'd answered my prayers."

I cocked my head to one side and smiled up at him. "Pretty sure of yourself, weren't you?"

"No, not of myself. But I knew that your anger showed that you still cared. What I didn't know was how to get you to recognize the fact." He leaned back against the sofa, and I rested my head on his shoulder.

"So where do we go from here?"

"That, my dear, is up to God and you."

"I'm under contract to the state of Oregon until May first."

"Being a pastor's wife is a difficult job. Are you sure you want to risk it?"

"Is that a proposal?"

"No!" He shot to his feet and turned to face me. "This is." Dropping onto one knee, he clasped my hands. "Chloe Celeste Chamberlain, will you marry me?"

"Yes!"

"In June?"

"Yes! Yes! Yes!"

Seizing the opportunity, he lifted me to my feet and twirled me around the parlor. When he lowered me to my feet, I took a step backward. "Before we can make it official, you will, of course, need to ask my father for my hand in marriage."

"Only your hand? I love all of you, woman, from the soles of your stinky feet—"

I blinked in surprise. "My feet aren't stinky!"

"To—" He grasped a curl on the top of my head and stretched it out straight. "—your kinky carrot top."

"Kinky? Carrot top!" I cuffed his arm. "Don't you ever—"

He chuckled and trapped my hands in his once more. "Seriously, there is so much to say. So much we need to discuss. I hardly know where to start." His eyes searched mine.

"When must you return to Chicago?"

"New Year's Day."

"That's more than a week away." I smiled and relaxed. "We have plenty of time."

We have time, I thought, *time to laugh, to love, to work, to sing, to play, to share, and most important, time to dream*. A warm glow stirred within me as I recalled the promise that had seen me through so many crises and disappointments.

"Delight thyself also in the Lord; and he shall give thee the desires of thine heart. Commit thy way unto the Lord; trust also in him; and he shall bring it to pass. . . . Rest in the Lord, and wait patiently for him." I closed my eyes, content and at peace. "God willing, we have plenty of time."

There's no gray in a black-and-white issue

She Said No
by Kay Rizzo

From the beginning, the physical side of Heather and Josh's relationship threatened to push them over the edge of reason. Though Christians, each viewed their growing intimacy differently. When their ideas collided, two lives were severely damaged in the emotional wreckage of a criminal act—date rape.

She Said No, by Kay Rizzo, confronts a difficult subject with uncanny insight and needful honesty. Its message could salvage or help protect the lives and relationships of those who may be at risk.

Paper. $10.95/Cdn$15.90.
Prices subject to change without notice.

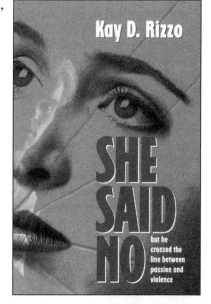

Kay D. Rizzo

SHE SAID NO

but he crossed the line between passion and violence

Books You Just Can't Put Down
from Pacific Press